Dysfunctional
DIARY OF A FLIGHT ATTENDANT

The Queen of Sky Blog

Dysfunctional
DIARY OF A ∧FLIGHT ATTENDANT

The Queen of Sky Blog

— a novel in blog format —

ELLEN SIMONETTI

To my mother

And with special thanks to Caroline Shearer, Gina Baker, and all of my blog readers who encouraged me and rooted for me along the way.

A Note to Readers

This book was inspired by the author's own blog, bearing a similar title, and the experiences that surrounded it. However, *Diary of a Dysfunctional Flight Attendant* is a work of fiction and no real persons, websites, or companies are portrayed within it. Names, characters, places, and incidents are either the product of the author's imagination or are used fictitiously. Any resemblance to actual persons, living or dead, events, locales, media outlets, or airlines is entirely coincidental. In addition, all photos are used ficticiously. Faces have been changed. No real people are portrayed.

Thank you for your attention. Now sit back, relax, and enjoy the book!

Contents

BlogAcres Member Profile 9

January
Introducing the Queen of Sky 11

February
Back on the Market 29

March
The Fly Girl and the Man of Mystery 49

April
Clear Air Turbulence 73

May
Mystery Unveiled 97

June
My Life in the Airport 119

July
Vacation! 143

August
The Normal Grind 165

September
The Queen is Dethroned 189

October
Media Storm 203

November
The Clouds Open 225

BlogAcres Member Profile:
Queen of Sky

Age: 29

Gender: Female

Occupation: International Flight Attendant/Student

Location: Quirksville, Texas

Blog Name: Diary of a Flight Attendant

Email: queenofsky@blogacres.com

Interests: Acupuncture, Airplanes, Astrology, Cheese, Cooking, Dancing, Daydreaming, Dial-up Internet, Eating, Flying, Food, Happiness, Infatuation, Internet Dating, Irony, Italians, Jetlag, Karma, Knights in Shining Armor, Lounging, Muffins, Napping, Nudity, Olives, Outdoors, Package Size, PMS, Reiki, Rowing, Royalty, Salsa, Sarcasm, Self Respect, Sleeping, Stewardesses, Traveling, Twenties, Web Surfing, Wine

About Me: I take classes at an acupuncture school one day a week (this is my first trimester), and the rest of the time I'm a flight attendant for Anonymous International Airlines. I've been flying for over seven years now, thus have plenty of stories to tell of the glamorous and exciting life of a sky diva! OK, I lied—actually I have plenty of stories to tell of what the life of a flight attendant is *really* like.

Favorite Quote: "Buh-bye!"

JANUARY

Introducing the Queen of Sky

Blog Virgin

Filed in ABOUT ME on Wednesday, 01/12

Wow. My very first blog entry! This is EXCITING!!! My horoscope said I would have a liberating experience today, and this must be it! After all, what could be more liberating than publishing a diary on the web?

Speaking of horoscopes, last week I ordered my annual "Astrological Forecast Report" from AstroWizards.com and have been awaiting its arrival with bated breath. I'm eager to see what it says, since I'm not sure where my life is headed right now. My job is great at times (like when I'm lying by the pool in some tropical country and getting paid for it), but incredibly frustrating at others (like when I'm stuck in my base city or—even worse—stuck on an airplane). And, meanwhile, the whole airline industry is in the toilet.

Then there's the matter of my non-existent love life. Even before it was non-existent, it was less than satisfactory. In fact, last year was such a rough year that I've decided from now on I need to be prepared for any possible bumps in the road. That's where the "Astrological Forecast Report" comes in. Between watching the stars and writing this blog, I'm hoping to make sense of things. (Which, might I point out, is a better way to deal with problems than popping pills, like a lot of my cohorts do.)

Anyway, today the report finally arrived and I tore it open greedily. I've summarized my forecast below...

Work: Mixed reviews here. One part of the report says things are going well and I'll get some kind of upgrade or promotion (unlikely, since I don't ever plan to fly the lead flight attendant position), while later on it talks about an abrupt change.

Personal Development: Here the report talks about inner and outer transformation. That's good, I guess.

Home: This part doesn't sound that great. It says there will be "matters that need attention." I just hope part of my ceiling doesn't collapse again.

Family: Says something about problems with my "mother or other female figures." Very strange, because my mother died last year. Needless to say, this prediction worries me.

Finally, and most importantly, there's the part about my **Love Life.** Some good and some bad stuff here, too. At first the report mentions an "unusual encounter," but later in the year it talks about disillusionment. And towards the end it says I should just have fun. Talk about mixed messages.

Well, all in all, not exactly what I wanted to hear. Let's hope the mixed forecasts lean in my favor. I signed up for Astro Wizards' daily horoscopes online, so I'll be getting updates as I go.

Anyway, I'm still very enthused about this new blog. I've got class all day tomorrow at the local acupuncture school, but will try to post something when I get home. Off to bed now...

Buh-bye!
—Queen of Sky

The Fringes
Filed in MISC. on Thursday, 01/13

Tonight in my lecture class I looked around and noticed a few things about my fellow acupuncture students.

In the first row, there was a middle-aged white lady with a bejeweled turban balanced atop her head. Directly in front of me, sat two roundish, mullet-haired pupils clad in matching plaid shirts and cargo pants. I spent the entire class trying to figure out if they were male or female. To my left hunched a skinny guy who periodically hummed some kind of mantra, and across the aisle hovered a tiny bird-like woman whose nervous tick caused her to spontaneously shake her head throughout class.

Eying these characters, I suddenly realized that by enrolling in this school I had joined the very FRINGES of society.

Anyhow, school really kicked my butt today. I can't believe I signed up for nine hours of classes in one day. And the worst part is, I have three hours of Qigong (Chinese yoga) at 9am, an hour at which I should be catching up on my well-needed beauty rest.

OK, enough griping. The way the airline industry is going, I need to find another career ASAP. So what, if it means wearing a turban and not shaving my armpits!

Santiago!
Filed in LIFE OF LEISURE on Friday, 01/14

At 7:30 this morning, as I was contentedly snoozing away in my big cozy bed, my cell phone went off. (Hate it when that happens!) I quickly glanced at the caller ID. It was my friend Gloria, the Hot Cuban Mama, and there was only one thing she could be calling about at that hour—a swap. Without a second thought, I turned the phone off, rolled over, and went back to sleep.

That girl amazes me. She's a single mother with three kids, but she never seems to suffer a shortage of men. Of course she *does* have a smokin' bod, which helps. And believe me, she flaunts it every chance she gets. She even has her uniform dresses tailored to hug her every cocoa curve. Who knew pea-green polyester could look so hot!?

Gloria is presently dating a married pilot, and the only chance she gets to see him is on layovers, so, of course, she always tries to fly with him. But that's her prob, not mine. I only help her out if and when it's convenient to me. If I did favors for everybody all the time, I would be flying crappy trips five days a week. You've got to look out for numero uno in this business.

Following my normal routine, I got up around eleven, showered, and finally checked my messages a little after noon.

"Hi, Elena. It's Gloria. How are you? I was hoping you could help me out." There was a hint of guilt trip in her tone. "My boyfriend John is on your Santiago trip on Sunday. Would you be willing to swap my Rome today for your Santiago on Sunday? Gracias, nena. I really appreciate it."

Santiago? I mused, perplexed. *Could it be that I got my swap?*

I quickly logged onto the Anonymous International Airlines (AIA) system to investigate. When I pulled up my monthly schedule for January, I discovered a Santiago trip on the 16th. I had put in a blind swap for the trip, never thinking I would get it.

Anyway, I am soooo excited! I haven't been to Santiago since last summer, and it's one of my favorite trips. I was originally supposed to go to Rome on Saturday, but that trip is very tiring. Twenty-four hours is not enough time to get two nights sleep and do everything I want to do. In Santiago we have thirty-six hours (and no jetlag—minimal time difference), which leaves plenty of time to sleep, drink lots of wine, eat lots of sea bass, party hard, and get my legs waxed and hair cut to boot!

I called Gloria back and left her a message to say sorry, but I didn't have enough notice and really wanted to do that Santiago trip anyway. She should know that as an out-of-base commuter I need at least a day's advance notice. There was no way that I could get from Texas to my East Coast base city at this point.

As I was ending my message, I remembered that I had been planning to ask the cute catering guy in Rome, Giancarlo, for some restaurant recommendations this week. I've managed to finagle a two-day layover there at the end of the month, and my girlfriend Christine, who has never been to Rome before, is coming with me.

Christine is a petite and very cute Chinese girl. We were in flight attendant training together, so I've known her for a while now. She's actually a year older than me but looks about five years younger. Unfortunately, though, she has low self-esteem and is always overcritical of herself, which tends to scare guys off.

I amended my message and asked Gloria to get the info for me, plus the name of a good club for a Thursday night, and possibly Giancarlo's phone number. :-)

That guy is a real hottie. One day in the back galley on the 767, we were complaining to the tall, buffed, olive-skinned Italian god that we had no coffee stirs for the flight. Giancarlo replied that they had none in stock in Rome, but then generously offered to come with us on the flight and stir everyone's coffee with his finger. We chuckled, and he headed off toward the front of the airplane.

"I'd rather he stir the coffee with his other appendage," one of the older flight attendants remarked after he left.

"Yeah, he can stir my coffee any day!" her friend quipped.

We had a good laugh over that one.

The Home Wrecker
Filed in LIFE OF LEISURE on Saturday, 01/15

I was so tired today I slept 'til noon. Am apparently still recovering from the double Caracas trip I did last weekend—uggh! And class the other day didn't help matters.

The only productive thing I did today was call my friend Christine to discuss our Rome trip later this month. The conversation quickly digressed, though.

"Guess who's on my Santiago trip tomorrow?" I said, itching to gossip.

"I don't know, who?"

"Gloria's boyfriend," I stated dramatically.

"Oh." She sounded immensely disappointed.

"Guess who wanted to swap with me to be on that trip?"

"Let me guess—Gloria?"

"Yep."

"You know, I flew with her boyfriend recently, and he told me he had just adopted a little Korean girl with his wife." Christine was adopted herself, so I could tell this really irked her.

"Uh-oh..."

"What Gloria and John are doing is *not right*," she added indignantly.

"Oh, well. Why is it she always has guys lapping at her feet, and we can't even get a date?"

"You're right, Elena. That's quite a prize she's got there—a married man with a new baby. Where do I sign up?"

"You got me there, Christine," I conceded. "I am *not* a home wrecker—not now, not ever!"

"Hear, hear, girlfriend. It's girls like her that give us flight attendants a bad name."

After agreeing on that last point, we gossiped about a few other things, like AIA's rumored up-coming pay cuts and the trips we were flying next month. We never really did discuss Rome.

Oh, well. It's time now to do some laundry and get ready for my trip tomorrow.

Toodles, y'all!

The Party Crew
Filed in FLIGHT BLOGS on Wednesday, 01/19

Hi, everybody. The Queen of Sky is back in the building.

I got in from Chile this morning, but by the time I got home to Texas it was afternoon. I've been catnapping all day in airports, airplanes, and finally in my own bed. Am pooped, of course. Working two all-nighters in one week will do that to you.

Anyway, it was a good trip...reminded me of the good old days (mostly pre-9/11) when I used to fly Santiago all the time. The best part was the crew—a fun, party crew. :-)

Setting the mood for the trip was the lead flight attendant, Barbara—one of my favorites. I used to fly with Barbara to Santiago all the time, since she always flew weekends like me. She's a warm, generous and motherly black lady. I LOVE her. She always has a smile on her face and a kind word to say to everyone. Plus, she likes to party. She makes some of the best airplane sangria (aka "crew punch") for the crew bus in Santiago—her own secret recipe.

Another party-hard crewmember was one of my fellow Spanish speakers, Nancy. Nancy is American but grew up in Mexico. Her father was an ambassador or diplomat or something like that, so she speaks Spanish like a native. I, on the other hand, speak Spanish like a gringo.

I've flown a lot with Nancy, too. She's probably in her late thirties, average looking, but keeps her bod in top shape. She has a couple of kids at home and thus prefers to spend as little time as possible in her hotel room on the layover. Layovers are her only chance to go out and party. Nancy consistently out-parties me, in fact, no matter that I'm ten years her junior. On more than one occasion, I've had to leave her at the club because

I was wiped and she wanted to keep going. One time I almost had to hop a cab back to the hotel by myself, because she was *busy*. (Luckily one of the pilots offered to accompany me.)

The funny thing is, Nancy always ends up cozying up with some pilot by the end of the night. And she doesn't even bother to take her wedding ring off.

My theories about her domestic situation flip-flop back and forth. At times I think she's bored in her marriage and just looking for some fun. At other times, though, I am quite sure she's on the prowl for husband numero dos. I have noticed that she never brings her husband on trips with her.

The exception to the party crew was Jeffrey, the third and final Spanish-speaking flight attendant on the crew. Jeffrey is a tall, blond, quiet 40-something Mormon who commutes from Utah. He learned Spanish as a missionary somewhere in South America. Nowadays he has five kids, including three teenagers, back in Salt Lake. But, unlike Nancy, we never see him once we get to the hotel. When someone asks him what he did on the layover, he gives his standard response: "I took a hot bath, read, and then I ordered room service. My layovers are the only peace and quiet I get. If you had five kids at home you would understand."

Anyway, Monday, the evening of our arrival in Santiago, I planned to meet up with the crew in the crew room on the third floor of the hotel for some wine and snacks. But first I needed to stock up on goodies at the local grocery store.

One of my favorite things about traveling to foreign countries is visiting their supermarkets. I love supermarkets in general, but especially foreign supermarkets.

I eagerly walked the four blocks to the store, ignoring various cat-calls along the way. (Haven't these men ever seen a six-foot-tall blond before?) Then I stopped to withdraw cash from the ATM machine at the store's entrance and realized I didn't know the exchange rate and had left my currency conversion printout back at the hotel. I finally decided it was something like 700 pesos to the dollar and took out 35,000.

That should last me through dinner, I thought, setting off through the store.

I started off with the produce. The peaches and plums were looking very nice, so I snagged some for a snack the next day and for the flight home. Then I spied the avocados. They were quite ripe and irresistible. I put two in my basket, as well, and made my way to the dairy section. I always have to have a little cheese with my wine. Not to mention olives and mixed nuts. I picked up the latter on my way to my final stop, the wine aisle.

As I rounded the corner, I spotted my captain, Frank, his eyes transfixed on the cabernets. Normally I don't recognize my pilots out of uniform, but this one was particularly round and white-haired, like an airline Santa Claus, so he was hard to miss. I wasn't sure whether he recognized me at first, but he faked it pretty well.

Captain Claus had picked out several nice reds, which I eyed skeptically. Here's a news flash: pilots are notoriously cheap. They usually bring the one-dollar bottles of wine to the crew room but only drink the *good* wine that other people have brought. Captain Claus seemed like the jolly, generous sort, however, so I decided to give him the benefit of the doubt.

On the way back to the hotel, the sun was starting to set behind the skyscrapers and the Andes Mountains beyond. It was a beautiful sight. The summer sun had cleared out most of the smog that plagues this Southern Hemisphere city, leaving the air hot and dry but breathable for a change.

I made a quick pit stop in my room, then headed down to the crew room, arriving around 8pm. After greeting my crewmembers and pouring myself a glass of wine, I popped my Ricky Martin CD into the stereo, and the fun was underway!

All eight of my crewmembers who showed up at the party went to dinner. This was unusual, since usually half of the crew complained that they were full after all the cheese and snacks in the crew room and bowed out of going to dinner.

Luckily the crew took my suggestion and picked a very nice seafood restaurant that I had been to several times. Some of the girls, myself included, didn't want a big group, so we reserved two tables of four. I ended up at the table with two pilots and one male flight attendant. John, Gloria's boyfriend, was one of the pilots at my table.

John is a pretty handsome guy, in a Waspy sort of way, in his late thirties. He had mentioned during dinner that he commuted from South Carolina, so I figured he was still with his wife. But then, when he stepped out to call Gloria between courses, Captain Claus informed me that John was presently going through a divorce, and in the meantime staying with his parents back in SC.

OK, I won't pass judgment, I thought. *He seems like a nice guy.*

After our delicious seafood dinner (I had sea bass, of course, in a creamy seafood sauce), we cabbed over to Suecia, the nightclub district, for a little late-night boogying. This is my favorite part of Santiago, besides the food and wine. I just LOVE that Latin dance music. I can dance to it all night!

At the club I eyed John and Nancy dancing dangerously close. It didn't look that innocent to me, but I was too busy shaking my booty to care. We piled into cabs back to the hotel around 2:30am. John and Nancy were notably absent.

The next morning my phone rang at 11am, waking me from a deep sleep. It was Adele, one of my late-night-partying crewmembers.

"Let's go get waxed! Be downstairs in half an hour!"

I couldn't understand how she could be so peppy. I felt like I had been hit by a truck.

"Whoa! I need a little more time than that to get ready," I tried to protest. But the voice on the other end was firm.

"I have an appointment at noon," Adele said. "I've got to wash up myself, but I'm gonna do a PTT—puss, tush, and tits."

Adele was a heavy-set, spunky black lady. I was informed on the flight down that she and Barbara were members of the "Bald Cats Club"... i.e., they liked to get it ALL waxed off. I, on the other hand, can't even bear the *thought* of hot wax near my privates. I just get my legs done.

But Gloria the Hot Cuban Mama goes to yet another extreme. Not only is she a member of the Bald Cats Club, but she once took her husband to get his BALLS waxed on a layover in Argentina! :-O

They got divorced shortly thereafter...

A Typical Day at Home with the Queen of Sky
Filed in LIFE OF LEISURE on Friday, 01/21

9:45am: Phone rings waking me up.
Am too lazy to get up and answer it.

9:50-11:45am: Lie in bed thinking about what I'm going to write in my blog today. (First sign of a blogging addiction.)

11:45am: My rowing coach leaves a message about rowing tomorrow. I am still too lazy to get up and answer the phone.

12:00pm: Call back rowing coach. We are on for tomorrow morning.

12:15pm: Turn on computer to see how many people have visited my blog since my last log in. (I'm such a Blog Whore!) It was less than 20, in case you were wondering.

12:30pm: Shower, dry off, note the usual tufts of hair on backs of thighs that I somehow missed shaving.

1pm: Call my friend Victor, a lawyer from the Caribbean. (He wanted his blog name to be Mr. X. I told him that would not do.) We talk for an hour and a half about various topics, including my blog. I tell him to read it, since I may be writing about my sexcapades soon.

"You having sex?" He sounds puzzled.

"Well, not recently..."

Then he proceeds to go on and on about how we could have a good time if I gave him a shot...sex on demand...no commitment...yaddah, yaddah.

I have heard it all many times before...and from many men...and in many languages.

"Sorry, you missed my slutty phase," I reply, unfazed.

Then he tells me I should add more psychoanalysis to my blog. Like why I do what I do.

"People don't want to read a psychology textbook," I respond.

I may, however, add more parentheses about my various neuroses.

He also says I should add plenty of details about my sexcapades...like crooked dicks, fetishes, and how I not only felt like a hooker when in bed with one guy, but a pack animal, as well.

I tell him he is probably right about that, but I want to keep my blog rated "PG-13", not "XXX."

The conversation ends with us both deciding *not* to go salsa dancing tonight (the original premise for the call), as the weather is blah and neither of us particularly feels like it.

I mention to him that we could have lunch or dinner next week some time to discuss my blog some more. (Neurosis #1: At times, slightly narcissistic/vain.)

2:30pm: Finally eat breakfast/lunch. I was so hungry while talking to Victor that I almost ate the phone. I munch on some rye crisps with butter and chestnut cream (aka crema di marroni... addictive... looks like Nutella, tastes like maple.) Then I heat up some homemade chicken vegetable soup and a sweet potato.

3:55pm: Dr. Phil wraps up and I gear up to watch Oprah's 50th birthday special. (I might as well be a housewife—I watch Dr. Phil and Oprah daily.)

4:15pm: I am regretfully interrupted from Oprah by a call from my friend Samantha from Germany. (I let her pick her own blog name. She said she didn't like her very Spanish name growing up, so she would always tell guys her name was Samantha. When they called for her, her dad would declare angrily: "There's no Samantha here!" and hang up on them. So the poor girl didn't have any dates in high school. I thought that was kind of funny.)

She complains about her normal stuff... job, Germany, in-laws. She contemplates setting up a blog just to vent about her German in-laws.

"Sure, someone will read it," I tell her. "People read my crap."

4:45pm: Tune back in to Oprah in time for the end.

Dance to Tina Turner's tribute, then start crying when little African children send Oprah their greetings.

5:05pm: Start laundry.

5:20pm: Purchase pajamas from ValeriesSecret.com.

$9 for shipping! What a rip-off!

5:40pm: Purchase Flip the Fluffy Beige Pup phone cover from CellCuties.com for my new flip-top cell phone.

I pray to the consumer god that it fits my phone.

$9 for shipping! What a rip-off!

6:00pm: Check laundry.

6:15-7:15pm: Write this entry and post on blog. :-)

Amount of meaningful things accomplished today: ZERO, ZIP, NADA. Amount of time spent online today: TOO MUCH.

Packing My Bags
Filed in MISC. on Saturday, 01/22

Well, I'm off to R-r-r-roma tomorrow. Should be fun. Christine is excited, too. I just hope she gets on the flights. Airline people travel standby when we travel for pleasure, in case you didn't know.

I'll give you all a full report on my return. The only bad news is Gloria said she scored Giancarlo the hot caterer's number for me, but then somehow "misplaced" it—yeah, right!

Run Ragged in Roma
Filed in LAYOVERS on Thursday, 01/27

The Queen of Sky got back from Rome last night, totally exhausted, then had to drag herself out of bed this morning for a full day of acupuncture school. Trust me, it was not pretty. (I ended up coming home at lunch and napping through my Chinese massage class.)

In any case, letting Christine come on my trip with me may not have been such a good idea after all. It totally wore me out. Here's the trip report as promised...

Since Christine had never been to Rome before, she went to the Vatican the day we got in (Monday) while I was taking my post-flight nap. Then later, we went to dinner with Ricky, another flight attendant on my crew, and a queen of a different sort.

Ricky is a tall, dark, and handsome hottie from Argentina. If he weren't gay he would be totally up my alley. He normally always flies with his partner in crime, a 20-something Colombian diva named Consuela (nick-named "Miss Colombia"). They're inseparable, like a Latin Will and Grace.

Anyway, for dinner we went to my standard layover restaurant, il Pomodoro, up the street from the hotel by the Villa Borghese. As we were being seated, I spotted Luigi, my slightly chubby but extremely friendly regular waiter. He rushed over to greet me. ("Ciao, bella! Come stai?") and whisked us to a table in his section.

I love Italians. They're always so flattering. Plus, they're my peeps.

The dinner was good, as usual. We had mixed bruschetta and focaccia bread as an appetizer and then I had the grilled chicken, which came with veggies and a little salad. Was not in the mood for pasta. Christine and I split a fabulous tiramisu for dessert, which Luigi told us he had made himself. Then he brought us three shots of Limoncello to cap it all off. Perfetto!

After dinner Christine and I didn't feel up to going dancing, mainly because it was so cold and we were tired. Plus, I was feeling like crap. My lower back was killing me. Instead we went to an internet cafe so Christine could email a friend to put in her monthly schedule bids for her. After that we had a cup of tea at the Café de Paris and ogled at the handsome patrons. In the end we didn't get to bed until after 1am.

The next morning, after my meager night's sleep (I can only ever sleep four hours at night on my layovers in Europe—it's called jetlag), I went out and got some coffee and fresh pizza for breakfast while Christine was showering. Then we headed out to see the sights.

First we descended the Spanish Steps, then hit some stores (winter sales!), and then found our way through Rome's maze-like streets to the nearby Trevi Fountain.

As we were throwing our coins into the fountain, it began to snow.

"Wow, how neat... snow in Rome!" we gushed.

We were told later that it hadn't snowed there in fifteen years. Unfortunately, though, the snow quickly turned to rain—a cold, bitter rain that penetrated my bones. We stopped to shop, then to have a cappuccino, but the cold rain did not let up. We made our way to the Pantheon and the Piazza Navona, but by then I was so cold that we took a cab to the quaint area of Trastevere for lunch. I wasn't in the best of moods. (Neurosis #2: Tendency to bitch and moan when tired, hungry, PMSing, or any time things aren't going my way.) The damp cold and my damp mood persisted, so after a quick bite of pizza we grabbed a cab back to the hotel.

We had dinner that night with Ricky again. This time I let him pick the restaurant, which ended up being a mistake. The place he chose was a tourist trap with crappy food. I had some kind of pasta with radicchio and gorgonzola, but it tasted more like bitter purple cabbage and Roquefort in a watery sauce. Not a good combo. (Neurosis #3: Am a bit of a food snob.) In my opinion, if I can cook better than the chef can, the restaurant is not worth eating at.

During dinner I told Ricky that if I was not married in five years he would have to somehow, someway father my child.

"No problema, mi amorrrrr," he replied with a wink. "Consuela might be a little jealous, though."

The next morning bright and early, our crew van whisked us back to the airport and the moment I had been waiting for the whole trip finally arrived: it was time for my pre-flight catering check with Giancarlo, the hot caterer.

Giancarlo came back to the back galley just as we were getting ready to board. When he saw me, he shot me a little wink. I swiftly set my sugar cups aside and tried my best to get my flirt on. But that little wink was all I got. We checked the meal counts together and he left.

Oh, well. Too much of a player, anyway.

Christine had better luck than I did. She got a seat in business class going home, as she had coming over. I was so tired I was ready to fight her for that seat. (As usual, I had only slept four hours that night.)

Then, after the lunch service, she came back to the back galley to tell us that the man sitting next to her was trying to pick her up. He told her about his houses in the US and Canada. He described what he expected from a relationship and asked her what she expected. He bought two Hermes scarves from me and Ricky as we passed through the cabin selling Duty Free, just to impress her.

"But he didn't buy anything for me," she complained.

The old ladies working in business class found out that Christine's seatmate was a millionaire. We were all excited for her. She had found her coveted Sugar Daddy (every flight attendant's dream).

But Christine was not convinced.

"He's too old," she whined.

Christine is thirty. Her sugar daddy wanna-be was forty-nine.

Meanwhile, in the back galley an Italian priest was trying to pick up Ricky.

No one was trying to pick up the Queen of Sky. (Neurosis #4: Jealous of gay men and kept women.)

Well, that's the end of that story. I'm pooped and off to bed.

Buona notte!
—Queen of Sky

Down in the Dumps
Filed in LAYOVERS on Friday, 01/28

Between classes yesterday I called Christine. She didn't answer, so I left a message. She has yet to return my call. That's odd. I know she's off today, and she usually calls me back right away.

Then, this afternoon I checked my email and saw that my Czech ex-boyfriend Mitch had written me with some FABULOUS news—fabulous for *him*, that is...

> *Hi Elena!*
> *Just to let you know the happy news.*
> *I am happily married with beautiful Slovakian girl.*
> *I wish you all happiness that we have.*
> *Bye!*
> *Mitch & Susana*

Well, that made me depressed. I didn't even know he was engaged. Here I am in a dating slump, having just been through the worst year of my life (will get to that later), and I hear that my ex is living the good life. (Neurosis #5: Jealous of exes.)

Oh well, good for him. He was a nice guy, but I was too young (21) and we were just not meant for each other. We lived together for three years, which was plenty of time to discover that we had some major cultural and communication issues. But that's beyond the scope of this blog.

I'm going to go drown in self pity now. :-(

Becoming the Queen of Sky
Filed in MISC. on Saturday, 01/29

Mood: Better than yesterday.

I'm sure you all are curious to know what I did before I ascended to my celestial throne. Well, becoming the Queen of Sky took time and lots of hard work. (Yeah, right!) OK, actually it just took me a while to realize that it was my birthright to be a sky queen (and not just a sky waitress)...

Eight years ago I was working as a travel agent in Miami and dating my (now newly wed) ex-boyfriend Mitch. After two years as a travel agent, I was tired of the long hours and poor pay, so I decided to try for a more "glamorous" vocation.

Yep—you guessed it—my highest aspiration at the time was to be a flight attendant, aka stewardess, sky goddess, sky waitress, sky mattress, trolley dolly, etc.

I swiftly applied with a major airline and a couple of minor ones. The one that called me first was Reich International Airways, a charter based out of Miami. They needed German speakers. I had been an exchange student in Switzerland in high school and also worked in Germany for a stint, thus had a rusty knowledge of German.

I have to say, thinking back to my days at that crappy little carrier really makes me appreciate what I have now. In fact, compared to Reich, Anonymous International treats me like a queen—and that's not saying much!

Reich flew mostly L-1011s (wide-bodies configured with 345 coach seats) to Europe and sometimes South America. These were not long-range aircraft, so we had to stop in Gander, Newfoundland, to refuel each way to and from Europe. At Reich we didn't get crew breaks, so we worked long and hard. Plus, being a charter airline, there was never an empty seat on our flights. You really had to be an insomniac to work there.

I did mostly two-day layovers in Paris or five-day layovers in Frankfurt. But once I was sent to Gander, Newfoundland, to do turnarounds (over and back with no layover) to England and Ireland. They sent me for a few days but ended up extending my stay in Gander by about two weeks. That was the way things worked at Reich.

And when we got back to Miami, we were always supposed to check in with Crew Scheduling before going home. I learned fast to duck out before Scheduling saw me, otherwise they would send me out on another seven-day trip the next day. Once they called me at home when I had just gotten in from a trip to give me a four-day Paris trip the next day. I was so upset—I didn't even have 24 hours at home.

I started screening my calls after that.

The rule at Reich was that crewmembers could take any drinks off the aircraft for our layovers except alcohol. Of course that was the first thing we took! What else was there to do in Gander, Newfoundland, for two weeks? One could only eat so much salmon and see so many moose and mussel farms. Needless to say, Reich flight attendants were a misfit bunch of partiers and alcoholics, both young and old.

The heads of the In-flight department were all lesbians, so it was known that to get any decent trips you had to suck some chucha. I guess that's why I never got any good trips.

There were plenty of cheating dramas at Reich, too. A girlfriend of mine started dating a Reich pilot while he was still living with another Reich flight attendant. That was big gossip around the L-1011 galleys. When you only have 300 flight attendants (vs. 15,000-plus, like at my present employer), everyone knows everyone else's business and word travels fast.

That pilot ended up marrying my girlfriend after Reich shut down, but only under the condition that she quit flying. I tried to tell her that he had cheated on her on various occasions. But she married him anyway, and last I saw her, she had a belly as big as a watermelon.

I've heard and seen too many stories like that. Thus, I would never date a pilot. Will do more pilot-bashing in later entries. (Neurosis #6: Judgmental, tendency to stereotype.)

Anyhow, after I was there four months, Reich was grounded by the FAA. Apparently, they had been flying one of their airplanes across "the pond" (Atlantic) with a cracked windshield. There were various other infractions, but what it boiled down to was the company was shut down because the children of the deceased owner were disputing who should run the company, until one of them called the FAA and put a permanent end to the argument.

Or something like that.

There was a big expose on *60 Minutes* or *20/20*.

I didn't care. I just wanted my money. Only got a fraction of what they owed me for my last month of service from the bankruptcy proceedings.

But it was all for the better... I ended up getting hired immediately thereafter by my present airline. And it was here at Anonymous International that I took my proper place as the Queen of Sky. (Though sometimes it's hard to feel regal when I'm picking up people's trash.)

There are a few things I miss about Reich, like the excitement of never knowing where I might end up or for how long. I guess my most exotic layover was in Palermo, Sicily. Or Recife, Brazil—but that one was too short to do or see anything. In any case, the charter lifestyle was definitely not conducive to holding down a good relationship. I had just moved in with Mitch at the time, and I seriously doubt our relationship would have lasted as long as it did if Reich hadn't gone out of business.

Update
Filed in MISC. on Sunday, 01/30

The Queen of Sky's next trip is to Bogotá next Friday. It's a short layover, so I won't have time to get into trouble or get kidnapped.

Speaking of Colombia, when I was eighteen years old I had quite an adventure down there. I ended up driving halfway across the country with a Colombian named Juan and his two brothers.

But that was a long time ago. I don't do stupid things like that anymore.

BTW, Christine still hasn't returned my call. I think she's mad at me for some reason. (Neurosis #7/8: Tendency to overanalyze things/Irrational fear of abandonment.) Hmmm... I just hope that trip didn't ruin our friendship. Two years ago we went to Machu Picchu together and had a great time. But we were *both* on vacation then.

"I never take people on layovers with me," Ricky had told me during the flight back from Rome. "It's too much stress. And I need my beauty sleep."

I have to say I agree with him now.

Anyhow, I have enabled comments on my blog, so now you can tell me what you think about all my misadventures.

Until we meet again... happy blogging!
—Her Mile Highness the Queen of Sky

FEBRUARY

Back on the Market

Deep Stuff
Filed in MISC. on Tuesday, 02/01

Well, today is a sad day for me. It's my mother's birthday. In case I haven't mentioned it before, my mother died last year. And today I started going through some boxes of her stuff—stuff that I had packed and hauled back from Atlanta myself a couple of months back. And it made me depressed... especially the pictures.

Last March my mother retired from her job as a transcriptionist at an Atlanta hospital and began selling real estate. She was really excited about her new career. It was around that same time I first remember her mentioning to me that she had pulled something in her neck.

I had vacation in May and went to Spain so that I could brush up on my Spanish. While I was over there, my mother emailed me to tell me that the pain in her neck had gotten worse. She now thought it was a slipped disk. I didn't think anything of it. Told her to go to a chiropractor. Meanwhile I was having a great time in España, meeting men named Roberto, Diego, Jorge, etc.

At the end of May I finally made it to Atlanta from Madrid after a standby nightmare. I got bumped off Anonymous Airlines, forcing me to take a Spanish carrier to NY. That flight arrived late, leaving no way for me to get home to Texas that night. So it was either head to Atlanta or pay for a hotel in NY. I chose Atlanta.

When I got in around midnight, I hitched a ride with another passenger to my mother's place in Midtown. My mother said she couldn't pick me up, because it hurt her neck too much to drive.

The next day I drove her to the chiropractor. She was in a lot of pain, especially when sitting down. At one point I looked into her eyes and got scared. Her pupils were totally dilated.

That night I flew home to Texas. Then I returned to Madrid for work a couple of days later. When I turned on my cell phone upon arriving back in the US, there was a message from my mother.

She was in the hospital.

The pain in her neck had gotten to the point where she couldn't stand it anymore. She had asked her neighbor to drive her to the hospital. Once there, the doctors had done some x-rays and found that the excruciating pain was caused by a tumor pressing on her spinal cord.

It was stage IV cancer.

I saved the message in complete shock. It took a minute or two for the words to sink in. Then the devastation hit.

To make a long, sad story short, I ended up staying with my mother and taking care of her in Atlanta all summer. She had surgery to remove several vertebrae in her neck and then radiation treatments, but the oncologist recommended against chemo. When I finally asked for her prognosis in July, I was shocked to hear the doctor say six months or less.

My mother wanted more tests. The tests confirmed what the doctor said. The cancer continued to spread rapidly.

By the end of August, I was at the end of my rope—stressed out, flying full-time and receiving no help taking care of my mother. (I'm an only child and my parents divorced when I was five.) The pain in her neck returned, and she started taking morphine. It was then that she told me she didn't want to be alone when I went on trips. Since there was no one else who could stay with her and I couldn't afford to take indefinite time off, I had to put her in a hospice care center run by nuns.

My mother was in denial the whole time. She said she would get better and accused me of trying to throw her away when I put her in the hospice.

I didn't fly at all the first two weeks of September (took time off without pay) so that I could visit her every day.

She went downhill extremely rapidly. Apparently the cancer had spread to her brain. One day she could walk and talk and the next day she was practically a vegetable. All she could do at the end was moan.

On September 14, I was supposed to go to Barcelona but I called Crew Scheduling to tell them I couldn't make it. The doctor had told me the day before that my mother had less than five days to live. And when I looked at her in the bed, struggling so hard to breathe, her heart beating so rapidly, I knew I couldn't leave.

She died less than an hour later. I was at her bedside.

Looking through my mother's pictures today, I realized sadly how little quality time we had actually spent together over the years. There was one particularly poignant photo I couldn't put down: My mother stood on a tour boat in the middle of an icy lake, a huge glacier looming behind her. A beam of light shone down on her from above. She looked radiant. It was the year before she died. We were in Anchorage, Alaska—the only AIA layover she ever went on with me.

Well, writing this has made me sad, so I am going to say goodnight. I sure hope this is a better year.

New Year's Resolution
Filed in MISC. on Wednesday, 02/02

Hi, all. I hope yesterday's entry didn't depress you too much. This is a new year, and I have high hopes for it (despite my astrological forecast).

I spent New Year's Eve in the airport in Lima, Peru this year. Perhaps not the best place to start the year.

Then on January 1st, I was stuck in a hotel room in Bustling Base City watching the *Queer Eye for the Straight Guy* marathon. (Needed to catch up—don't have cable at home.)

After watching about three episodes, I realized I don't do anything they tell the scruffy straight guys to do, including using cleanser and moisturizer on my face.

Hence my New Year's Resolution is:

—To take better care of my skin—

I think I can handle that one.

No dieting, weight loss, or any of that crap. I prefer to fluctuate like the tides and the seasons.

Anyhow, after five episodes of *Queer Eye* I was all queered out. I will never have their fashion sense or design sense.

In fact, my taste is so bad that my gay friend Jesse, a fellow AIA flight attendant and Quirksville resident, said to me one day, "God Elena, you could almost be a lesbian!"

A Typical Day Going to Work for the Queen of Sky
Filed in COMMUTING on Friday, 02/04

I was thinking last night about how I think about my blog way too much. It's like my baby. And today I was very worried about it since I was leaving town. So here I am at a computer in the airport in Bustling Base City to check on my baby blog before my flight to Bogotá.

My "Day at Home with the Queen of Sky" was quite a popular entry, so I wrote this one on the plane this morning:

A Typical Day Going to Work with the Queen of Sky

6:00am: Alarm goes off.

6:10am: Crawl out of bed cursing (am not a morning person).

6:15am: Shower, dry hair, apply makeup to the beat of my samba CD.

6:45am: Look through closet to pick out uniform pieces with the least holes and stains in them.

7:00am: Sniff collection of black work shoes to find the least stinky pair.

7:05am: Shove as much crap as possible into my tote bag (it wouldn't close) and my roll-aboard, even though I'm only leaving on a two-day trip.

7:10am: Look at clock—realize that I am running late, as usual.

7:15am: Water one-and-only plant, turn down heat, shut off lights, run out door with bags in tow.

7:25am: Chuckle when I read "Drop Bush Not Bombs" bumper sticker on a car in front of me on my drive to the airport.

7:45am: Reach airport via employee parking lot bus. For the first time in months, actually check in on time for my commuter flight :-)

7:50am: Highlight of my day: pass through airport security.

7:55am: Purchase and devour potato, egg, and cheese breakfast taco on way to gate.

8:00am: Greet gate agent and pilot commuters waiting at gate.

8:15am: Board commuter flight bound for Bustling Base City.

8:20am: Switch from my first class seat to a whole row in the back of coach, to the surprise of my first class seatmate. (A little airplane math: three coach seats are greater than or equal to one domestic first class seat.)

8:40am: Put down notebook, lie down for a nap in my three seats.

Flight Blog: Bogotá
Filed in FLIGHT BLOGS on Saturday, 02/05

On the way to Bogotá yesterday, the Queen of Sky was working in the back of the 757 with a slightly bitchy Brazilian queen whom we shall call Silvio. Silvio's motto regarding passengers is, "This is *my* house and you are *my* guests." (In other words, SIT DOWN AND SHUT UP!)

After the service, Silvio and I were gossiping in the back galley about other flight attendants. He told me that another Brazilian guy we both knew had had a sex change operation and was now going to fly as a woman.

He had me going for a good ten minutes.

"Just kidding!" he finally squealed, getting a big kick out of himself.

Actually, I have flown with a transsexual flight attendant before. I just thought he/she was a big girl like me. It wasn't until after the trip that I heard what his/her receding hairline and fake breasts were really all about. (He/she always wore a scarf, so his/her Adam's apple was not visible.)

The Queen of Sky is so clueless sometimes.

Anyhow, I hate the 757. I always hit my head on the video screens, and passengers always get mad at us because the overhead bins fill up within ten minutes of boarding. Especially on Latin America flights, where passengers try to bring on everything but the kitchen sink... well, sometimes that, too.

And the Queen of Sky, not being particularly empathetic, somehow is always the one who has to rip the overstuffed bag from the innocent passengers' trembling clutches and drag it to the front door to check it.

I'll have you know I have never won any customer service awards. In fact, I am that flight attendant you asked for a cup of water on your flight to Europe last summer... the one you're still waiting for.

Sorry, I have a very short memory.

There have been studies about the effects of high altitude radiation on the body wherein they have found that flying shrinks your brain.

Plus, the Queen of Sky is so tired from commuting to work at the crack of dawn the day of her trip that she cannot be bothered with your frivolous requests.

Anyhow, back to my trip. Our hotel van in Bogotá had bulletproof windows. And when we arrived at the hotel, a dog sniffed our bags for explosives. Made me feel very secure. (Not!) Actually, I'm surprised we don't have an armed escort there, like we do in Lima.

On the way back from Bogotá today, the Queen of Sky was sitting on the so-called Sharon Stone jumpseat in the mid-galley area. The jumpseat got its name from the fact that you are facing the first row of coach passengers, and any slight movement will give those passengers a free show if you are wearing a skirt.

And of course the Queen of Sky was wearing a skirt.

In the first row, directly in front of my jumpseat, sat a redneck wearing a trucker hat that read "Alabama."

He had raised a fuss during boarding when there was no room directly over his head for his bags. I told him there was plenty of space in the back.

"You know how it is when you're tryin' to get off," he said.

I did not like his tone.

"Oh, well," I replied unconcerned, turning back to the boarding door.

Julie, the girl working with me, was more empathetic and put his bag in first class for him.

I was going to let the bags incident slide, but then, during the flight, I caught said redneck trying to look up my skirt. I thought it was my imagination, but Silvio and Julie said they noticed it, too. Not only that, he was constantly grabbing his "goods."

Silvio said he had copped a feel of Mr. Redneck's "goods" when he passed him in the aisle on the way to the lav. He had been checking out Mr. Redneck's goods since the beginning of the flight. I told Silvio he could have him. The Queen of Sky does not like white trash.

I was going to say something rather politically incorrect here about the reason gringo males travel alone to South America (in my experience, it is usually to find hookers or pick up their mail- or internet-order brides). But then, after the flight yesterday, I saw said redneck in the crew and diplomat line in US Immigration, and overheard him declare to the crewmembers in front of him, "Ah'm a *dip-lo-mat*."

If that is what US diplomats look and act like, I think our country is in trouble. But then again, we're *already* in trouble with the world community... but I'm not going to go there. This is a *strictly* non-political blog.

Hasta luego...
—Queen of Sky

P.S. Thanks to each of my five commenters for all of your positive words! Glad you enjoy my blog!

Back on the Market
Filed in MEN on Sunday, 02/06

Hi, all. Here's an interesting and little-known fact about the Queen of Sky: she's into internet dating.

In fact, I've been a fan of internet dating since long before it was mainstream and acceptable. I have even been known to internet-date on my layovers.

A couple of years back, I was flying to Santiago, Chile, almost every weekend. Thirty-six hours is a long time to kill, and one can only drink so much wine and eat so much sea bass. Plus, I had no social life at home, so I figured I might as well have one on my layovers. After a quick Web search, I found a Latin American dating site (RedCupido.com) and added my profile with a picture. (Slightly altered version follows...)

Name: Queen of Sky
Sex: Not Lately
Age: 29
Sign: Scorpio with Sagittarius rising
City where you live: Quirksville, Texas
Country where you live: USA
Height: Taller than most Latin men, i.e., 6 feet (183 cm), 6'3" in heels.
Weight: Fluctuates wildly
Eye color: Grey
Hair color: Blond (natural)
Present occupation: Celestial royalty
How do you describe yourself? I'm a fun-loving and easygoing American flight attendant who flies to South America often. Am in desperate need of a handsome gentleman to show me around Santiago. ;-)
Hobbies: sleeping, eating, dancing, traveling, blogging, cyberdating.
Describe the person you are looking for: Romantic, stable, a gentleman, intelligent, generous, honest, fun-loving, tall, dark and handsome, car owner, willing to show a naïve six-foot tall blond flight attendant around his city.
Type of relationship you are seeking: Friendship and maybe more ;-)

Adding the picture to the profile was a mistake, though, because I got way too many replies. So many that I couldn't answer them all. So, I took the picture off.

At the same time, I decided to change my city of residence to read Santiago, because as a resident of the US, I was getting emails from large numbers of guys who just wanted a ticket to the States.

When men responded to my profile, I would immediately check their profile to see if they met my minimum age and height requirements (age: 25-40; height: at least 5'10"). If not, they got automatically deleted. If they *did* meet my standards, though, I would swiftly request a picture. If they didn't send one, they got deleted, too. The mistake the Queen of Sky made was judging candidates based upon one lone photo.

I had five cyber dates in Santiago. There would have been more, but I quit while I was ahead (or behind, in this case). Each time one of my dates showed up in the lobby of my hotel, I was unfailingly disappointed.

A couple of them had really bad teeth. (They weren't smiling in their pictures.)

One, I'm pretty sure, was on drugs.

Another was way too short. Definitely lied about his height. Not to mention the fact that Queen of Sky's crew, who was seated in the lobby at the time of his arrival, had an adverse reaction to him.

"He looked retarded!" Erica, a Chilean girl on the crew, exclaimed after I quickly got rid of my date. I sent him home to change and then avoided his calls for the rest of the layover.

Most of these guys were poor students with no wheels. No good for a layover man. The Queen of Sky needed someone to take her OUT. So, finally (actually sooner rather than later), I abandoned my internet man-hunt in Chile.

Well, now, after an extended dry spell (haven't dated anyone since before my mom got sick last year), I have decided to try dating on layovers again. But *certainly* not in Chile. This month I've managed to get two trips to Buenos Aires, Argentina, on my schedule. Since I've only been to B.A. a couple of times, I don't know my way around well. I *definitely* need a guide. Accordingly, I've once again put my profile on Red Cupido, this time changing my "city of residence" to Buenos Aires.

Time to sit back and wait for the flypaper to catch some flies....

Daily Horoscope

Filed in MISC. on Sunday, 02/06

Hmmm. After I posted that last entry, I checked my daily horoscope on AstroWizards.com and got a little concerned. This aspect was mentioned in my forecast report, too. I hope it's not an omen for my newest foray into online dating...

Unusual Encounters

Today you could find yourself encountering unusual or nontraditional social contacts or romantic situations. Technology may play a role in initiating these encounters. This could take the form of a strong and unique attraction between you and a stranger, but you may be torn between maintaining your independence and succumbing to your desires. Any relationships that begin under this influence are likely to be volatile and/or short-lived.

Aspect: Venus trine Uranus
Period of Influence: 2/05–2/07
Courtesy of Astro Wizards

I especially loved the "and/or" at the end... uggh!

Caught One
Filed in Life of Leisure on Monday, 02/07

Double hmmm. Today I got an email from a cyber-suitor in Buenos Aires. He claims to be an Italian engineer by the name of Maurizio.

I immediately checked his Red Cupido profile to make sure that he met the minimum requirements. He did, so I quickly requested pictures. The Queen of Sky does not waste time with these things. To my surprise, a couple hours later there was a whole photo album from my cyber Romeo.

I opened the album eagerly and was greeted by images of a 30-something Italian-looking man with a slight receding hairline. He looks average—above average, actually. Medium brown hair, physically fit (a plus, since the Queen of Sky does not like fat guys), and a certain twinkle of intrigue in his eyes—OK, maybe that last bit is just wishful thinking on my part. ;-)

I emailed him back and told him I would be in Buenos Aires on the 10th and 11th to see if he wanted to meet. I like to try to meet my internet dates ASAP to see if we have any real-life chemistry. Have been disappointed too many times. Not that I have any big expectations for this guy—just want somebody normal to show me around.

Anyway, keep your fingers crossed for me and hope that my horoscope is wrong!

My Skills
Filed in ABOUT ME on Wednesday, 02/09

I'm presently in the flight attendant lounge in Bustling Base City, waiting for my flight to Argentina. Am bored...

THINGS I HAVE SKILLS AT:

Cooking
Dancing
Sleeping
Eating
Certain sexual positions

THINGS I HAVE *NO* SKILLS AT:

Cleaning
Brown-nosing
Butt-kissing
Decorating
Picking out clothes
Shopping
My job
Diplomacy
Any sexual positions where I have to do some work

I guess I have a lot less skills than I thought! :-O

Buenos Aires
Filed in LAYOVERS on Saturday, 02/12

Well, the Queen of Sky got back from Buenos Aires this morning. It was a pretty uneventful nine-hour flight today. But uneventful is good in this business. And we had three-hour rest breaks in flight, which made it all the better. :-)

Anyhow, the layover in B.A. was interesting, to say the least...

Thursday, upon arriving at the Hotel Imperial in Buenos Aires, I called my internet date, Maurizio, to see if he wanted to meet up the next day. He didn't answer, so I left a message.

After making this important call, I took my well-deserved post-all-nighter nap. (The Queen of Sky needs a good five hours snooze time after an all-nighter.) Then I showered and made a quick supermarket run. Needed to pick up a few things for my layover munchies, plus, of course, some fabulously cheap Argentine wine.

Maurizio returned my call that evening, just as I was about to go meet my crew for a little wine tasting in the captain's room. He explained in his broken Spanish that he had been on his sailboat earlier in the day.

"Oh, that's nice," I replied, wondering if he was just saying that to impress me.

"Yes, I go sail when I can."

"So would you like to meet tomorrow for lunch?" the Queen of Sky inquired, not wanting to beat around the bush. The crew party was calling my name, after all.

"Yes, that's fine."

"Like noon?"

"Bene. OK." He sounded eager to please—a definite plus.

"Good, so why don't you call me when you get to the lobby of the Imperial and then I will come down."

"You come down to the lobby? OK. Va bene. Until then."

"OK, until tomorrow noon. Call my room when you get to the hotel," I repeated to confirm.

When I hung up I realized that I forgot to tell him that there were two Imperials in Buenos Aires.

Oh well, he'll figure it out, I thought.

The next day I went downstairs to look for my date, since it was a little past noon and I hadn't heard from him. On the way down I caught a glimpse of myself in the elevator mirrors and noted one of the professional aviator's occupational hazards: perma-bags under the eyes.

I look like an insomniac. Lovely.

The Queen of Sky entered the glistening lobby just in time to witness a flustered, slightly balding Italian man rush through the revolving door.

I hoped this was Maurizio. If it was, he looked better than in his pictures—now that's a first! In fact, he reminded me vaguely of a young Marlon Brando.

He walked directly toward me.

"Reina de los Cielos (Queen of the Skies)?"

"Sí."

"Maurizio Mascherato. Pleasure to meet you." Sweat was dripping from his forehead. He quickly wiped it away in an effort to compose himself.

I put out my hand for a formal shake. Maurizio ignored the hand and planted a kiss on my cheek. I noted that he was an inch or two shorter than me but quickly flashed back to all of the tall A-holes that I had dated. Plus, I was wearing heels, so I had to cut him a little slack.

"I'm sorry I'm late. I went to the other Imperial first." He seemed genuinely apologetic.

"Oops, that was my fault," the Queen of Sky confessed.

Maurizio was very courteous. I could tell he had class. And, even more importantly, he had a car!

So off we went.

He took me on a quick tour of B.A., including Evita's tomb, which I had requested to see. Then he took me to lunch at the yacht club. I was impressed.

Finally, an internet date that's not a loser!

During lunch, Maurizio told me he was working for a huge international diplomacy and aid organization (whose name I won't mention here). He had been dispatched to Argentina after the economic crisis to monitor things.

The Queen of Sky found Maurizio strangely and mysteriously attractive. After all, he is not the normal type I go for. Normally I go for sleazy Latin men—the sleazier, the better. Plus I typically require that my dates be at least tall enough to see me eye to eye.

"When are you coming back?" Maurizio inquired when he dropped me off back at the hotel.

"Next Wednesday."

"Oh, I will be in Washington next week."

Sure, I thought. *I guess he's not interested.*

But I was wrong.

When I arrived home this afternoon, I quickly checked my emails before crashing. Surprisingly, there was a message from Maurizio in my inbox:

Ciao Reina,
How are you? How was your trip back to the USA? I enjoyed meeting you and look forward to seeing you again soon. Did you like me?
Kisses,
Maurizio

Short and to the point. The Queen of Sky likes a man who knows what he wants.

Today
Filed in LIFE OF LEISURE on Sunday, 02/13

Howdy, all! Just another day in the "Life of Leisure" today. Around 2pm, I finally pried myself up from my computer, looked outside and realized the sun was shining and it was a beautiful day here in Texas. So I went down to the lake to have a row. I know I'm slow, but today a canoe passed me as I was leisurely rowing along. That's pretty bad!

This evening I went to the student clinic at my acupuncture school. I feel like I am coming down with a cold, so my classmate, whom I shall call

Steve, stuck some needles in my sinuses and in my chin, hands and ankles. Then he gave me a massage, which I rather liked. Steve seems to always end up being my partner in the Chinese massage class we have together. I am kind of attracted to him, but he is married with two kids, and I DON'T GO THERE!

Hmmm... anyway, Maurizio and I have been emailing back and forth since I got back from B.A. We'll see where this goes. Am leaning toward a "let's just be friends" approach, since I am pessimistic about all relationships nowadays.

Speaking of relationships, yesterday I tried to contact Christine by both phone *and* email. She hasn't responded to either. Am upset about that. I wish she would at least tell me what I did.

V-Day
Filed in MEN on Monday, 02/14

Happy Valentine's Day, everybody!!!

I received a very sweet e-card from Maurizio this morning. There was a bouquet of flowers and a big smiling cupid. It was very cute. I am going to try to get another Buenos Aires trip next month, since Maurizio said he would be out of town most of the rest of February.

Anyway, today I'm driving down to San Antonio to see my father, who is in town from back East for a music convention.

Lots of love,
—Q of S

Over My Head
Filed in LIFE OF LEISURE on Tuesday, 02/15

OK, so the Queen of Sky just spent a small fortune on a new used Honda CRV. Have been spending money (that I do not have) like water lately. Bought some EXPENSIVE new furniture last month.

As soon as I can figure out how, I am going to put a PayPal link on my blog to accept donations to my "car and furniture fund" from my generous and undemanding benefactors.

What I really need is a GAY SUGAR DADDY.

Please forward this to anyone you know with those credentials. Thanks in advance!

Life of Leisure
Filed in LIFE OF LEISURE on Tuesday, 02/15

BTW, the Queen of Sky was supposed to go to Argentina today but got a paid trip drop. In other words, Scheduling dropped the trip from my schedule and I still got paid for it! (We get three such elective paid days off a year.) Therefore, I can continue my Life of Leisure uninterrupted for a while longer. Maurizio wasn't going to be in Buenos Aires this week, anyway. Plus, this saves me from missing my acupuncture classes two weeks in a row.

It's a good thing I don't have to fly very often, otherwise I might really dislike my job. :-P

Next trip: Lima on the 26th—which means I have over a week off! Woohoo!!!

A Riddle
Filed in LIFE OF LEISURE on Thursday, 02/17

Riddle: How many flight attendants does it take to hook up a DVD player?
Answer: Three, plus one engineer.

The Queen of Sky bought a new TV and DVD player last week, but it has been just sitting on the floor in her living room, since her techie neighbor told her she needed to buy some cables to hook it up. Well, I finally got the cables and then could not figure out how to hook them up. I now had the cables I had just bought plus the cables that came with the DVD player.

When the Queen of Sky's friend Monica came over the other night, she took one look at all those cables and exclaimed (in her little tiny voice): "We'd better not try it, because something might blow up!"

Monica is a cute little redheaded flight attendant with that itsy bitsy voice that men go nuts for. She looks about 25 but is actually 40-something. (I'm envious!)

The next day, the Queen of Sky's friend Kim the Fireball (like Monica and Queen of Sky, another AIA flight attendant who prefers to reside in Quirksville rather than Bustling Base City) came over and after various attempts to hook the TV to the DVD/VCR and many a foul word, there was still no picture on the screen. So, we gave up.

Finally, last night the Queen of Sky's lawyer/engineer friend Victor the Jamaican Sensation came over. He took one look at all those cables, plugged in the ones I had bought, and it was good to go.

That is, in my experience, the only thing men are good for—hooking up cables and fixing things around the house. After my ex and I split, of course everything in my apartment started breaking... the doorbell, the garbage disposal, etc. I'll have you know that most of those things are still broken today, some five years later.   :-O

My Skills 2
Filed in ABOUT ME on Sunday, 02/20

MORE SKILLS THAT I HAVE:

>Foreign Language
>Blogging (newly discovered!)
>Coke-can opening

MORE SKILLS I DO *NOT* HAVE:

>Hairstyling
>Customer service
>Announcement-making
>Organization

Mood: BLOATED
Filed in LIFE OF LEISURE on Tuesday, 02/22

Last night the Queen of Sky went to dinner with some friends. I slurped down a Mexican martini and gobbled a basket of chips or two before dinner arrived.

A chile relleno and an enchilada later, I was positively stuffed. But this did not stop me from inviting my friends over to my place for a slice of my freshly baked cake.

The only person who took me up on my offer was Monica, as the rest were too full, painfully rubbing their stomachs.

Anyway, she followed me home in my new CRV and I directed her to park in front of my building, as my two cars are now taking up my two spaces. (Gotta sell my old piece o' junk.)

When we got inside, I eagerly sliced into the vanilla cake iced with Peruvian dulce de leche and almonds and filled with cherries and chocolate. After a few bites of the rich cake, however, we both felt like were going to throw up. But that didn't stop us from making out on my new sofa. She stuck her tongue in my mouth, and it still tasted of chocolate and caramel...

JUST KIDDING!   :-P

That was for all you guys out there with your lesbian flight attendant fantasies. ;-)

Monica left after eating most of her cake, and I then sat in front of my computer trying to digest and log onto my blog for TWO HOURS!!! (Apparently BlogAcres' server was down.)

Finally I gave up and went to bed.

Slutgirl's Relationship Question
Filed in MISC. on Friday, 02/25

Slutgirl posed this question on her blog last week:

Is it better to...

    a) Have a relationship in which you are totally secure, yet have grown bored and no longer feel any passion...

  or

    b) Take the bad that comes with the good, to put up with the heartache and BS that seems to come as part of the package in being head-over-heels in love?

A happy medium would be nice.

Queen of Sky's answer:

    c) None of the above.
       The Queen of Sky prefers to be alone and happy rather than with someone and miserable.

To fill the relationship void, you can either surround yourself with:

    a) gay men
    b) cats
    c) inflatable men
    d) boxes of bonbons and petit fours

  or

    e) all of the above

On the Job
Filed in MY LIFE IN THE AIRPORT on Saturday, 02/26

The Queen of Sky is finally back at work today.

Am sitting in the flight attendant lounge in Bustling Base City trying to covertly write this entry.

looks around to see if anyone is watching her

It's Saturday, so there aren't too many old bags in the lounge today. All of the old bags like to fly weekdays.

Anyway, my head is presently spinning, as I got up at 6am today to come to work and have been sitting here for the last hour putting swap requests into the computer for next month. Tonight is the first round of swaps. Most likely after spending an hour putting in those damn swaps, I won't get anything anyway.

My schedule is OK for next month—I have a Lima and a Phoenix/San Juan trip—but I need to swap off of all three of my one-day trips, as they are very inconvenient for out-of-base commuting. Also, I would like to get at least one Buenos Aires trip so that Maurizio and I can finally have our second date.

Well, I have to go now and put on my lesbian prison guard uniform and grab a bite to eat before briefing.

Am going to Lima today to get my furry legs waxed and scruffy hair trimmed (and eat a ceviche in between).

Hasta la vista!
—Q of S

Flight Blog: Lima
Filed in FLIGHT BLOGS on Monday, 02/28

Well, the Queen of Sky had a successful trip to Lima. The crew was nice and we had an uneventful trip down. The flight was not full, which is almost unheard of nowadays. Everyone on the crew seemed to be coming down with something, though.

One F/A (flight attendant) had a terrible headache, so I offered her some reiki (energy healing). I stood over her in the mid galley with my hands on her head for about fifteen minutes, to the confused looks of passers-by. Afterward she said the sinus pressure in her forehead was much relieved.

In any case, let me say something here about crew punch. On South America and sometimes Spain trips, it's traditional to have "crew punch" (aka jungle juice, sangria, etc.) on the crew bus from the airport to the hotel upon arrival in the layover city. As one of the designated Spanish speakers on the crew, Queen of Sky took it upon herself to perform the miraculous feat of turning water to wine (punch) this trip. At the end of the flight, she deplaned with two large water bottles full of the mysterious red liquid.

Some crews have even been known to hold "airplane sangria contests," where flight attendants in the front, mid *and* aft galleys make a batch of the potent poison to later be judged on the way to the hotel. Actually, this rarely happens at my airline, but I understand from my friend Kim that it was quite a frequent occurrence at the original Pan Am, where she got her start.

Oh, the other thing I wanted to mention from that flight to Lima was the Queen of Sky's announcements. The Queen of Sky, as you may or may not know, is a Spanish speaker at her airline. But she's not a great public speaker and sometimes gets flustered while making PAs (public address announcements).

This flight was one of those times.

Upon landing in Lima, the Queen of Sky did not have her PA book out and consequently garbled half of her Spanish announcements.

Oh well, I'm sure they got the picture.

"Damas y caballeros, bienvenidos al tercer mundo. Esperamos que sus maletas llegaron tambien...yaddah, yaddah, garble, garble...La Reina de los Cielos y toda la tripulación les agradecen volar con Anonymous International Airlines."

Well, I will write about my layover tomorrow. Right now I have to put in for more swaps since I got none the first round. Am keeping my fingers crossed for a Buenos Aires trip to come my way...

MARCH

*The Fly Girl and
the Man of Mystery*

A Typical Lima Layover
Filed in LAYOVERS on Tuesday, 03/01

This is about how the Queen of Sky's Lima layover went this week:

Sat. 11:45pm: Depart Lima airport for hotel, pass jungle juice around the crew bus.

Sun. 1am: Crawl into bed at my hotel for the night.

Sun. 5am: Awaken to the sound of neighbor who is either talking loudly on the phone, singing, yelling, or all of the above.

Sun. 5:30am: Go back to sleep.

Sun. 6am: Awaken again after dreaming that my loud neighbor is trying to get into my room. Actually, he was trying to get into *his* room.

Sun. 9:45am: My alarm goes off, awakening me from a SOUND sleep. Shower and rush to get ready before breakfast buffet ends at 10:30am.

Sun. 10:15am: Queen of Sky joins the rest of her crew (minus pilots) at breakfast. The free breakfast buffet is one of the perks of this layover. It features Peruvian tamales, miso soup, vegetable tempura, various fruits and pastries, fresh juices, and omelets made to order. My crew said the pilots were there earlier. Normally if the pilots don't show up for the free breakfast (remember, pilots are notoriously cheap), it can only mean one thing in a South American country: they were at the hooker bar WAY too late the night before.

Sun. 10:50am: After gorging herself at breakfast, Queen of Sky makes arrangements to meet some of her crew at 4pm for a late lunch.

Sun. 11:00am: Go downstairs to salon to have my hair cut. Show hairdresser pic from *Celebrity Hairstyles* magazine. Actually, I wanted to bring my Valerie's Secret catalog, but figured my fine hair would never hold a sexy lingerie-model hairstyle.

Sun. 11:55am: Depart salon with new do. It is cute, but the Queen of Sky is still adjusting to it. Total spent: $15, *including* tip!!!

Sun. 12:15pm: Enter Sofia Bubenstein salon for leg waxing.

Sun. 12:20pm: Wince in pain and bite lip as legs are waxed. Total spent: $20.

Sun. 1pm: Hit supermarket. Buy Peruvian wine and tamale, plus plenty of fruit to eat on the flight home.

Sun. 2pm: After returning to hotel to drop off groceries and "freshen up," head back out in the beautiful sunny 80-something-degree day for a walk down to the mall overlooking the ocean.

Sun. 2:30pm: Have chair massage at the mall: 10 minutes for 10 soles (about $3). What a deal! Purchase and eat slightly stale churro (Peruvian doughnut) on the way out of the mall. Walk back to hotel scoping out the chifas (Peruvian Chinese restaurants) on the way. My crew had been talking about eating at a chifa for lunch later.

Sun. 3:30pm: Run into one of my crew at computer downstairs. He says he will not be joining me for late lunch.

Sun. 4:05pm: Finally one person from Queen of Sky's crew shows up just to say that she is still full from the breakfast buffet and will not be joining me for lunch. A little disgruntled, the Queen of Sky heads to *chifa* to dine alone.

Sun. 4:20pm: Queen of Sky eats Peruvian Chinese food. First course: Some kind of gingery noodle soup. Second: Fried fish filet with rice and french fries (should have ordered the fried rice.) Third: Some kind of fruit salad, probably out of a can. Verdict: The soup was good, might come back to try the fried rice. Total spent: $6 (an expensive lunch in Peru).

Sun. 5:30pm: Head back to hotel for nap before pick-up.

Sun. 10pm: Wake-up call.

Sun. 11:05pm: Have coffee and cookies downstairs with crew before loading on crew bus to airport.

Mon. 1am: Depart Lima for USA. Spend the whole six-and-a-half-hour flight exchanging girlie magazines with the crew, gossiping, drinking jasmine tea, and just TRYING TO STAY AWAKE! We don't get a crew rest on this flight (officially), because it is less than eight hours. It is one of the worst flights in the AIA system for every flight attendant's worst enemy: FATIGUE. (Oh yeah, I forgot to mention that we served the passengers at some point, too.)

Mon. 7:40am: Arrive in USA, head straight for crew lounge, and take nap before catching a 1pm flight home.

Mon. 7pm: Queen of Sky is still recovering from losing a night's sleep.

P.S. Good news, all! I got a trip to Buenos Aires for this weekend, and Maurizio has confirmed that he will be in town. ;-) Stay tuned...

Misc. Notes
Filed in LIFE OF LEISURE on Thursday, 03/03

I decided to skip my Chinese massage class today, because I realized today is March 3rd, and I have not paid my bills. Am leaving tomorrow for three and a half days, and my three days off just seem to have flown by. The only thing I have accomplished thus far is my laundry (yesterday) and making scones (Tuesday). I just did three hours of Qigong (like Tai Chi), and it's nice to go to that massage class afterward and get worked on a little, but today I just have too much to do to get ready for my Buenos Aires trip tomorrow.

Meanwhile, yesterday I received an email from that mysterious Italian engineer/diplomat, Maurizio. He says he has a surprise planned for me. Hmm. Am skeptical, but we shall see...

Great Second Impression
Filed in LAYOVERS on Monday, 03/07

Well, the Queen of Sky got home this morning from Argentina exhausted, as usual.

All I can say about my second date with Maurizio is WOW!

He picked Queen of Sky up at the Imperial on Friday night, presenting her with a delicate bouquet of multi-colored roses.

"Roses for a rose," he said with a little chivalrous bow. (10 points, plus 5 for flattery.)

Our first stop was the marina, where he took me to see his sailboat. Very nice. We shared a glass of champagne onboard. And he didn't try anything. (30 points—10 for the boat, 5 for the champagne, and 15 for being a gentleman.)

Then he took me to his apartment where he presented me with a printed menu of the four-course meal that he was going to prepare for me. (Another 10 points—nice surprise.) At the bottom of the menu, he had signed his name as "Count Maurizio Mascherato." Queen of Sky was needless to say impressed—could he be a real count?! (If true, plus 50 points.) I tried to act blasé about it, though, pretending that I didn't see his title.

Anyhow, after a fabulous dinner and more champagne and then wine—Italian, of course—Maurizio was a complete gentleman and asked me if I wanted him to take me back to the hotel. The Queen of Sky declined with a wink, and a passionate, though slightly awkward and somewhat sloppy make-out session on his sofa followed...

There was the clumsy first kiss, during which Queen of Sky could not help but giggle (it was the champagne!); then my nervous admission that I was on my cycle, so there would definitely be no panty-prying or other below-the-belt antics. The latter statement was followed by more giggling, this time from Maurizio. Luckily, the rest went quite smoothly. ;-) (Bonus points.)

Screw "just friends" ... must try to get another trip to B.A. ASAP!

Déjà Vu
Filed in MY LIFE IN THE AIRPORT on Wednesday, 03/09

Here I am again in the international flight attendant lounge in Bustling Base City. The Queen of Sky is surrounded by a bunch of dried up old southern belles who are flying their weekday Europe trips today.

My back is bothering me today. I think it was that three-hour Qigong workout yesterday. I have been having various health problems since my mother died last summer and lately it has been my kidneys. The good news is I can get some antibiotics at the pharmacy in Lima as soon as I get in (I think the pharmacy next to the hotel is open 24 hours). Normally I would go to my naturopath or acupuncturist or reiki practitioner, but the Queen of Sky is flying for six days straight now, so all that is out of the question this week.

Not much else to report here. A supervisor is standing behind me so I have to go...

Lima

Filed in LAYOVERS on Thursday, 03/10

Hello, all, or Hola a todos, as they say down here...

I am here in Lima at the hotel. Just went to the pharmacy next door, and they gave me some antibiotics and recommended that I also purchase some cat's claw (uña de gato, a Peruvian herb) for urinary tract inflammation. I opted to get the tea form at the supermarket, which is where I am headed next.

Last night when we got to the hotel, I joined the crew for a drink at the bar on the fifth floor. Probably not the best idea for my kidneys. In any case, one of the girls on the crew (woman, actually—she is 49 and has a teenage daughter) showed up with her Peruvian "friend" who is 29 and looks about 15. Anyway, good for her. If she is happy, the Queen of Sky says go for it and have fun! Like Demi Moore and Ashton Coochie or whatever his name is.

The problem is girlfriend is talking about trying to bring Boy Toy back to the States. The Queen of Sky has been trying to talk her out of this and will continue to do so tonight on the six-and-a-half-hour flight home. (The Queen of Sky tried to import a Spanish boy toy once, and it was a *complete* disaster!)

The pilots did not show up last night for a drink. A couple of the flight attendants said they overheard them planning to meet downstairs, which of course meant they were headed for Aguardiente, the hooker bar. Surprise, surprise.

Apparently a cargo airline pilot died at our hotel a couple of months ago after popping some Viagra and picking up a hooker at Aguardiente. Hope he had a smile on his face.

Nelly the Panamanian Powerhouse/Party Animal, the other Spanish speaker on my crew, said he died in room 1010, which was another girl on the crew's room last night. Needless to say, that girl was a little freaked.

OK, well now I am blabbing. Need to get going, am meeting Nelly at 2pm for lunch at the Queen of Sky's favorite cevichería on the planet: Alfresco.

Hasta lueguito,
—Q of S

Feel Like Crap
Filed in MISC. on Friday, 03/11

8:25am

Queen of Sky just got in from Lima and is heading to her commuter hotel now here in Bustling Base City because she has to go to Phoenix tomorrow. Will have to sell food on that flight... should be loads of fun. *sarcastic smirk*

Am going to go pass out now...

In the Airport Again
Filed in MY LIFE IN THE AIRPORT on Saturday, 03/12

Here I am again in the airport in Bustling Base City. Yesterday morning after coming in from Lima, I went to my commuter hotel where I slept until 6pm. Then I caught up on all of my favorite cable shows (*Food 911, Queer Eye, The Anna Nicole Smith Show,* etc.), since I don't have cable at home. Stayed up far too late watching TV and then tossed and turned all night on rock-hard bed at Dumpy Commuter Hotel. Queen of Sky suspects that the last guest in her room had set up a meth lab in the bathroom, as there were some strange stains in the toilet.

This morning, for some reason, I woke up at 8:30am. I didn't have to be back at the airport until 3:15pm, so I decided to call downstairs to the front desk to request a late checkout.

"Twelve o'clock," the desk clerk stated firmly.

"Fine," said the Queen of Sky.

I was almost back to sleep when the maid knocked on the door around 9:30am. I didn't answer.

Fifteen minutes later, the phone rang. It was the front desk. They wanted to know if Her Mile Highness would be checking out today.

"Yes, they already told me I could check out late," a perturbed Queen of Sky replied.

And of course I never got back to sleep.

Anyway, I only have one leg to Phoenix today and then two legs tomorrow to San Juan, so I guess I will survive. Although I have to sell food on the Phoenix legs... :-P Oh JOY!

Luckily, I had brought some Peruvian food with me to heat up in my room for dinner last night. I had rice and lima beans and a tamale. Unfortunately, though, I had claimed my avocados, one of which was perfectly ripe, when I came in yesterday, and the Customs agents subsequently nabbed them from me. Should have just smuggled them in. :-(

However, last night when I was craving fresh fruit, I realized I had forgotten about the Texas pink grapefruit in my tote bag. Good thing Customs didn't screen my bag.

Anyway, gotta go—nosy people around... don't want them reading over my shoulder. :-P

The Queen of Sky Sells Food
Filed in FLIGHT BLOGS on Monday, 03/14

Some of you may have heard about the recent initiative to sell food on board certain airlines' domestic flights. Well, the Queen of Sky had the *privilege* to work two of these flights this weekend. And let me just say one thing about food for sale...

IT SUCKS!!!

Yesterday on the way to Phoenix on a 767 (widebody), we were only staffed with three in the back to sell food to some 180 passengers. A girl from the front had to come back to help us. It was a disaster. First, the Queen of Sky's handheld cashier was not accepting credit cards, then people kept asking the Queen of Sky for things that were not on her cart, and she had to subsequently drag her HEAVY cart back to the galley to fetch them. Not to mention the brake on the cart was not working, so the cart was rather cumbersome.

At one point, a passenger complained angrily to the Queen of Sky as follows:

"How many more times are you going to hit me with that damn cart?!"

As is her custom when a passenger raises his voice at her, the Queen of Sky raised hers right back:

"I'm sorry. I am in a bad mood. This is the first time I've sold food, and people keep asking me for stuff that is not on my cart."

Disgruntled passenger: "Well, I am in a bad mood now, too!"

Q of S: "Well, I didn't do it on purpose." (Yeah, right.)

About fifteen minutes into the service, the Queen of Sky was still attending the *first* row. She spied the endless rows of coach seats stretching ahead of her and her mood worsened.

Let me make a comment here about passengers. American passengers are very demanding. Although there is no language barrier with them, the Queen of Sky finds them more difficult to deal with than most foreign passengers. They seem to think that the $50 they paid for their round-trip ticket to Florida entitles them to first-class royal service.

The Queen of Sky says WAKE UP and look around you! Your low fare has resulted from my PAY CUT and STAFFING CUTS. That means I am getting paid less and less to do more and more work! >:-(

I always see those arrogant business travelers in the airports rolling their eyes and complaining about the poor service of the minimum wage workers in the food court. These people have obviously *never* had a minimum wage job. Otherwise, they would appreciate the fact that YOU GET WHAT YOU PAY FOR!!!

OK, Queen of Sky is going to get off her soapbox now and go try to take a nap before her flight to San Juan this afternoon. As you can tell, all this sleep deprivation has made me cranky.

Anyway, the moral of the day is: TREAT YOUR FLIGHT ATTENDANTS AS YOU WISH TO BE TREATED, and maybe then they will not hit you with their beverage cart when you lean over to tie your shoes.

Spring Has Sprung
Filed in LIFE OF LEISURE on Tuesday, 03/15

Well, the Queen of Sky finally got home from flying six days straight today. She arrived in her quirky little Central Texas city this afternoon to find that spring had sprung. The birds were singing, the sun was shining, people were out biking and walking, and the trees were budding with bright green.

The Queen of Sky, on the other hand, looked as if she'd been hit by a spring tornado. Her hose were ripped to shreds, her hair tangled and greasy, her feet and whole body stinky, and her uniform looked (and smelled) like it could work a flight by itself.

The Queen of Sky stopped at Whole Foods on the way home from the airport, still in uniform. She tried to hide her wings and ID badge, though, because she had a sneaking fear that people in the grocery store might start asking her for pillows and blankets or more coffee and Coke.

Believe you me, the last thing the Queen of Sky wants to see for the next couple of days is the inside of an airplane or airport!

Last night in San Juan, the Queen of Sky and her crew gathered at the bar by the ocean at their *fabulous* hotel. Her Mile Highness had a $12 salad and a piña colada. And at the end of the evening, the captain was nice enough to pick up the tab. (Exception to the cheap pilot rule.) I told him that if I'd known he was buying, I would've ordered the $17 shrimp salad! :-O

Unfortunately, though, we had to leave the next morning soon after sunrise. What a waste! We used to have long layovers in San Juan, but they, along with most of our long Latin America layovers, are a thing of the past.

We used to call them the Anonymous Airlines Dream Vacations. *sigh*

Anyway, Queen of Sky is going to go collapse now.

Happy Belated St. Paddy's Day!
Filed in LIFE OF LEISURE on Friday, 03/18

The Queen of Sky was a bad girl and cut acupuncture class last night to go out with two redheaded flight attendants (Kim and Monica) for St. Paddy's day. We headed downtown in my mini SUV and circled and circled looking for parking. Finally Monica said she knew a garage connected to a Thai restaurant where, if we say we are eating there, we can park for free. So we tried it. Pulled a ticket and the gate went up.

There was an outdoor St. Paddy's festival taking place on Fourth Street. Lots of people, beer, and a band whose lead singer was wearing a kilt playing on the stage.

We opted to get some food and settled on a local tapas bar.

Kim was wearing a green and white shirt that read "Forever Irish," and Monica had on green flip-flops and earrings. The only green item that Queen of Sky could find in her closet, however, was a green sports bra, so I opted for a lone green heart earring (the other having mysteriously disappeared) in one ear and a shamrock earring in the other.

The three of us were lined up at the bar sipping wine and nibbling (OK, gobbling) tapas. Queen of Sky told Monica that she should sit at the end, since Her Mile Highness is very unapproachable. In fact, if anyone tries to speak to Queen of Sky in a bar, she simply growls at them in response. However, Monica didn't move, preferring to sit in the middle.

On the other side sat feisty little Kim, who started a conversation with the guy to her left. Pretty soon, Monica and Queen of Sky looked over, and the guy was giving Kim a back rub. Don't really know what transpired in between.

Anyway, Kim refused to tell the guy what we did for a living, and afterward we joked about all the things we had told guys in bars over the years when they asked what we did for a living. Heh, heh, heh...the best was Kim's career as a "she-spy." And when she lived in DC, she and her girlfriend used to tell men they were legislative aides for made-up legislators! :-D

Anyway, I told the girls it would have to be an early night as I had to get up at 6am to come to Bustling Base City (where I now sit) and then fly to Milan this afternoon. So we left the bar around 9:30pm.

I received a call as we were walking to the car. It was my friend Victor... Somehow I missed his call and was trying to call him back when we ran right into the very same Victor in the middle of Fifth Street!

"I was just trying to call you," he said.

I had called Victor at 6:30pm to tell him that I was heading downtown with the girls for the festivities. He was just now coming out to meet us—on Caribbean time, apparently!

Anyway, we parted ways, as Queen of Sky was about to turn into a pumpkin.

And it turns out Monica was right...we did *indeed* get free parking!

Flight Blog: Milan
Filed in FLIGHT BLOGS on Sunday, 03/20

Well, I just got in from Milan. It was a very successful layover. My main goal was accomplished: I found the new H&M (cheap Euro-trash clothes), although I got a rather late start yesterday and ended up only having about 40 minutes to shop. I made some spur-of-the-moment fashion decisions, which may not be a good thing when you have the fashion sense of a slug, as the Queen of Sky does.

Then, after H&M closed at 8pm, I made my way to the supermarket, where I loaded up on cheese and other goodies.

There are always hot guys in that supermarket. Too bad they always bring their girlfriends shopping with them. :-(

The thing about Milanese men is that they are frightfully über-fashionable, which can be quite intimidating for someone whose idea of a fashion statement is wearing a leopard print scarf with her airline uniform overcoat, aka "the refugee coat". (As an aside, my friend Ricky says that even *his* gaydar doesn't work in Italy.)

After the supermarket, I headed to the restaurant I had spied next door. The sign said they specialized in seafood. Seafood is the Queen of Sky's favorite. So I decided to give it a shot and was not disappointed. In fact, I had an all-out feast.

The waiter recommended the house mixed antipasti to start, which consisted of seemingly endless little plates of a variety of seafood dishes... fried anchovies, stewed squid over soft polenta, octopus salad, shrimp and white bean salad, marinated fish. And then, when I thought the feast had ended, he brought me a little plate of baked mussels and scallops. Next I ordered spaghetti with clams. By the time that arrived, I had already sucked through most of my half-bottle of pinot grigio.

There was a group of little Italian ladies at the table next to me. My meal pretty much mirrored theirs, except they ordered a second course of fried seafood plus a pizza after the pasta first course. Then I ordered the dessert they were having—a slice of panettone served warm and drenched in some kind of liqueur. And, of course, ice cream on top.

Finally, the waiter brought me some after-dinner liqueurs to try, including limoncello—my favorite! I was already tipsy, but that put me over the edge. Queen of Sky stumbled back to the hotel after that.

OK, I've gotta run... am making myself hungry writing this, plus my friend Kim just came over to remind me that my flight home leaves in 30 minutes...

Ciao!
—Q of S

Commuter Update
Filed in COMMUTING on Sunday, 03/20

I got bumped off my commuter flight home, and now I have to hang around this *%@#! BBC airport until 8pm!

Kim got on the flight, because there was one seat left and she is senior to me. That's how things work at the airlines: Seniority rules!

Queen of Sky is going to surf the blogosphere now until her head starts throbbing, which shouldn't be long at this point. I have been up for about twenty hours now, as I was wide awake this morning at 4am in Milan (10pm Bustling Base City time) and couldn't go back to sleep due to jetlag, as usual.

Tah!

Senior Mamas
Filed in MISC. on Monday, 03/21

Hello again. Tonight I want to clarify something.

You may have wondered why Queen of Sky did not "hang" with her crew in Milan the other day. Let me explain something about international crews (at least at my airline anyway).

Airline bidding goes by seniority. Therefore, the more senior flight attendants get their choice of flights before the more junior ones like me. I have seven years of seniority, but that is a drop in the bucket at my airline.

61

And, of course, most flight attendants prefer to fly to Europe rather than to some place like Shreveport, Louisiana, or Buffalo, New York, in the dead of winter. Hence, international crews tend to be very senior (20-plus years seniority) and OLD.

The exception is the language speakers. We have two or three language-of-destination speakers on each international flight (but in my opinion, we should have four or five, at least). In general, these flight attendants are much more junior, like me. (I am not an Italian speaker, though, just Spanish—I got a lucky swap for that Milan trip.)

Therefore, I am usually one of the only flight attendants out of the nine- or ten-person international crew who is still in her child-bearing years. And Queen of Sky doesn't always feel like hanging around women who could be her mother. Also, I don't like being the translator/tour guide for the rest of the crew.

One of the "senior mamas" (as we lovingly call them) on my trip to Milan this weekend asked me what time I was going to the grocery store, because she had never been there before and wanted to tag along with me.

"Whenever I wake up," said I.

Fortunately, Senior Mama made plans with some of the other old ladies.

Don't get me wrong, some of these old bags can be a lot of fun. Plus I have learned a lot from them over the years.

On the crew bus to the airport in Milan yesterday, a couple of them were talking about the good old days (back in the 70s) when they had just started flying. Back in those days, flight attendants had to share rooms on layovers. And these ladies said that, being junior, they always got stuck with the weirdos that no one else wanted to room with.

One of them had to room with a woman who liked to sleep with the window open—even though it was the middle of winter in Ann Arbor, Michigan, and a snow storm was blowing around outside!

Another said she once roomed with a flight attendant who every morning liked to do exercises in the nude. :-O

And they went on and on about how awful it was for two women to share a bathroom when they had a 4am report time.

One of the senior mamas (SMs) on my Milan crew this week was Bobbi. I used to fly with Bobbi quite a bit. We were both based in Miami when I first started with Anonymous Airlines.

Bobbi is quite the character. She used to be a Playboy bunny back in the day. And she *loves* to shock people—especially pilots.

She used to introduce herself to "the guys" in quite a unique way. Instead of the customary handshake, she would walk right up to them and shake their balls. Yes, their nuts.

You should have seen the looks on those poor pilots' faces. :-D

Queen of Sky was once at a captain's retirement party in Frankfurt with Bobbi. We were having a sit-down dinner at a nice German restaurant when Bobbi, in typical fashion, flashed the whole crew.

She was very proud of her knockers. And they were in great shape, so she had a right to be (although I suspect she had a little help).

I once heard a story about Bobbi's 50th birthday party. Her friends wanted to shock *her* for a change, so they got her a cake in the shape of an erect penis.

Well, Bobbi took one look at that cock-cake, and her eyes bugged out. She rushed over to it, pulled down her panties, and jumped right on top!

Now that's the kind of SM I love to fly with! But she is one of the rare few.

The other day during the flight back from Milan, one of the other SMs pointed out to me a stain on my "important part" on the front of my skirt.

"Well, I guess I will just have to find a good-looking guy to rub it off for me," I joked.

The two SMs working with me didn't even break a smile.

Anyway, c'est la vie. I get to fly to great places but often end up hanging out by myself.

I promise to post a more interesting entry tomorrow.

—Q of S

A Tale of Dining Blog Super Divas
Filed in LAYOVERS on Tuesday, 03/22

It was a warm summer's day in Lima, Peru. Just a hint of smog hung in the air. Two of everybody's favorite blog superheroines, Queen of Sky and Chucha Galore (aka Nelly the Panamanian Powerhouse—she decided to start her own highly entertaining blog, "Diary of a Rock 'n' Roll Wife," after I told her about mine), were on their way down the street to dine at the most decadent cevichería this side of Trujillo.

The natives gave the pair some strange looks as they passed. Apparently they had never seen Blog Super Divas before.

Upon reaching a busy intersection, Queen of Sky used her special powers to stop Third World traffic. Subsequently, the two divas crossed the road and climbed the steps on the other side to enter the inconspicuous little place with the orange awning—Alfresco.

Chucha Galore quickly put the waiter under her ample-bosomed Panamanian spell, and she and Queen of Sky were seated immediately. Chucha's spell soon wore off, though, as the two had to wait about 20 minutes (!) for the waiter to take their orders and bring them the customary fried corn kernels to snack on. But that was a small price to pay to dine at one of the best restaurants in Lima.

For the first course, Queen of Sky recommended the piqueo Costa Pacifico del sur. (Queen of Sky has had this as her entree once before.) When the plate arrived, both Queen and Chucha dove into the delicacies. The platter included: the world-famous ceviche mixto (marinated raw fish and seafood); one california roll; causa rellena (mashed Peruvian yellow potatoes, stuffed with crab); pulpo al olivo (octopus in olive sauce); ensalada de mariscos (seafood salad); tiradito Alfresco (raw fish fillets in Peruvian yellow pepper sauce); and finally, in the center, Peruvian large kernel corn and a sweet potato to complement the ceviche. Each delicacy was perched on top of an empty scallop shell. (Queen of Sky is drooling just thinking about that plate.)

When the waiter returned several minutes later to check on the two super divas, he found a large platter topped with a bunch of empty shells.

"I'll bring your entrees right out," he said, spying Chucha Galore and Queen of Sky licking their lips.

For the entree, Chucha had the picante de mariscos, a mixture of sea-food in a creamy pinkish sauce, served with rice and corn. Despite the name, it was not spicy.

Chucha was in heaven. She fiercely fought off Queen of Sky's fork when it came near her plate. But with her secret powers once again, Queen of Sky managed to skewer and devour a couple of Chucha's shrimps with-out her noticing.

Queen of Sky had chosen for her entree the brochetas de pescado, delicate fish kebabs with three different types of Peruvian white fish in an herb and butter sauce. As her garnish, she had chosen the large kernel corn sautéed with cumin. The dish was delightful and delectable. And light, compared to Chucha's cream-fest across the table.

Then, at the end of the magical feast, a mysterious Peruvian man came over to the table and paid the divas' check. This is when it pays to be famous super divas...

Yeah, right—that's a nice fantasy, anyway. ;-)

(Actually, the total bill was only about $30 for everything!)

Good News!
Filed in MISC. on Wednesday, 03/23

Good news, everybody... I had low hours this month, so I put in a pick-up for a trip to Buenos Aires. And I got one—tomorrow! YAY!!!

Need to email Maurizio ASAP. He and Queen of Sky have been instant messaging each other almost every day. He will be excited! :-D

Sleaze and Romance in Buenos Aires
Filed in LAYOVERS on Sunday, 03/27

Happy Easter, everybody!

Well, Queen of Sky's latest trip to B.A. did not get off to a great start. My commuter flight to Bustling Base City (BBC) was canceled Wednesday afternoon (mechanical, of course), leaving me to take the jumpseat on my back-up flight. This one cut it really close to my sign-in time. This left me no time to change into my uniform when I got to BBC. (I was commuting "incognito"—in regular clothes—that day.) Thus, I had to change into my lovely uniform in the airport bathroom. I felt like Super Girl...or Super "Stew", rather.

Anyway, I made it to BBC on time, thank goodness, but had to haul ass when we landed. Of course we parked at Concourse G, and I had to get all the way to Concourse Z in twenty minutes flat.

Not an easy task under any circumstances...and today, right in the middle of my treacherous trek, the stupid airport train broke down. Queen of Sky had to drag her trusty two-wheeled sidekick nearly half a mile beneath the terminal, and half of the moving sidewalks down there were broken as well!

Then, at the end of the long trek, Queen of Sky schlepped down one more flight of stairs and into her home away from home, the flight attendant lounge.

Ignoring the normal lounge bustle, I sprinted to the sign-in computer, where I swiftly typed in my employee number and password.

"YOUR SIGN IN HAS BEEN CONFIRMED AT 8:07PM. THANK YOU FOR BEING ON TIME," read the screen.

Phew! I just made it! I sighed with relief.

The computer automatically generated the rotation sheet for my trip. I scanned the crew list and cringed when I saw the pilots' names.

The captain, Bill, was a notorious sleazebag who had once offered to be Queen of Sky's sugar daddy, even though he is married to another flight attendant. Also on the crew were the notorious lovebirds, Gloria the Hot Cuban Mama and John the Married Pilot.

Well, should be an interesting trip, Queen of Sky mused.

I had a couple of minutes to spare before my briefing, so I quickly surveyed the room for anybody I knew.

The harshly lit lounge contained quite an assortment of people—young and old, fat and thin, short and tall, male and female, but mostly middle-aged, middle-weight, middle-height females. The one thing we all had in common was our hideous pea-green polyester garb.

Several pea-clad worker bees hunched over the mailboxes, shuffling through files. Others sat at the round school-cafeteria tables, eating from plastic and Styrofoam containers and gossiping with friends. Still others mulled about in front of the "Duty Desk," where supervisors are always available to answer flight attendants' pressing questions. Unfortunately, however, their answers can never be trusted.

The hubbub of the lounge reminded me of a high school reunion. Banners hung throughout the room, and a large cake and soft drinks lingered in one corner. Loud and overly animated conversations ambushed me from every side:

"Betsy! I haven't seen you in years! How have you been? Still living in Memphis?"

"Hey, girl! Long time no see! Where are you headed today?"

"Catherine! I'm flying with you today! We're gonna have fun! It's a great crew!"

"Harriet! Are you back in Bustling Base City now? We missed you! Are you still married? To the same guy?"

My ears rang as I navigated the room. Finally, I spied Ricky and Consuela at a table on the other side of the Duty Desk and went over to say a quick hi.

"Hola, mi amorrrr!" Ricky purred as I approached.

His uniform was perfectly tailored and his shirt starched and crisp. And he was wearing his signature "Cockroach Killer" shoes (so-named for the extra-pointy toes).

I kissed him on the cheek and then greeted "Miss Colombia" the same way. Her cleavage was about to pop out of her uniform dress, which she had had hemmed up to her mid-thighs. If she bent over in flight, she would give the whole cabin a free show.

"Hey, where are you guys headed today?"

"We're going to Chile," he said. "What about you?"

"Argentina," Queen of Sky replied, pronouncing the 'g' as a hard 'h', the Spanish way.

"Oh, you lucky thing!" He made a jealous face. "Say hi to my country-men for me. Those Chilean men are so feos (ugly)!"

"OK, I will!"—wink—"Well, have a good trip! No time to chat—gotta run to briefing. Hope to fly with you guys soon." I leaned over to kiss them both goodbye. "Cuidate (take care), Consuela. Try to keep him out of trouble on the layover!"

"Girrrrl, I'm the one that has to keep *her* out of trouble!" Ricky retorted, throwing his girlfiend a dirty look.

In a flash, I turned and disappeared down the hall to my briefing room.

Captain Bill was standing next to the door when I entered. He shot me a wink as I took my seat on the long side of the table opposite Gloria. Gloria waved at me, trying not to interrupt the captain's briefing speech.

"I'm Bill, but y'all can call me el jefe grande..."

Upon hearing his introduction, which I had heard so many times before, I flashed back a trip to Chile we had flown together a year or two before. Captain Bill had a habit of practicing his very poor Spanish during his onboard announcements. That particular time, after takeoff in Chile, he was trying to tell the passengers that we were hauling thousands of pounds of salmon back to the US (cargo is big business out of Chile), but instead announced at an ear-numbing volume that we were flying at 30,000 feet in a 3,000-pound salmon.

As I was chuckling under my breath, "el jefe grande" handed a sheet to the lead flight attendant, Bridget. Bridget was a wiry older woman who looked quite stern. She had a puckered, weathered face with too much makeup and hair a very unnatural shade of red (think: Ronald McDonald).

Bridget rolled her eyes when she saw the sheet. Then she passed it around the table at Captain Bill's request.

Normally the captain gives the lead flight attendant a list of the cockpit crew's names. This time, instead of just the normal printout, Captain Bill had printed a picture of three Anonymous Airlines pilots in the cockpit in their uniforms, smiling at the camera. Upon closer inspection, however, you saw that the pilots were actually Harrison Ford, Tom Cruise, and Kevin Costner. Bill had superimposed their faces onto the photo and then printed his crew's names below.

As the sheet went around the table, laughter and merriment consumed the tiny room. The only person left with a straight face was the lead, Bridget.

After Captain Bill's traditional speech about the weather and flight time, he made one last request—demand, actually—before exiting the room:

"Don't forget to make the sangria!"

Prim and proper Bridget gave him *the look*, eyeballing him squarely over the gold rim of her reading glasses. She reminded Queen of Sky of her fourth grade English teacher.

"There will be no sangria on this trip!" she snapped.

Uggh. It only takes one bad apple to spoil the crew! I silently lamented.

On the flight down to Buenos Aires I was working in the back with Gloria. I debated whether I should tell her about John's tryst with Nancy in Santiago a couple of months back. I finally decided not to, since I had no hard evidence—I had only seen them dancing. Plus, Gloria was not exactly innocent. She was quite the player herself. I had known her to juggle five guys at one time. And besides, John had started seeing Gloria while he was still with his wife, so infidelity was already a given in his case.

Mid-flight, after the meal service, Queen of Sky went up to the cockpit (and the only time I go up there is if I really need something) to ask if "the guys" had change for a $20 because we needed it for our duty-free sales. John had change, which he graciously handed to me. Immediately thereafter, Captain Bill swiveled around in his seat and bellowed:

"I'll make him give you that $20 bill right back if you show us your tits right now."

Such a classy guy!

So of course Her Mile Highness made her royal exit from the cockpit.

Then, on the crew bus to the hotel (sans crew punch), Captain Bill sat right next to me and offered ever so generously:

"Elena, if you wanna make a little extra cash on the layover, you can come to my room."

I grimaced at the thought.

"I really don't need much..." he added, misinterpreting my disgust.

"Sorry, I've already got plans," I replied with a contemptuous laugh, sparing myself more details.

How could anyone take such a sleazeball seriously?

But that wasn't the end of it. As we were waiting for our rooms at the Imperial, Queen of Sky overheard the disgruntled captain (by this time he had tried to make the moves on every girl on the crew) arrogantly declare:

"I don't need you girls. I can get a hooker and a beer for $10!"

He continued happily about how the worse the economy got in Argentina, the younger and prettier and cheaper the girls got.

Gross, but typical of a pilot.

Anyway, Gloria and John said they were going to a tango show and invited me and Maurizio to join them. But when I called Maurizio, he had other plans for la Reina de los Cielos. He wanted to take me to a very chic restaurant. But first we went to a wine bar and got a little tipsy and groped each other a little. :-O

After a nice dinner accompanied by not-so-nice music (poor renditions of Sinatra songs in Spanish), we went back to the hotel. As we entered my room, Captain Sleaze was coming out of his across the hall. I ducked through the door quickly, hoping he didn't see me.

Well, I'm going to stop here, since this is a PG-13 blog. But let me just say that some *very* good things happened in room 715 that night (think: snorkeling gear).

But then the next day at lunch, Maurizio caught me off guard.

He was watching me very intensely as I gobbled my pumpkin gnocchi.

"Elena," he began. "It takes me a little bit to fall in love..." He paused for a deep breath. "... but I *love* you."

I was floored. Had no idea what to say. It was, after all, only our third date!

"I love you, too" was finally my slightly forced response.

I still don't know what to think of all this. Am reeling. And then of course Captain Sleaze told the whole crew on the bus back to the airport that night that Queen of Sky had "gotten busy" on the layover.

I made sure to respond loud enough for everybody to hear:

"Well, at least I didn't have to pay for it!"

Today's Soapbox:
Low Carb Carbohydrates
Filed in MISC. on Monday, 03/28

Queen of Sky was at Whole Foods tonight and noticed with chagrin the number of low carb products that have crept up, even there at her favorite supermarket—Carb Blockers, Low Carb Cleanse, etc.

WHAT HAS THIS WORLD COME TO?

Queen of Sky is tired of hearing people talk about their low carb diets.

A couple of weeks ago, as you may recall, Queen of Sky had the misfortune to work a Food for Sale flight at Anonymous Airlines. Well, approximately 45 minutes into the food sale service, Queen of Sky was not even a quarter done with the cabin, and some bald-headed, middle-aged guy had the nerve to ask her if she had anything "Atkins" on her cart.

Queen of Sky just looked at him.

Oh, how she wished this had been the gentleman she had hit three times with her cart already as she passed up and down the aisle fetching stuff from the galley!

After a couple minutes of silence with Queen of Sky glaring at him angrily, the man finally said:

"Well, I guess this salad will be OK."

Queen of Sky snatched his credit card from his hand and moved on to her next customer.

I have no sympathy for these people, since I myself do *not* diet. Unless you count the All Carb Diet that I sometimes subscribe to.

The All Carb Diet is very easy to follow in Italy, where one eats bread, pasta, rice, *and* pizza in some combination at every meal.

So explain this: Why are the Italians so much thinner than us?

In Queen of Sky's expert opinion, gathered from serving food and drinks to people the world over inside a long metal tube that shoots through the air, the answer is simple: SODA.

That's what it all boils down to, folks. I have noticed that the Italians drink only wine and water with their meals, while Americans (and many Latin Americans) drink can after can of SODA.

And it doesn't matter if it is diet or not—the effect seems to be the same.

In fact, Queen of Sky secretly suspects that diet soda contains enough toxins to take out a whole city. Forget bioterrorism—Americans are already poisoning themselves. Al Qaeda should drop the suicide bombings and just buy stock in American soft drink companies.

OK, now Queen of Sky is rambling.

Anyway, bottom line is this, soda kills, not carbs—after all, soda is not one of the four food groups, whereas chips and salsa are, regardless of what you might think. (We in Texas have known the latter for a long time.)

In conclusion, *please* listen to the Queen of Sky and BRING BACK THE CARBS, AMERICA!!!!

Monday, Monday
Filed in MISC. on Tuesday, 03/29

Queen of Sky can't play today because she has to study for her finals at the acupuncture school this week. And—uggh!—there sure are a lot of charts to memorize here. Plus, I need to find some friends to practice my Chinese face massage on... any volunteers?

Acupuncture School Dropout
Filed in MISC. on Thursday, 03/31

Well, the tests went well, but now that the trimester is over, I have pretty much decided that acupuncture school is not for me. That school drained me—maybe because I had nine hours of classes in one day. But besides that, I was not *passionate* about the subject matter.

I found it interesting, don't get me wrong, but in my three-hour evening lecture class I was always much more concerned with writing blog entries and trying to figure out my classmates' genders than paying attention to the teacher. To make matters worse, Queen of Sky always ate dinner right before that class, thus experiencing a major sinking spell during the lecture.

Anyhow, there has to be something else out there for me. Something I can be passionate about *and* use to supplement my income. Plus, the way the airline industry is going nowadays, I may not have a job a year from now. All this Coke-can-popping is starting to get to me anyway. And besides, Her Mile Highness can't reign the skies forever.

Need a Plan B. Have been thinking of looking into cooking school, and now may be the time.

Maurizio Update:

Well, my mysterious diplomat connected his web cam tonight for our nightly chat. That was INTERESTING, to say the least! He gave Queen of Sky a little show at one point. ;-)

I have managed to get another trip to B.A. next month, so looks like our little romance will continue. :-)

APRIL

Clear Air Turbulence

Early Saturday
Filed in LIFE OF LEISURE on Saturday, 04/02

I guess you are all wondering where Queen of Sky has been today.

Well, I got up at the CRACK OF DAWN (7:30) to go to an Italian class over at the University of Quirksville. I've decided that I need to learn Italian so that Maurizio and I can communicate easier. Right now we speak Spanish to each other, which can get confusing, since it's neither of our native tongues. Plus, if I can get my Italian good enough, I'll be able to fly the Italian routes at Anonymous International. :-)

Anyhow, the class ended at noon, about the time Queen of Sky is usually getting up. So, with the whole day ahead of her still, she headed to Container Store, Cost Plus, and Pier One. Queen of Sky needs some accent pieces for her new $3,000 couch that was finally delivered last week.

Unfortunately, though, Queen of Sky doesn't trust her own taste, so will wait until next week and drag Kim (who is currently somewhere in South America) back to the above stores with her.

I liked some of the stuff at Pier One and Cost Plus but don't know if wicker will go with my new modern chocolate faux-suede couch.

Any gay guys out there that can give the Queen of Sky some advice?

Back to Work
Filed in LIFE OF LEISURE on Sunday, 04/03

Sigh

Queen of Sky's life of leisure is coming to a temporary end tomorrow, because she has to return to work. :-(Just checked the weather in Lima for this weekend, and it says 80 degrees and partly cloudy. Not bad.

It's about time for me to get my hair cut again. Am also going to stock up on antibiotics while I'm there. And, of course, I will make my regular trip to Alfresco for some FABULOUS Peruvian seafood.

Work, Work, Work
Filed in MY LIFE IN THE AIRPORT on Monday, 04/04

Well, here Queen of Sky is at the airport in Bustling Base City. Queen of Sky's friend Jesse was on the flight to work with her this morning. However, she didn't have time to talk to him much before the flight, since she arrived at the gate five minutes prior to departure, due to the fact that her breakfast taco place had changed ownership and now tacos cost $3 instead of

$2—what a rip-off! Her Mile Highness had to drag her trusty two-wheeled sidekick "Valigia" all the way down to the cafe by Gate 10 to get a croissant, and the line was very long.

Anyway, after a brief chat with Jesse, I boarded and headed to the back of the airplane for my nap. Jesse sat somewhere toward the front. I was expecting to see him after the flight, but by the time I deplaned, he had taken off like a queer running late for a Cher concert. (Who knows—maybe he was.)

Queen of Sky wasn't through telling him about her blog, but oh well.

There sure is a lot of commotion in the flight attendant lounge today. I was going to try to take a nap since I didn't get much sleep on the airplane this morning, but with all this noise, it's unlikely I'll be able to.

While I was in the restroom a minute ago, I spotted my old friend Christine fixing her hair. I walked over and greeted her warmly. All I got was a frigid "hey," and she ducked into one of the stalls. I guess she's still mad at me. She has yet to return any of my numerous calls or emails.

Presently I can hear this crazy lady I've flown with before at the computers opposite me. She has a high-pitched squealy voice, kind of like nails on a chalkboard. I can't remember exactly why, but I know that the lady is crazy and that I can't stand her. I think Crazy Lady might have yelled at me with her squealy voice on a flight to Europe one time. Don't know... just remember I don't like her.

Anyway, all the commotion is about the new bidding system that we're getting July 1. There are tables set up throughout the lounge with people to assist with our questions. Queen of Sky would like to point out that none of the flight attendants want this new system, but since Anonymous Airlines flight attendants are non-unionized, we have no say in the matter.

Methinks a lot of people are going to be upset when it is implemented. Change is never a good thing to flight attendants, especially senior ones.

Anyway, am going to look for some earplugs now and try to take a nap before my briefing at three-something.

Latah!

Layover La-La Land
Filed in LAYOVERS on Tuesday, 04/05

Hi, all. Queen of sky is here in Lima having a relaxing layover. It's one of those layovers where she does her normal routine: sleeps until she's hungry, then eats until she's tired.

Got up this morning and ate breakfast with the crew. The free breakfast buffet was quite sparse today. They didn't replenish much... like the vegetable tempura and the Japanese fish, both of which Queen of Sky got the last piece of when she came down at ten o'clock.

Anyway, the crew was having too good a time together. Somehow pilots and hooker bars came up in the conversation, and the captain said pilots and hookers are "two peas in a pod." Then the copilot told us a story about the time he went to Aguardiente (the nearest hooker bar) and saw his captain with a girl on each arm. The copilot had told one of the girls there that was "harassing" him that he was a salesman, but when Captain Lush spotted him and waved enthusiastically at him, the girl proclaimed:

"You know him? You're no salesman, then—you're a pilot for American Airlines!"

We got a good laugh out of that. (Note: We don't fly for American.)

Anyhow, after breakfast Queen of Sky went back to her room and tried to go back to sleep. I lounged around until 2pm, and then went to the grocery store along with another girl on my crew who wanted me to translate every little thing for her... how annoying!

Well, am hungry again now... so off to find some grub!

Layover La-La Land, Continued
Filed in LAYOVERS on Tuesday, 04/05

5:14pm

Well, Queen of Sky is still here in Lima at the hotel. I just saw the captain in the lobby. He informed me that pick-up has been pushed back two hours tonight due to a late-arriving aircraft. That leaves more time to sleep and eat and SHOP!

Earlier, Queen of Sky went for a walk to look for food and finally decided she wasn't in the mood for ceviche, so went to a vegetarian place next to the hotel that Chucha Galore had recommended one time.

It was very good. I had a Peruvian dish (lomo saltado) made with soy meat instead of beef and a Peruvian large kernel corn salad (tried to avoid the tomatoes, which were the only raw item in the salad... for those of you who do not travel to Third World countries, you can get many things, including intestinal parasites, from raw produce.)

That reminds me of the conversation we were having at breakfast this morning about all the Third World diseases we have had that have stumped our First World doctors. I have had scabies (a skin mite like body lice where you itch all over), a parasite from Mexico whom I affectionately named Pedro, plus various forms of diarrhea and the complications thereof. We decided collectively that we are better off going to the pharmacist in Lima and describing our symptoms than going to a doctor back home. The pharmacists in Third World countries seem to be pretty keen at recognizing Third World diseases—rashes, different forms of diarrhea, parasites, infections, etc.

Well, speaking of pharmacies, I just went to the pharmacy next door and stocked up on antibiotics. A girl on my crew told me to get some "Z-packs." I have no idea what they are, but I bought two of them for $15 a pop. Apparently they are high doses of antibiotics that you take in three doses instead of for a week or two. Anyway, Queen of Sky is not normally the Queen of Antibiotics—in fact she usually avoids them like the plague—but this recurrent kidney infection has made her paranoid.

OK, Queen of Sky is rambling once again and needs to go to the night market to buy some junky jewelry and then take a nap before pick-up (which is now at 1am!!! Yuk!). It's a true all-nighter tonight, so one must be prepared!

Pooped!
Filed in MY LIFE IN THE AIRPORT on Wednesday, 04/06

10:07am

Queen of Sky just got in from Lima. One word... POOPED!

Queen of Sky's flight was almost quarantined by US Customs this morning, as there were two sick passengers aboard. One of them, a little Japanese Peruvian lady on her way to Japan, turned out to be just constipated. The other, a young gringo male, was puking and dry-heaving the whole flight. The paramedics that met the flight said it was only food poisoning, though. Hopefully they are right and it was nothing communicable. If not, Queen of Sky now has enough antibiotics to kill every bacterium from here to Lima and back, so she is not worried.

I told my crew before landing that if we got quarantined, I would take one Z-pack immediately and then would auction off my extra one to the highest bidder.

Bidding starts at $50! Cash only—and payment up front!

Well, I'm going to take a nap now before my flight home at noon. Nighty-night! *lunges for lounge chair*

—Q of S

Not Much to Tell
Filed in LIFE of LEISURE on Thursday, 04/07

Hmm. Not much going on around here. Slept like twelve hours last night and could have slept like twelve more. :-O

Queen of Sky didn't sleep well the night before her Lima trip, nor the night she spent in Lima, and then of course, lost a night's sleep on the way home. So it will take a while to catch up. Meanwhile, this sleep deprivation has caused my kidneys to feel a little iffy again. If they still feel iffy tomorrow, I will begin taking the refill antibiotics I got in Lima.

In other news, I got a pick-up for a Buenos Aires trip this Monday. I was surprised to get that trip but had left the request active in the computer, and the day of my Lima trip (last Monday) I happened to check my schedule, and there it was!

I can't wait!

The Queen of Sky's Résumé
Filed in ABOUT ME on Friday, 04/08

It has come to the Queen of Sky's attention that some of her readers do not think she is reaching her full potential in her present position as a grumpy flight attendant.

Therefore, she has decided to post her résumé (C.V.) and wait confidently for the job offers to come rolling in...

QUEEN OF SKY
69 Skymattress Ln.
Quirksville, TX 76969

AGE: 29
BIRTHDAY: Nov. 21
SEX: Infrequently

OBJECTIVE: To find a job where I have to do less work than I do now, have more days off per month (at least fifteen), get paid more, and travel less.

LOCATION: I am willing to relocate to California, Hawaii, the French Riviera, or a quaint sun-drenched isle where the men are handsome and the food divine.

EDUCATION
B.A. Spanish, minor Journalism, University of Quirksville

WORK EXPERIENCE
Presently: Flight Attendant
Job Description: Making passengers miserable, ruining people's joy of travel, slacking off whenever possible.

Before That: Travel Agent
Job Description: Screwing up clients' travel arrangements, slacking off whenever possible.

A Really Long Time Ago: Various odd jobs, including: Waitress, Assistant Tuba Salesgirl, Frozen Yogurt Server, Airline Cargo Reservations Agent, IRS Temporary Data Entry Clerk, Hotel Front Desk Clerk.
Job Description: Living paycheck to paycheck, trying to scrape by, slacking off whenever possible.

SKILLS
Blogging, slacking off, eating, sleeping, cooking, some massage, some sexual positions (where no work is involved), dancing, margarita-making.

Languages: Swiss German, Beer Hall German, Airplane Spanish, Bedroom Italian.

REFERENCES: None. (So don't bother asking.)

—Q of S :-)

Today's Doings
Filed in LIFE OF LEISURE on Saturday, 04/09

Queen of Sky has been cooking up a storm today. She bought a bunch of fresh veggies at Whole Foods yesterday and starting cooking them today after her Italian class.

First, there was broccoli, which Queen of Sky ate with a homemade béchamel sauce. Then asparagus, steamed and then sautéed in olive oil with spring onions. Then Queen of Sky made a big pot of pasta, and for the sauce dumped a bunch of olive oil (Italian) in the pan and then three chopped cloves of garlic, a whole peeled and chopped tomato, some canned Italian tuna, whole peperoncini (Italian dried hot peppers), and some of the asparagus. I had a little feast after I tossed the pasta in the sauce... a very tasty feast. Now for dessert I'm going to have a baked organic sweet potato. So, once again Queen of Sky is sticking to her All-Carb diet. :-D

But after today's internet purchases, which included an itsy bitsy bikini from ValeriesSecret.com, Queen of Sky should be working on losing her pooch (aka cushion for the pushin'). Oh well, guess I will wait until the bikini is delivered to cut the pasta and start exercising.

Other recent internet purchases of Queen of Sky's include: a bumper sticker that reads "My other car is a broom"; monogrammed cami and boy short PJ set; tropical flowered pants (the last two items also from Valerie's Secret). Queen of Sky hopes these items are of better quality than the PJs she ordered from VS a couple of months ago. >:-(

BTW, I have decided, upon reviewing my blog entries, to change the title of this blog from "Diary of a Flight Attendant" to "Diary of a DYSFUNC-TIONAL Flight Attendant." Methinks the latter is more appropriate.

OK, gonna watch the finale of "The Apprentice" (recorded it) and eat my sweet potato now...

e-Learning
Filed in LIFE OF LEISURE on Sunday, 04/10

Grrrrr! Queen of Sky just spent the last three hours completing an e-learning course for work to learn about the new bidding system we're getting in July. Upon completion, however, she realized that the course was not mandatory, as she had thought.

>:-(<<— Grumpy Queen of Sky

Am going to log off now, as my eyes are about to bug out from looking at this damn monitor too long. :-(

On a positive note, tomorrow I make my long-awaited return to Buenos Aires. :-D

Update when I get back...

The Countess of Sky
Filed in LAYOVERS on Thursday, 04/14

Don't cry for Queen of Sky, Argentiiiiiiina!

I got home from Buenos Aires this morning. (Actually, it was afternoon by the time I got back to Texas .) 'Twas another eventful layover in the "Paris of South America."

My friend Ricky was on the crew, and when we arrived at the hotel in B.A. on Thursday, I warned him not to get a room next to mine, as Maurizio would be coming over that night and was very loud (think: opera-singer).

Consequently, Ricky marched right up to the front desk and demanded, "Give me a room next to hers!"

He told me he would be listening through the wall, cheering, "You *go*, girrrrl!"

Anyhow, Maurizio did indeed come over that night and took Queen of Sky to a fancy restaurant, where he refused to let her pay, as usual. And afterward he did indeed come back to her hotel room for a little love-romp—rrrrROW! He leaves little to be desired in the bedroom. He does have a few fetishes, though, but I won't go into those here. ;-)

Maurizio is quite a catch. Dare I say, too good to be true.

This trip he told me some stories about the life of a Venetian blueblood. He said they still have arranged marriages in Venice, and that his grand-parents had picked out a wife for him when he was a child. :-O But when he grew up, he declined her hand. Actually, the poor girl waited for him for a long time and then finally married someone else.

Anyway, on the flight back to the States last night, I asked Ricky if he had heard any noises coming from my room on the layover.

"No, I didn't hear any operas," he said. "What about you? Did you hear any*thang* from *my* room?"

"You had company, too?"

"Of course, honey! I went to the clubs and met some *manzzzz*."

After congratulating him, I assured him that the only thing I heard from his room was him singing along to a Britney Spears video right before pick-up time.

A little while later we started talking about what we had done on the layover. I pulled out the custom-made leather jacket that Maurizio had bought for me earlier that day. I donned it proudly and strutted around the galley as Ricky sat on the jumpseat admiring it. I told him that I was hopefully gonna have to change my nom de plume to "Countess of Sky."

"You better get your claws into *this* one, girrrrl!" he replied.

The Deluge and a Drunken Christmas in Madrid
Filed in LAYOVERS on Friday, 04/15

Queen of Sky woke up this morning at 7:30 to what sounded like someone pouring buckets of water outside her window. It was in fact rain. The thunder and lightning proved that.

I just saw on the news that someone's house was struck by lightning and went up in flames. Around here in downtown, we got about two inches of rain, but apparently north of here they got five inches!!!

Anyway, I am just glad my patio didn't overflow into the house. Although my floor *could* use some washing. (Don't do floors...or anything else, for that matter!)

Well, this afternoon I got a rather random phone call:

"Hi...this is Renee. I flew with you to Madrid at Christmas."

Ahh, Queen of Sky remembers that layover well...

The whole crew met in one of the pilots' rooms for a little crew party. Everyone brought something... food, wine, etc. One pilot had even brought four bottles of champagne. We expected to stay in, assuming that everything was closed on Christmas day.

Well, much boozing later, we came to find out that there *was* a restaurant open near our hotel. We made a reservation and headed over.

At the restaurant, Queen of Sky started drinking white wine (earlier she had been drinking a nice rioja and champagne). The white wine the waiter brought was so good that Her Mile Highness almost skipped dinner and ordered a bottle of that wine and a straw. But, alas, she ended up ordering some codfish, which was not that cheap, BTW.

Anyhow, at the end of the dinner, a drunk Queen of Sky was trying to recruit people to go downtown with her to party some more. Unfortunately, no one complied. But that turned out to be a good thing. When Queen of Sky stumbled back into her hotel room, her head was spinning and she passed out cold on the bed.

The next morning at pick-up, the whole crew (at least all the flight attendants) had a pained expression on their faces, including the Queen of Sky, who had awoken thinking that she was going to puke. (I am not a puker, so for me to reach that point there must have been some serious drinking going on.)

Poor Renee was the worst off on the crew. She was puking the whole nine-hour flight home. Finally she realized it probably wasn't the alcohol, but the steak she had eaten at dinner that made her so sick.

Queen of Sky has never felt so crappy flying home, except maybe in the olden days when she used to fly Madrid out of New York. (Those were some party crews!) But that's another story.

Also, apparently at dinner the lead flight attendant (who was seated at the other end of the *long* table from me, out of my line of vision) had been all over the recently divorced copilot. Back at the hotel, one of the other crewmembers spotted her getting off the elevator with him at his floor.

This was quite the galley gossip around the airplane the next day, and it finally got back to the girl in question.

"I don't remember getting to my room last night," she said. "I woke up completely clothed."

After further probing, she admitted she couldn't remember getting off at the copilot's floor, either. But her panties *were* still in place when she woke up. (That was the first thing we asked, of course.)

In any case, she finally marched up to the cockpit to set the record straight.

"He said I *didn't* go to his room," she naively told us afterward.

Likely story, we chuckled to ourselves.

Anyway, turns out Renee has a layover tomorrow in Queen of Sky's central Texas city. Am going to take her to lunch and perhaps to the outlet mall. No chance of a repeat of Madrid, though, since I'm taking antibiotics once again. :-P

Daily Horoscope
Filed in MISC. on Saturday, 04/16

Hmmm... this does not bode well...

Emotional Deprivation

This is a sobering period for your emotions. You feel deprived, with the likely result of excessive worry and depression. Sorrow and disappointment abound in your life right now. The source of your troubles may be your mother or other female figures in your life. Depression can lead to vulnerability to illness during this time. There is a tendency to suffer from physical complaints, including digestive ailments, chronic conditions, and problems with the hands and feet. Your domestic environment may seem restrictive, restrained, or lacking emotional content altogether. How well you cope with the circumstances of this influence will be determined by your level of maturity.

Aspect: Saturn opposing Moon
Period of Influence: 4/14 – 5/11
Courtesy of Astro Wizards

Busy Sunday
Filed in *LIFE OF LEISURE* on Sunday, 04/17

Queen of Sky is busy being social today. Am going to dinner now with some friends, then have to do laundry. Earlier I showed Renee (the flight attendant in town on a layover) around town and helped her choose the right area to live in if she decides to move here. It was very hot today, so we mostly stayed inside my air-conditioned mini SUV.

   Gotta go now...

Hasta lueguito,
—Q of S

ASK QUEEN OF SKY A QUESTION!!!
Filed in *ABOUT ME* on Sunday, 04/17

(borrowed from Honeymelon—check out her blog)
I want everyone who reads this to ask me three questions, no more and no less. Ask me anything you want. Really. I'll answer anything. Then I want you to go to your journal, copy and paste this, allowing your friends (including me) to ask you anything. Leave your questions in the comments below.

P.S. Am off to Milan tomorrow... will answer your questions when I get back.

Back Home Again
Filed in *MISC.* on Monday, 04/18

Well, I got up at six o'clock this morning, as normal, to go to work. In fact, it wasn't until I got all the way to Bustling Base City and was trying to catch a nap in the flight attendant lounge that things became abnormal.

   I had turned off my cell phone while I was in the lounge chair, but the bustle and PAs in the lounge prohibited me from sleeping. I finally gave up and turned my cell phone back on to prepare to send some naughty phone-cam pics to Maurizio.

There was a message.

It was my uncle. He said my 96-year-old grandmother had passed away this morning.

I took a moment to compose myself and called him back. He said the funeral will be Saturday in North Carolina. I broke down after the call and went to find a supervisor with tears streaming down my face. The supervisor took me off my Milan trip, and I caught the first flight back home to Texas.

But first I had to do the terrible task of calling my siblings to notify them of the death.

I hadn't seen my grandmother in over a year. She had Alzheimer's and was in a nursing home outside of Atlanta. She didn't recognize me when I last went to visit and just sat around seeming to wonder why she was still here. It was very sad.

She was my maternal grandmother. Her death today is painfully ironic, since my mother used to always joke that Grandma would outlive her, and in the end she did.

Anyway, that is my sad news.

OK, I'm going to go be depressed now...

Tough Decisions
Filed in MISC. on Tuesday, 04/19

So I have one day to figure out how to get all the way from Texas to North Carolina for my grandmother's funeral. I checked the flights out of Quirksville, and of course this week is spring break at the local university, and all the flights are full. I found out that I do *not* get a confirmed space ticket to go to a relative's funeral on Anonymous, just a higher priority standby ticket, so it looks like I won't be going. In fact, unless I leave today, the chances of me making it to the funeral on time are about one in a thousand. The only flight that would get me there early enough tomorrow is still not early enough if you count the two-hour drive from the airport to the town where the funeral will be held. And chances are I won't get on that flight anyway.

Hmm... decisions, decisions...

P.S. Thanks, everybody, for all of your condolences!

Update
Filed in LIFE OF LEISURE on Wednesday, 04/20

Well, this morning when I awoke to my alarm at four o'clock (!!!), I was really not feeling well. I felt like crap, actually. My sides were throbbing and I felt feverish, which meant that my kidneys had flared up again. I tried to drag myself out of bed but was unable to. Consequently, I decided *not* to attempt to make it to my grandmother's funeral.

I called my doctor's office this afternoon to make an appointment, since the antibiotics I've been taking on and off don't seem to be resolving my problems. Hopefully I haven't screwed myself up with all this self-medicating.

Anyway, this is all very depressing... Oh, and I forgot to mention that I haven't heard from Maurizio since I got back from Argentina a week ago. Strange. He usually responds to my emails right away.

Well, coming up next I will answer some of your questions. Hopefully that will cheer me up a little... but for now, I'm going to take a nap.

First Questions Answered!
Filed in ABOUT ME on Wednesday, 04/20

OK, Q of Sky will answer at least one person's questions every day. First up, MandiMAC...

From MandiMAC on 04/17:

1. **What's your dream vacation?**
    Queen of Sky's dream vacation is lounging on a beach in Tahiti (or anywhere for that matter) with a really HOT and SEXY guy who is really into ME and ONLY ME!!!

2. **What was your worst flight?**
    Worst flight? Hmmm... there have been so many. But the time I had a group of Spanish teenagers aboard the all-nighter to Madrid ranks among my top ten worst flights of all times. They wouldn't sit down or shut up the whole flight and stood right by our crew rest seats talking loudly ALL night.   >:-(Badly behaved passengers make for an ANGRY Queen of Sky!

3. **How long do you plan to fly?**
    Until I find my sugar daddy, and then I'm outta here! (Kidding.) Actually, I'll probably be one of those old bags that flies until she's 80. :-O

Romulus' Questions Answered!
Filed in ABOUT ME on Thursday, 04/21

From romulus on 04/18:

1. **If you could pick three songs to describe yourself, what would they be?**
    - Livin' la Vida Loca
    - Like a Virgin
    - I Will Survive

2. **If you could pick one person to spill coffee on, who would it be?**
    You.

3. **Does the "Mile High Club" exist?**
    Why do you think they call me "Her Mile Highness"!!?? :-O ;-)

Spinster's Questions Answered!
Filed in ABOUT ME on Thursday, 04/21

From Spinster on 04/19:

1. **Where were you born?**
    Queen of Sky was born in Boringham, North Carolina.

2. **Where do you live now?**
    Q of S lives in Quirksville (aka KeepItWeird), Texas.

3. **Are you a pilot, or learning to fly, or would you like to?**
    No, no, and no.

Those weren't very original questions, Spinster.

Mood: ANGRY!
Filed in MISC. on Friday, 04/22

So today Queen of Sky went to the doctor (or nurse practitioner, rather) to get a prescription for antibiotics.

Anyhow, the nurse practitioner at first told me that I just had back strain. I told her this was not the case. I know the difference between back strain and throbbing kidneys.

So then she tested my urine and confirmed that there was something going on there.

"We will send it for a culture, which will take two to three days, and then I can prescribe the right antibiotics for you," she said. "In the meantime, I am referring you to a urologist. The referral will take four to five days."

Then she sent Queen of Sky home with a prescription for painkillers. Queen of Sky took this to the pharmacy, and they told her that the prescription was for a 30-day supply, and that this was WAY too much, as this particular medication causes liver damage if you take it for more than three consecutive days.

Great, I thought. *My liver is going to fall out and my kidneys will still be throbbing.*

Then the pharmacist said they should have given me an interim prescription of antibiotics, even if they didn't know the exact type of infection. So, I called my nurse practitioner back at 1pm to ask for some antibiotics. Of course I had to leave a message.

And no one ever called me back.

Needless to say, Queen of Sky is ANGRY right now. I would have been better off flying to South America and self-medicating... plus it's a lot cheaper... no co-pays, etc.

Meanwhile, I've decided to give up yoga for the time being, as my back will never heal if I'm constantly straining it, bending forward and backward and twisting. And I may be calling in sick for my trip to Spain this Monday.

The good news is, today Queen of Sky sold her POS (piece of sh*t) car. (Remember, I bought a new one a couple of months back.) Bubba, Bubba, and Bubba drove down from Redneck County and gave Queen of Sky $1200 cash. Whoopee!!!

Time for some shopping!!!

OK, now I'm rambling again. I smell my freshly baked scones in the next room, and it's time to sample them. Neighbors upstairs are stomping around. Maybe they are trying to tell Queen of Sky her music is too loud. It's only 10pm. Hmmm...

Sunil's Questions Answered
Filed in ABOUT ME on Saturday, 04/23

From sunil on 04/17:

1. **Would you ever give your life for a stranger?**
   Ummm, let me think about that one... NO! Queen of Sky will be the first one down the slide in the event of an emergency landing. :-O

2. **Where would you like to live?**
   Hmm. Someone has not been following Queen of Sky's blog very closely—tsk,tsk!
   Queen of Sky already spelled out the places she would like to live in her résumé a couple of weeks ago: If not Texas, then California, Hawaii, the French Riviera, or a quaint sun-drenched isle where the men are handsome and the food divine!

3. **What's your favorite color?**
   Purple and orange. These are on Queen of Sky's coat of arms.

Chucha Galore's Questions Answered!
Filed in ABOUT ME on Sunday, 04/24

From ChuchaGalore on 04/18:
1. **How does it feel to be a young, sexy, blond, international flight attendant?**
   Not as glamorous as it sounds.

2. **If you were to donate an organ, which one it would be and why?**
   I would like to auction off my kidneys to the highest bidder... or heck, I'll just give them away! They've been problematic of late, anyway. Must have been all that crew sangria!!!

3. **What's the best place to do it in the plane?**
   No place. I think this is where you and I differ, Chucha. Queen of Sky only "does it" in large, plush, cozy beds! (And she only does two positions, at that!)

   (I was joking before when I said that's how I got my nickname.)

Incompetent Doctor's Office and Calling in Sick
Filed in MISC. on Monday, 04/25

Uggh. I'm still feeling feverish and achy. Yesterday I called Incompetent Doctor's Office about five times, just trying to get my test results from the other day. When the nurse finally called me back, she admitted that my urine sample had been inadvertently discarded rather than sent to the lab. So she prescribed me some different antibiotics. Two a day for ten days. As soon as I started taking them, I felt better. In fact, yesterday I felt pretty good.

But this morning when I woke up, my back was feeling iffy again. I really wanted to go to Barcelona, but I didn't want to strain myself. Plus, Barcelona just wouldn't be the same without being able to have a glass of wine or sangria with my tapas. So, Queen of Sky made an executive decision and called in sick for the trip.

Am just going to rest until my trip to Lima on Monday. Meanwhile, Incompetent Doctor's Office is supposed to refer me to a urologist. Fun, fun, fun.

Anyhow, up next, Q of S will answer the "Sugar Daddy" questions. ;-)

Queen of Sky's Sugar Daddy Profile
Filed in ABOUT ME on Tuesday, 04/26

OK, enough with the depressing stuff. Queen of Sky is still in her underpants (has been in her underpants all day). Finished watching *American Idol* and *The Bachelor*, so now I have time to play. Here are the long-awaited answers to cali-whatever's questions (who BTW did not read the three-question rule):

From calinativo on 4/22
Describe the following requirements of your sugar daddy:

1. **How much sugar should the daddy make annually to keep Q of S in the lifestyle she is accustomed?**
    A lot.

2. **What age and physical requirements exist (height, weight, hair or not)? Please provide a range.**
    Prefer over 6' (183cm), nice build (although a *little* cushion for the pushin' is acceptable... Q of S has some of her own), hair is negotiable, foreign accent a must.

    In addition, he must be handsome and debonair. ;-)

    I forgot to mention the age range is 20-40, though Queen of Sky is a *bit* flexible on that.

2a. **Are the physical requirements negotiable based on the amount of sugar provided to Q of S annually?**
No.

3. **Can the sugar daddy be married, engaged, have girlfriend(s)?**
Absolutely not... and NO KIDS, PLEASE!!!

3a. **Is his domestic status negotiable based on the annual amount of sugar provided to Q of S?**
NO!

4. **What can the sugar daddy expect in return ?**
A thank you card... or random postcards from Q of S's layovers—you choose!

5. **Finally, can the sugar daddy be a sugar mamma?**
No, but he *definitely* can be a gay man. In fact, this is the perfect scenario for Queen of Sky—the Gay Sugar Daddy.

6. **Assuming the person meets the above requirements, where do they apply for the position?**
Send Queen of Sky your address, and she will send you the full application and her bank account number.
Note: Anyone can apply for Queen of Sky's "Anonymous Generous Benefactor" position. For the benefits thereof, see #4 above.

Honeymelon's Questions Answered
Filed in ABOUT ME on Wednesday, 04/27

OK, here is the last round of questions, folks:

From Honeymelon on 04/18

1. **What's the best part of being a flight attendant?**
Free flights; traveling to international destinations and getting paid for it; only working twelve days a month; not having to work with the same people all the time; shopping in foreign lands; getting great haircuts for $12 in Peru; eating fabulous seafood and drinking fabulous wines in Spain; buying fresh mozzarella and pinot grigio at $4 a bottle in Italy; a different man in every port; I could go on and on...

2. **What's your favorite movie?**

   Best movies I have seen recently were *About Schmidt* and *Lost in Translation*. *Lost in Translation* was like a bunch of my layovers and vacations tied together, but I liked the ending better in *About Schmidt*. That movie had a really good message (about the importance of priorities), not to mention it was hilarious!

3. **What's the best place you've ever traveled to?**

   For work, probably Rio. Talk about a *beautiful* city. Only problem is all the prostitutes and poverty.

   Best place I've traveled to on my own was probably the south of Spain. I had a great time there.

Good News and Bad
Filed in MISC. on Friday, 04/29

First, the good news. Queen of Sky is feeling almost back to her old self after four full days on the new antibiotics. Back is still stiff, but no longer achy. However, after being on various antibiotics for the past month, Queen of Sky has a sneaking suspicion that there is a nasty YEAST INFECTION in the near future with her name on it—YUK!!!

Guess the only way to avoid it now is for Queen of Sky to toss herself into a big vat of yogurt!

More good news: Queen of Sky swapped her Lima on Monday for a Buenos Aires tomorrow.

Now the bad news... I still haven't heard from Maurizio. I just sent him another email to tell him I will be in his neck of the woods again the day after tomorrow. We'll see if he responds. But it looks like Her Mile Highness will have to go this one alone. :-(

Commuter Stories
Filed in MY LIFE IN THE AIRPORT on Saturday, 04/30

This afternoon I had almost gotten to the airport when I realized that I had not put a uniform shirt or sweater in my bag. (Queen of Sky was commuting in regular clothes today.)

I quickly turned around and headed back home. Then I realized I was already running late and going all the way home would surely make me miss my flight. And the next flight (my back-up) was full.

So I turned back around and set off for the airport again.

As I was running to my gate, I heard my name called out behind me. I spun around. There sat two other Anonymous Airline commuters leisurely having breakfast.

"Don't worry, Elena, the flight is delayed," one of them said.

I told them about my uniform dilemma, and they said it shouldn't be a problem. There were plenty of shirts in Lost and Found in the flight attendant lounge.

One of these commuters was a pilot, the other a flight attendant, whom I shall call Veronica.

Veronica is a mess. She's very attractive (former swimsuit model), and guys go nuts for her, but there always seems to be some drama going on in her life. She's a single mother and flight attendant, which is a bad enough combination to start with.

She was dating a guy in Finland (!!!—sounds like something I would do) and got pregnant and kept the baby. Probably not the best decision.

The Finnish guy, of course, dumped her after that.

The most recent drama has been Veronica's several-years-long affair with a married pilot. (They met on a Rio trip—go figure.) Not only is he married, but he has three kids to boot—a real win-win situation.

These are stories I hear everyday... dumb blonds (or brunettes or redheads) and married pilots who promise to leave their wives for them. And then the dumb blond (or brunette or redhead) is always the one that gets dumped in the end.

Well, Veronica got dumped by her married pilot a while back, but he is still on her mind. She showed us a book today that he had recently given her, entitled *The Purpose-Driven Life*. Maybe he was trying to tell her something.

Ya think?

Anyway, I can't be too hard on Veronica because she's from a broken home, and I know what that's like.

Presently Her Mile Highness is sitting in the flight attendant lounge, having picked out the least-stinky uniform pieces from the lost and found. Earlier in the bathroom I overheard a flight attendant I commute with talking about the flight from Europe a week or two ago that had to make an emergency landing in Iceland because of a note the crew found scribbled on a napkin in the lav that said "Bomb on board" and the date.

She was working that flight. She said they had to prepare for an evacuation—every flight attendant's nightmare. And they did indeed evacuate, but on air stairs rather than on the slides.

"Seven and a half minutes," she announced.

That was the time it took for them to evacuate the almost 200 passengers down the stairs.

Oh, by the way, I did finally receive an email from Maurizio this morning. He apologized for not responding sooner, saying that he has been in Honduras or Guatemala—somewhere remote, anyway, where he didn't have email access. He says he is now home in Italy and unfortunately cannot meet me in B.A. tomorrow, but if I get a trip to Europe in the next few weeks he can meet me anywhere on the Continent.

That should be pretty easy to do. I'm gonna try to get a two-day layover in Barcelona. I saw it in the bid packet for next month. :-)

Well, nothing much else going on. There was some gossip on the flight to work this morning about what will happen if Anonymous Airlines files bankruptcy. We are all looking for other jobs, second careers, etc. Queen of Sky needs to call the culinary school next week again to request a catalog, since they never sent it to her. She needs to get started on a back-up career, since there is currently no sugar daddy in sight (except possibly Maurizio... but only time will tell if he is the real deal).

Well, that's all the gossip I have for now...

Until we meet again,
—Q of S

MAY

Mystery Unveiled

The Witches of Recoleta
Filed in LAYOVERS on Tuesday, 05/03

Hi, all. Guess who's back in da 'hood? Yup, Queen of Sky. Got back from Argentina this morning.

It actually ended up being an OK trip, even though I didn't have my Italian suitor to wine and dine and romance me. :-(

On Sunday, the day we arrived, after a brief nap, Nancy (the pilot-crazed flight attendant—pilot-crazed *married* flight attendant, to be more specific) and I went tango dancing. That was fun, even though I didn't know what I was doing. I am a proficient Latin dancer, but the tango is not in my repertoire. Luckily, though, there were some little old men at the dance hall who had no problem showing Queen of Sky how to whirl about sultrily on the dance floor.

Later I had dinner with the whole crew at a nice buffet restaurant that's a crew favorite. Ever since the Argentine currency crashed, the prices there are unbelievable—especially for food. We paid about $4 each for the huge dinner buffet, which included freshly grilled meats (although Queen of Sky only ate the chicken—she doesn't eat anything with more than two legs) *and* UNLIMITED wine!!! This is pilot paradise—they don't even have to pretend to offer to pay for our meals, it's so cheap here! (BTW, of course during dinner Nancy was flirting heavily with the captain, who was also married.)

On Monday I was feeling like a little alone time, so I walked over to Recoleta, an artsy area, to check out the street vendors. But I ended up getting sucked into the fortune tellers.

First I consulted a palm reader and was very unimpressed by her talents.

"I see an O... I see a T," said the witchy-looking lady with a scarf wrapped around her head for effect. "You are going to meet someone with these initials."

Yeah, right, I thought. *I could have done a better job reading my own hand with a palmistry book!*

Then I hit a tarot card reader. But fifteen minutes later and another $5 poorer, I was equally unimpressed.

That bruja didn't even count her cards right! I remarked to myself, after watching her deal the cards into piles to form a circle.

The problem? She only made eleven piles instead of the customary twelve. And then she gave me a rather gloomy and far-fetched reading. She said my whole life was going to change soon, and all because of something innocent. I asked her if it involved Maurizio. She said no. I asked her if it would be a change for the better. She said she couldn't tell me that.

Arggh! All I wanted was to hear about my bright future and whether I would drive into the sunset with Maurizio.

Afterward I walked back to the hotel through the brisk air (it's fall in the southern hemisphere), slightly miffed at wasting my money.

Well, not much else to report from the trip, except some MAJOR personality conflicts on the crew on the way home. A couple of senior mamas had a power struggle during the meal service in business class (and all through the flight, actually). Who cares who does meals and who does drinks, as long as it all gets done! Queen of Sky couldn't wait to land.

Good Swapping Karma
Filed in LIFE OF LEISURE on Wednesday, 05/04

Ah, Madrid! My friend Victor and I were talking about that fab city last night at dinner. Victor was stationed there many years ago when he was in the army. Apparently he has some *very* fond memories...

"Hmmm... There was Maria and Isabel and Maria and Graciela and... Maria," he wistfully reminisced. "Man, those were the days! I'd like to go back over there and look some of them up." A peaceful smile washed across his face as he touched his jaw nostalgically.

I hated to be the one to burst his bubble (well, not really).

"They're probably all married with six kids and twenty-six grandkids by now, Victor," I said.

His brow furrowed and his smile turned to a frown.

"Hmmm... you're probably right."

Victor's stories inspired Queen of Sky's own wistful reminiscences about Madrid. But not about any handsome Spaniards she had romanced—no, she would rather forget them.

Q of S's fondest memories of Madrid are of a much more palatable nature: tapas, to be exact.

I began to recount nostalgically the six-month span some years ago when I was based in New York. Back then I used to fly to Madrid four or five times a month, and we used to go downtown for tapas every trip.

One time a frisky Spanish flight attendant took Q of S to a bunch of his favorite tapas bars. At the end of the night, however, he tried to have Her Mile Highness for dessert. Nonetheless, Señor Frisky's fabulous tapas route later became the basis for Q of S's own route.

"You've been to a real tapas bar, right, Victor?" I inquired.

"Yeah, I think so. Like that place Sevilla on Fifth Street, right?"

"Not exactly. In Madrid, each little tapas bar specializes in a certain dish, like codfish croquettes or garlic shrimp or Spanish omelets," I explained. "And what you do is nibble on a little plate of tapas and sip a little tiny glass of beer or wine. Sometimes they just give you a little shot glass. It's fun! Then you start the whole thing over again at the next place."

Q of S became glassy-eyed (and drooly-mouthed) just thinking about her beloved tapas route.

"Elena, do you ever think about anything besides food?" Victor asked, amused.

"Yes. Sometimes I think about wine."

It must have been karma, because this morning at 8:15, Queen of Sky got a phone call (which I wouldn't have answered, except I thought it was Maurizio. He knows not to call me before 10am, but sometimes when he's on the other side of the globe, he miscalculates the time difference.).

I leapt out of bed and grabbed the phone eagerly. But when I heard a female voice on the other end of the line, my hopes were instantly dashed.

Why would anyone call and wake me up such an ungodly hour!? Q of S mused angrily.

Alas, it was Gloria (I should have known) asking me if I would swap my Lima tomorrow (her boyfriend is on it, of course) for her Madrid on Sunday.

CLARO QUE SI!!!! (OF COURSE I WILL!!!!)

So, I will get to do my tapas route in Madrid on Sunday. :-) Only thing is, I really needed to get my hair cut in Lima, but I have another trip there later this month, so no need to worry. I swapped with another flight attendant earlier this month to give her Memorial Day weekend off, so apparently this is my karmic payback.

Namaste!

Happy Cinco!!!!
Filed in LIFE OF LEISURE on Thursday, 05/05

HAPPY CINCO DE MAYO, EVERYONE!!!!

I have one more day of antibiotics, so drink some margaritas for me!!!

—Q of S

P.S. The 5th of May is actually not celebrated in Mexico, just in the States. The holiday there is the 16th of September (Mexican independence day).

Queen of Sky's Shopping Spree
Filed in LIFE OF LEISURE on Friday, 05/06

Well, Queen of Sky was feeling good yesterday, so she headed to the mall, which put her in an even better mood.

First, she hit Express, where she spent $400 on cute little sun dresses for her possible vacation in Italy this summer. Express sure is a lot more expensive than H&M, but their stuff is more feminine.

Then Queen of Sky was hungry, so she headed to the Ruby's all-you-can-eat buffet in the mall. Possibly not the best idea when swimsuits were next on my list of things to buy. A couple of plates of fried chicken, veggies, and pecan pie later, I headed to a teenybopper skate store to check out their bikinis.

First off, Queen of Sky was the oldest person in the store, so people looked at her a little oddly. Then, as Queen of Sky was perusing the itsy-bitsy bikinis, she spotted the exact same bikini she had gotten from ValeriesSecret.com the week before. It was the same price ($82), the only difference was there was no $14 shipping & handling fee!!! (I was a little pissed at that, since of course they had sent it in a regular mail envelope, and now I am going to send it back because it didn't look quite as sexy on me as it did on Gisele the rubber band.)

Anyhow, several trips to the dressing room later, I finally found the perfect suit. They even had the top in extra-large. It makes Queen of Sky look voluptuous but not ridiculous. Unfortunately, it was $100. But it has a paisley top that is reversible. On the other side it's denim, to match the bottom. And the bottom has a paisley belt to match the top. In any case, Queen of Sky was smitten... made me look like Ursula Andress in whatever Bond film she was in. (I will try to post a picture of it soon if I can figure out how.)

So, new shopping total, $500-plus. :-O

Next, Queen of Sky bought some $7 sunglasses at Payless, then ducked out of the mall before she could max out her credit cards.

Then she headed to Sprawlmart to stock up on flip-flops and toiletries. Queen of Sky got the last pair of flip-flops that light up as you walk (in extra-large... OK, I have HUMONGO feet). Upon leaving the shoe section, I overheard a little girl exclaim to her mother as I passed:

"Look how tall that lady is!"

I was wearing my heels so must have appeared about six foot four (over 190 cm).

Then I spied some really cute cami and panty sets in the underwear section. I bought one set that says "Princess" and another that says "Hottie."

Needless to say, Queen of Sky spent another $100 easily in Sprawlmart.

Queen of Sky was in a good mood from all this shopping. She had found her Italy wardrobe and bathing suit and even some cute PJs to boot! She decided to make one more stop before heading home—Kohl's, a discount department store. Queen of Sky usually buys her work shoes there. But today she had no luck. There were only summer shoes in stock. I did find some really cute little bracelets with rhinestone initials, so I bought seven or eight of those. Have birthday gifts taken care of for the next year! (Another $60 spent!)

Queen of Sky is afraid to add up the total money spent yesterday, and today she is having shopper's remorse. Will head back to Express to return one of the $60 dresses (totally see-through, and the pale pink totally washed me out), plus a jeans skirt ($58 is way too much to pay for a simple denim skirt!) and an orange shirt that is frankly too orange. Queen of Sky is also contemplating returning the little white sundress that is also totally see-through, though it fits like a glove and is very sexy. However, how often does one get the occasion to wear a sexy white dress?

Anyhow, that's the scoop. Back is bothering me a little today... must have overdone it yesterday trying on all that stuff. :-O

Need to do laundry and take that stuff back to the mall now...

Move over Giselle, Move over Kate Moss...
Filed in LIFE OF LEISURE on Saturday, 05/07

... this white girl's got *curves*!!!

OK, I finally figured out how to use my mother's digital camera (and auto-timer) and found the right cable to hook it up to my computer. However, my PhotoShop is not working, so I could only do minimal edits here. Could not remove love handles, cushion for the pushin', etc.

Whaddya think? Should Queen of Sky keep this one? It was $100, but Queen of Sky thinks she might be able to wear this on her vacation in Italy this summer (am taking an Italian course in Rome and then going to meet Maurizio on his home turf in Venice).

Back to Work
Filed in MY LIFE IN THE AIRPORT on Sunday, 05/08

Queen of Sky got an extra two hours of sleep this morning in her *own* bed. :-) Very happy about that.

Anonymous International added another flight this month from Quirksville to Bustling Base City, so Queen of Sky was able to take a flight at 10am rather than 8am to come to work. This still left a back-up flight before my sign-in time, which is all I need to keep from getting in trouble if things go wrong (flight cancellations, weather delays, etc.), which they often do.

Presently I'm sitting in the flight attendant lounge in Bustling Base City. I just found out that with the new bidding system that goes into effect in July, I will have six "access days" on my schedule per month. That's six days on call... >:-(

I haven't been on reserve (on call) for more than six years!!! That *really* bites!!!!

Anyway, only have an hour left before briefing to go to Madrid. The weather is looking iffy over there... cold and rainy, so Queen of Sky may not be able to do her tapas route after all. :-(

Back in Bustling Base City
Filed in MY LIFE IN THE AIRPORT on Tuesday, 05/10

Well, Queen of Sky just got in from Madrid. Tried to take a nap here in the flight attendant lounge, but the two loudest flight attendants at Anonymous Airlines were having a very LIVELY conversation right outside the sleep room. Plus, the guy on the lounge chair next to me was snoring loudly.

I am too lazy to go all the way over to Concourse X now to see if I can get on the 5:30pm flight back to Quirksville. The flight is full, with five people standing by already and zero empty seats. Not good odds, plus Queen of Sky bought three bottles of wine and a bottle of olive oil and does not feel like schlepping that plus her trusty standard black two-wheeled sidekick Valigia all the way from Concourse Z.

Hmmm, guess Queen of Sky will go back in the sleep room for a few more hours and hope that chatty Doris and Debbi have abandoned their posts outside the door for their flights to Whoknowswhere and drooling Dave has woken himself up with his snoring by now.

Geez... it's always an adventure trying to get a little shut-eye around here!

Anyway, it was a good trip. I'll write about it later. The only bad part was that the lead flight attendant was very by-the-book. ("We'll be doing everything the Anonymous Airlines way.") Which meant that even though we were wide open on the way back, she insisted on splitting the crew rest breaks into three instead of two. Three breaks equal shorter breaks for everyone.

Thus, we only got to rest for one and a half hours instead of two and a quarter. And unfortunately I couldn't sleep for my break, as I kept thinking how short the break was and how as soon as I fell asleep, I would have to wake up. So of course I never fell asleep, and needless to say, am exhausted right now. Every flight attendant's worst enemy, fatigue plus jet lag, has caught up with me today. :-(

On that note, am going back to the sleep room now...

Hasta luego,
—Q of S

MADRID
Filed in LAYOVERS on Wednesday, 05/11

Queen of Sky promised a recount of her layover in Madrid, so here goes...

The flight to Madrid went smoothly. I was working in business class. There were only 27 passengers up there, so it was easy. But regardless, after the eight-hour all-night flight, I was exhausted.

It was cool and drizzly in Madrid when we exited the airport and made our way to the hotel van. We dropped our bags off with the driver and piled in.

On the ride to the hotel, half-asleep, I planned my layover... *I'll probably just go to the Corte Inglés* (big department/grocery store) *and the pharmacy after I wake up from my nap,* I thought. *It's not a good day to do my tapas route. Next time. I haven't really connected with anyone on the crew anyway. All a bunch of old bags, as usual on a Sunday Europe trip.*

But then as I was walking into the hotel, Valigia in tow, the captain turned to me and said, "So, Elena, are you going downtown to have tapas?"

I froze. I forgot I had mentioned my tapas route to him before we left Bustling Base City. Visions of myself and Old Fart (although nice) Captain on a "date" together flashed through my fatigued brain. Queen of Sky often seems to end up going out on the layover with the only straight male flight attendant on the crew. But going out alone with a pilot—that was much worse!

There are many flight attendants who love to hang out with pilots (like my friend Gloria), but I'm not one of them. I hate to generalize (not really), but Anonymous Airlines pilots tend to have "rich, arrogant American" plastered all over their faces. Plus, they are typically the two big no-nos: married *and* cheap. And they often prey upon innocent young flight attendants (which they mistakenly think I am).

Here's their typical strategy: remove wedding ring after getting to layover (after all, according to many pilots, your wedding vows don't count once you cross the ocean or the equator); invite youngest, most innocent-looking flight attendants out for drinks/dinner; try to get young, innocent flight attendants drunk (making sure to hide indented ring finger through course of the evening); do not pay for young, innocent flight attendants' dinners (thus saving money to buy flowers for wife when get home); and, finally, try to get young, innocent flight attendants back to your hotel room.

If the strategy doesn't work with the young, innocent flight attendants, or there are none on the crew (which is more often the case on international flights at Anonymous Airlines), then the pilots will use the strategy on the older, divorced, and/or horny flight attendants.

You would be surprised to know how often it works.

I finally muttered a "yes" to the captain after a long pause. In the meantime I realized that it would be me and *all three* pilots, not just the captain. That would be a little better.

Then, as we were standing around still waiting for our rooms (sometimes we have to wait HOURS in these *shockingly* inefficient European layover hotels), Libby, another flight attendant—and the only other crew member still in her child-bearing years—decided to join us for tapas, too.

So it actually ended up being fun.

Meanwhile, I stressed that I needed *at least* four hours of beauty sleep after an all-nighter, so the five of us met in the lobby for a drink at 6:30pm. About an hour later, after the pilots had recounted all of their newest dirty jokes, we took the subway downtown. From there we began our tapas bar crawl through the drizzly cold evening. The good thing about the weather was that the bars weren't as crowded as usual.

We started at the little codfish bar in front of the Corte Inglés by the Puerta del Sol. There we stood (there are no tables in this place), elbow-to-elbow with the local patrons, nibbling on codfish croquettes and fried chunks of cod and sipping mini-beers and shots of wine. The captain and some-body else complained about the bones in the fish, and Libby complained that it was too greasy. Too authentic for them, I guess.

Queen of Sky loves that place. But we were quickly off to the next locale.

"So what's next?" inquired the captain.

"Either the mushroom place, the shrimp place, or the potato place," I replied.

We decided collectively on the shrimp place, El Abuelo, and the little group shuffled across the plaza, past the Tio Pepe sign, right at one of the many Museos del Jamón and up the street to the little standing-room only bar filled with the odor of garlic, olive oil and, of course, shrimp.

To be continued...

Madrid, Part II
Filed in LAYOVERS on Thursday, 05/12

Let's see, where did Queen of Sky leave off?

Ah, yes... at a tapas bar in Madrid.

At the fragrant little bar, El Abuelo, the dysfunctional airline family munched on gambas al ajillo (garlic shrimp), sopping up the garlicky olive oil with their bread. This place won high praise from Queen of Sky's crew. Next up was the potato place, Las Bravas, across the way. There we partook of the famous patatas bravas (fried potatoes with spicy sauce) and a tortilla brava (Spanish omelet with spicy sauce) and, of course, olives. Queen of Sky had a nice glass of rioja to wash down all the garlic.

Next, the group headed around the corner to Abuelo II and had their vegetable course: pimientos de padrón (little mild fried peppers) and grilled asparagus with alioli (garlic mayonnaise). Good stuff. The group praised Queen of Sky's choices in tapas bars, although the captain had been to several of them before, too.

Finally, we crossed the Plaza Mayor in the rain and the cold wind and decided to forego the mushroom place (a crew favorite) because Her Mile Highness was whining that she wanted something hot to drink...like a mug of thick Spanish hot chocolate with churros (Spanish doughnuts)—YUM!

After some discussion and a near mutiny, the group followed Queen of Sky's lead and ended up at the Chocolatería San Something, a stone's throw from the Plaza Mayor and the Puerta del Sol.

There, one of the copilots and I had chocolate con churros, and the other two pilots had after-dinner drinks.

"I thought you said you weren't hungry anymore," the capitán said to Queen of Sky.

"No, I said I didn't want to eat any more garlic. I reached my quotient." (If you've ever had Spanish food, you know what I mean.)

I had a couple of sips of the copilot's Frangelico, which was the perfect chaser for my thick, rich hot chocolate. It was the perfect ending to the evening (although after all those churros, I thought I was going to puke).

We took the subway back to the hotel around 11pm, against Q of S's wishes. I had wanted to take a cab, rather than schlep the five blocks or so back from the subway to the hotel through the cold, wet night—plus I really needed to use the bathroom, if you know what I mean—but the pilots didn't want to cough up a few extra euros). Thus, we called it a night.

-THE END-

P.S. Queen of Sky didn't get home on Tuesday until midnight!!! My 9pm flight to Quirksville was delayed... Uggh! I spent about six hours in Bustling Base City airport!!! Might as well live there. :-P

10 Little Known Facts About the Queen of Sky
Filed in ABOUT ME on Friday, 05/13

1. Queen of Sky is a slob.
2. Queen of Sky has no fashion/decorating sense.
3. Queen of Sky recently had to purchase size 12 shoes. :-O (Q of S has a sinking suspicion her feet are still growing...they're normally a size 11.)
4. The good news is, if Q of S's feet are still growing, her boobs are too. Her friend Jesse asked her last month if she had gotten a boob job. Queen of Sky was flattered.
5. Queen of Sky is six feet tall, but does *not* play basketball or volley-ball, so please DON'T ask!
6. Queen of Sky is not athletic.

7. Queen of Sky likes to salsa dance. (Only with good dancers, PLEASE!!! Also, no midgets, please—i.e., anybody under 5'10".)
8. Queen of Sky lived with a hunky but lazy Czech man for three years.
9. Queen of Sky is now happily single.
10. Queen of Sky is thinking about getting a cat.

Booty Call Guy
Filed in MEN on Saturday, 05/14

Hmm. This evening I got a call from an old friend—Ralph, aka Booty Call Guy.

Ralph is a six-foot-tall beefy guy whose favorite pastimes (besides sex) are pumping iron and admiring himself in the mirror. He's a pretty good-looking guy, except for the nose, which looks horribly out of place. (He had a nose job, supposedly to correct a broken nose.) Actually, come to think of it, he has one other detracting physical factor: the dark carpet of hair that covers him from head to toe (think: gorilla). Ralph is one of those rarities at the airlines: a straight male flight attendant.

I call him Booty Call Guy because I once made the mistake of having a booty call with him after we flew a Madrid trip together a couple years ago. Every time I worked a trip after that, I met another flight attendant whom Ralph had "serviced." Turns out he had "serviced" at least half the single women at AIA—and a good portion of the married ones, too!

Queen of Sky does not share, so this was a no-brainer for her—buh-bye, Ralph! He didn't get the hint, though, and to this day still calls me, hoping in vain that I'll give it up again.

Anyway, as is his norm, the first thing Booty Call Guy inquired about was as to whether I was "gettin' any." I assured him that I was gettin' plenty. Nonetheless, he generously offered to fly from Bustling Base City to Quirksville to "take care of me" any time I needed him to.

"Thank you, Ralph. You're so thoughtful," Queen of Sky replied sar-castically. "Always looking out for my needs."

After a few minutes, BCG could tell he wasn't getting anywhere with me this evening, as usual. So he did what any self-respecting macho man under the circumstances would do—pulled a face-saving disappearing act.

"Well, I just called to say hi and bye," he announced, and hung up before I could respond.

BCG's phone call reminded me of our drive halfway across the country last October. Ralph, aka BCG, my semi-stalker, offered to drive with me from Atlanta to Texas so that I could bring some of my mother's things home with me. I was skeptical, because I knew all he was after was booty—my booty, that is. But in the end I let him come because he was furloughed and had nothing better to do. Plus he still had free flights privileges, so he could fly back home afterward.

I loaded up the rented mini van on my own because Ralph said he was just there to help me drive, and we left around 10am on the long drive to Texas. The topic of conversation for the whole drive was, of course, sex.

Sex was all Ralph ever thought about. Well, that and money.

He's been married three or four times before and has two grown children by two different women. He wants me to be wife numero cuatro (or cinco). I once asked him if he had ever been faithful to anyone he had dated, and there was a long pause. He came back with a story about some girl he used to sleep with, along with several others, but when they had decided to be exclusive, he had dropped the other women he was seeing.

I wasn't buying it.

The fact that he had not spoken to his mother back in South America for over six years (he says she owes him money) was enough to make me mark him off my list of potential boyfriends, let alone husbands.

Anyway, back to the drive. Ralph drove like a maniac—80-plus miles an hour, and swerving around to pass cars and trucks on the left and right. I should have just taken a Dramamine and passed out. On more than one occasion, a trucker or other vehicle came after us because Ralph cut them off.

He finally let me drive for a stretch so that he could give his road rage a rest. But after a couple of hours he got impatient, saying we would never make it to Texas that night with me driving.

So he took the wheel again and I held on for dear life.

We made it to Texas in ten hours. Quite a remarkable time, so I was glad Ralph had driven with me after all.

I told him I would take him on a tour of Quirksville the next day, but all he did from the moment we arrived in my city was complain. He was angry at me because I didn't want him to move in with me. He asked me what time the first flight in the morning to Bustling Base City was.

"Sorry, Ralph. I am not getting up at the crack of dawn to take you to the airport," Queen of Sky replied.

After we got to my place and unloaded all the stuff, I said goodnight to Ralph, went into my bedroom, and locked the door.

The next morning I asked Ralph how he had slept.

"Good—but I would have slept better if you had *given me some*! At least a *hand job* or something!"

He had such a way with words. Really knew how to talk to a lady.

Her Mile Highness took him to the airport, and that was that.

Sad Entry
Filed in MISC. on Sunday, 05/15

OK, every now and then you need to have a sad entry.

I know Mother's Day was last week, but I didn't want to depress people, since it was the first Mother's Day since my mother died. But then I was talking to another flight attendant this week about a colleague of ours who is dying of brain cancer, and I decided to do a tribute to my mother.

> *Dear Mother,*
>
> *I know we did not have an ideal mother-daughter relationship, though we had been trying to work on that in the past few years.*
> *I really wish things had turned out differently. I wish that disease had not come along when it did, just when things were getting better between us. I wish we had had more time together. There's so much I didn't know about you, so many trips we didn't take together, so many ways our relationship could have grown.*
> *Well, I don't know what else to say except I wish you were still here. Happy Belated Mother's Day. I love you.*
>
> *Your daughter always,*
> *Elena*

Can't Wait
Filed in MISC. on Monday, 05/16

Well, through some creative swapping and a little downright begging, I have managed to get a two-day Barcelona tomorrow. Maurizio is going to meet me there, so I am really excited! He says that is his favorite city, besides Venice, of course.

Well, I need to start packing now... :-D

My Life in the Airport
Filed in MY LIFE IN THE AIRPORT on Tuesday, 05/17

Here Queen of Sky sits, once again in Bustling Base City airport. Feels like I never left.

Today I'm heading east to Barcelona for some tapas, wine, and *amor.*
:-D

I once again took the 10am flight to work, which was nice except that it's on one of those mini-jets that are always packed to the gills. Today it was full of that four-letter word: KIDS.

In the row behind Queen of Sky sat a family of five, including two hyperactive kids and one screaming baby who crapped his diaper right after take-off.

Needless to say, there was no napping on that flight for Queen of Sky.

Well, there is a picture here in the flight attendant lounge of a flight attendant who was murdered a couple of weeks ago by her estranged husband at a dentist office. Truly sad and horrific. I remember her well from several Santiago trips together. She was a beautiful, classy woman and an excellent flight attendant. She was also one of the first black flight attendants hired at Anonymous International back in the 70s, according to Chucha Galore.

Hmm. So sad. I was going to leave a comment in the memorial book, but unfortunately it's not here this week. Last week I saw Barbara, my favorite ever-jolly lead flight attendant, standing by the memorial book wiping away tears. She was a close friend of the murdered woman.

I guess this entry ended kind of on a downer. Anyway, got to get ready for my briefing now...

Take care and stay safe,
—Q of S

Stood up in Spain
Filed in LAYOVERS on Wednesday, 05/18

Hi, all. I am really PEEVED right now. Am sitting here at an internet café in Barcelona, having just read an email from Maurizio. He didn't call me at the hotel earlier, so I decided to check my emails. Sure enough, he had sent me one:

> *Amore, I have bad news. There has been a conflict in Morocco, and I was sent here to help resolve it. I won't be able to come to Spain this week. I am very sorry.*
> *I love you.*
> *Baci,*
> *Maurizio*

Well, he could have at *least* called! I could have been waiting for him at the hotel all day. >:-(

Arrgh! This sure does ruin Queen of Sky's fabulous layover plans! (Granted, I did see something about a diplomatic conflict in some islands off the coast of Morocco in my perusing of the *Wall Street Observer* on the flight last night.)

Oh, well, I guess I will meet the crew downstairs for drinks tonight... just another ordinary Barcelona layover. :-(

Yours truly,
—Stood Up in Spain

The Backstreets of Barcelona
Filed in LAYOVERS on Saturday, 05/21

No, this entry has nothing to do with the Backstreet Boys, although Queen of Sky is sure she will start getting plenty of Googlers looking for just that.

Well, I got home late last night. My layover in Barcelona turned out OK, despite the crappy beginning. I met my crew for dinner, and we went to a local restaurant that had rabbit (yuk!) and snails (uggh!) on the menu. But we drank a lot of vino, so everything went down real smooth. I split a tasty paella with two of my crewmembers.

The next day five of us took the train to Montserrat to see the monastery perched high on a mountain. Very beautiful. But something I ate the night before wreaked havoc on my stomach, so I had to cut my excursion short and hightail it back to the hotel, leaving my crew behind.

Later that night Queen of Sky was feeling better and was hungry again. But since she had not found a "layover buddy" on the crew (i.e., someone to hang out with on the layover), she went out tapas bar crawling by her little self.

During the course of the evening, Q of S decided that the tapas bars in Madrid are better than in Barcelona, and cheaper, too. After eating, Q of S bought a bunch of stuff she didn't need, as usual, and even found a store open at 11 at night to buy two little flamenco dresses for her nieces, who both have birthdays next month. Those dresses are *too cute*... and they cost 25 euros for both (about $30)... woohoo!

On the way back to the hotel, I tried to enter the subway, but the entrance was closed. I assumed the whole system was closed, as it was about midnight on a Sunday night. Too cheap to hail a cab, I decided to walk back to the hotel.

Little did I know the kinds of neighborhoods I would have to traverse on the way from Ramblas back to Layover Hotel. Boy, some of those back alleys *smelled*!

At one point, I thought I was in the Middle East or South Asia. I had no idea how many Bangladeshis and Indians there were in Barcelona. (Hmmm, could be some good Indian food around those parts :-) although Q of S has pretty tasty Indian food back in Texas.) I finally made it back to the hotel unscathed around 1am.

Anyhow, that's about it. On the flight home from Barcelona yesterday, Q of S was standing at the boarding door and noticed a large number of handsome and buffed American men coming on board. When I asked them their seat numbers, without hesitation they replied, "I'm with *him*," and waved their hands rather effeminately at the gentleman in front of them.

I guess you all see where this is going... Yes, it was a group of gay cruisers. We had almost a whole airplane full of them. And, let me tell you, they drunk us dry! (Which is hard to do when you are sipping your girlie cocktail through a little coffee stir!) Q of S had to snatch a bourbon and coke out of some poor passenger's hands on final approach as he tried to sip the last ounce through his "straw." Apparently he was competing with Her Mile Highness for the title "Queen of Sky"!

Anyway, among them were some interesting characters. There was the gay couple wearing matching yellow striped shirts. ("Are they twins?" Q of S and her crew mused.) And there was a flamer in a hot pink skin-tight top.

Then there was the flight attendant in charge, a rather sassy black lady, who, upon noting the day's passenger load, declared:

"There's only *one* diva on board today, and it's *me*!"

And, finally, there was the sole male flight attendant on the trip, who was like a mini-celebrity among the male passengers. He might as well have signed autographs. :-O

(My friend Ricky will be pissed that he wasn't working that flight!)

In keeping with the mood aboard the ship that day, Q of S instructed the pilots on the new protocol before they left the gate:

"When you guys come out for your crew rest breaks later, you need to come out two at a time and holding hands."

Hee, hee, hee. :-D

We only had about five female passengers on the whole 767 that day, and the captain requested that we make sure one of them was sitting next to his crew rest seat.

Well, I'm gonna crash now...

Toodles!
—Q of S

The Soap Opera of My Life
Filed in MISC. on Sunday, 05/22

Queen of Sky needs a little help naming her personal soap opera. If my blog were a soap opera or a telenovela, what would it be called?

Here are some things I have come up with:

"The Flights of My Life"
"The Days of My Flights"
"As the World Flies"
"La Reina de los Cielos"

Any other suggestions?

Well, as you can see, Queen of Sky has *way* too much time on her hands.

Got to go pack now for three-day trip to NotSureWhere tomorrow. But first I need to check my horoscope.

Later, gators!

Daily Horoscope
Filed in MISC. on Sunday, 05/22

Confusing Energies
During this period you will be subjected to confusing and possibly down-right deceptive influences. This is not a good time to start new male relationships. In fact, a male in your life could be the cause of your present disillusions. Avoid get-rich-quick schemes and anything that seems too good to be true. Your energy will be low now and you may suffer from various health problems, ranging from infections to pulled muscles to lymphatic disorders. Avoid drugs and alcohol and all new medications during this time. Accidents or violent attacks are a real possibility. Be cautious, but not paranoid.

Aspect: Mars square Neptune
Period of Influence: 5/22-5/29
Courtesy of Astro Wizards

Geez, Astro Wizards! Can't you guys give me a break for once?!

My Life in the Airport Continues
Filed in MY LIFE IN THE AIRPORT on Monday, 05/23

Here Queen of Sky is in Bustling Base City once *again*. Today I'm going to Panama City, Panama, for a short (nine-hour) layover. The hotel is quite far from the airport (but is *really* fabulous—a five-star), so that means Q of S will only get about six hours sleep tonight. But tomorrow is another easy day, just two legs (Panama–BBC, then BBC–Tampa). All daytime flying—that's the best part.

Hmm, what else is new? Oh—I just ran into that hot mama, Gloria, here in the flight attendant lounge. She asked me about Maurizio, and I gave her the latest. Then she showed me some pics of her and John from different layovers together. She said the sex is *incredible*. :-P

"No wonder you two are always trying to fly together," Q of S replied with a wink, meanwhile secretly thinking, *Home wrecker!*

Where's the Glamour?
Filed in LAYOVERS on Wednesday, 05/25

Queen of Sky is once again sitting in the flight attendant lounge in Bustling Base City, totally exhausted, waiting for a flight home. Last night in Tampa, Q of S did not sleep well at Brand Name Hotel, which was, BTW, crawling with white trash. But it was Florida, so what did she expect?

Q of S went downstairs to the restaurant to get her 25 percent crew discount on dinner and was very disappointed in the seafood platter she ordered. The mahi-mahi was so over-cooked she mistook it for shoe leather.

Fresh Florida seafood, eh? What does it matter, if they don't know how prepare it?

Anyhow, the waiter comped Queen of Sky's key lime pie, which was also less than satisfactory. They actually used Cool Whip instead of whipped cream on top. Queen of Sky has had *much* better key lime pie in Quirksville.

OK, enough venting... as you can tell, Queen of Sky HATES Florida.

Anyway, right now I have to try to make my 5:30 flight home, which is full as usual.

Wish me luck!
—Q of S over and out

The Recovery
Filed in COMMUTING on Thursday, 05/26

Finally got back to Quirksville at MIDNIGHT last night! *&%#@!!! Got bumped off the 5:30pm Crappy Regional Carrier flight, as usual, then the 8pm flight was delayed, as usual, so I went over to the 9pm flight, which ended up with a mechanical! Uggh! Another lovely day commuting.

Queen of Sky is recovering today and will likely still be recovering on Monday when she has to hit the road (or sky) again. Luckily, this time she is once again flying to one of her favorite layover cities: Lima.

Disbelief
Filed in MEN on Friday, 05/27

OK, so here I was ready to give Maurizio one more chance, even after he stood me up in Barcelona. But then today I received an email that put my seventh sense (the liar sense) on HIGH alert. Now I know he lied to me about the reason he couldn't come to Spain last week. But that's just the *beginning*. Check this sh*t out...

> *Dear Friends,*
> *Maurizio has been in a terrible accident. He and his team fell off a cliff while climbing in the Alps last weekend. Maurizio will pull through, although he is currently in fairly bad condition. He is staying in room 666 at the Ospitale Catolico in Turin, but hopefully by next week he will be back home and will be able to respond to emails.*
> *Please pray for him.*
> *Cordially,*
> *Benedetta Mascherato, Countess of Cozze e Vongole*

I was copied in along with what looks like everyone else in Maurizio's address book. The email was written in both English and Italian.

At first I thought, *Oh, wasn't that nice of Maurizio's mother or sister to email his friends. How considerate.*

Then I remembered Maurizio telling me he is an only child. *raises eyebrow*

And his mother is Swedish and therefore would not be named Benedetta. *raises other eyebrow... smoke begins to pour from ears*

Too good to be true? I should have listened to my intuition. :-(And if he really *is* married, then that's the END of this love story, because the Queen of Sky is NOT a home wrecker!

Boy, am I SEETHING right now!

I Pity da Fool
Filed in MEN on Sunday, 05/29

Well, I am of course still hurt, upset, and LIVID about the whole Maurizio thing and have not decided what to do about it yet. I was really starting to fall for him, too. Hmm... anyhow, I think I will reserve judgment until he gets out of the hospital, so at least he has a chance to defend himself (as if there is a defense for what he did).

All I can say is that his friends had BETTER pray for him... They'd better pray that Queen of Sky doesn't drag him back up that mountain and toss him back down again!

I pity da fool that crosses the Queen of Sky! >:-(

P.S. Thanks to Slutgirl, Chucha Galore, and the rest for all of your creative revenge strategies! My favorite was the one involving superglue, two meat-balls, and one salami (Italian, of course). :-O

JUNE

My Life in the Airport

The Joys of Commuting
Filed in COMMUTING on Wednesday, 06/01

8:57am, Bustling Base City
Grunt. Queen of Sky is having a BAD morning.

The flight back from Lima went OK, but there was a ground delay in Lima because the captain decided to change his routing at the last minute. So we took off over half an hour late, around 1am. Then we arrived in BBC on time at 8am, which was bad news for me, because my Crappy Regional Carrier flight back to Quirksville was scheduled to depart at 8:17. But the flight was wide open today, so I decided to go for it anyway.

In a rush, I leapt over the wheelchair passengers, sprinted through Immigrations and Customs, and hightailed it over to Concourse X, all the while with a full bladder. The flight to Quirksville was still on the board, and, as CRC flights are *always* delayed, I figured I had a chance.

Q of S arrived at Gate X28, completely out of breath at 8:23. Normally CRC flights don't even start boarding until five minutes past departure time. But guess what? Apparently the only Crappy Regional Carrier flight that leaves on time is the 8:17am flight to Quirksville!!! :-(

The agent told Her Mile Highness the flight was gone, and she limped back over to Concourse Z where she now has to wait until noon for the next flight home. >:-(

OK, enough venting. Am PMSing and have been up all night, so am now going to search for a quiet lounge chair in which to nap. I was supposed to go to a birthday party this afternoon, but it doesn't look like I will make it.

Anyway, will post pics from the trip when I finally get home.

Layover Report
Filed in LAYOVERS on Thursday, 06/02

Home at last! Now, without further ado, here's the layover report as promised...

Well, I tried not to think about Maurizio at all (bastard!) on my trip this week, resolving to have a layover fit for a Queen. And succeed I did, in having a relaxing layover, if nothing else.

The night of our arrival (Memorial Day), Queen of Sky went downstairs for a drink with the crew, and they talked her into accompanying them to the casino down the street. Eric, one of the flight attendants, wanted to play roulette. We watched as he first lost $20, then put down another $20, and in the end was up $150 when Queen of Sky announced that she was about to turn into a pumpkin and left to get her beauty sleep. The other girls on the crew (Lori, Lacy and Lupe) wanted to hit another casino and try the slots on the way back to the hotel. Lacy lost $4, and we called it a night.

The following morning Queen of Sky had breakfast with the crew and then headed to the supermarket.

What did Queen of Sky buy, you ask? Well, she bought some Peruvian dulce de leche; Tacama Peruvian wine; her favorite tropical fruit, the chirimoya; some more perfectly ripe avocados (which she may or may not have smuggled into the US); a camu-camu (a tropical berry) yogurt drink; and some sweet potato chips.

After the successful supermarket run, I had a full-body massage and got my hair cut and styled in the salon next to the hotel. I never style my hair, because I'm lazy, so I took a pic before it went back to its normal stick-straight state.

Finally, after the aforementioned spa treatments, Queen of Sky went to her room to relax a while and then had a nice lunch (ceviche) followed by a nap before the all-night flight back to Bustling Base City. Some of the crew went to the tailor, but I once again forgot to bring the things I need altered. Oh well, will be back at least once next month.

Pics coming up...

Pics from Lima
Filed in PICS on Friday, 06/02

As Queen of Sky promised, here are some pics from her Lima layover this weekend.

From Bustling Base City to Lima
(Eric the gambler in the middle)

Freshly cut and styled

View from Queen of Sky's hotel room of beautiful Lima:
Kind of like LA, but poorer and dirtier. Same amount of smog, though.

My Home away from Home
Filed in MY LIFE IN THE AIRPORT on Saturday, 06/03

Well, here Queen of Sky sits in the flight attendant lounge in Bustling Base City airport. Seriously, I spend more time here than I do at home!

The Cat and the Sleeping Queen

Queen of Sky spent her one day off yesterday sleeping (slept like 12 hours... that Lima trip wiped me out—might as well have done a Europe trip!) and blog surfing (caught up on all my favorite blogs). The only thing that could disturb my peaceful slumber yesterday was a cat meowing very loudly at 8:30am behind my condo. I tried to ignore it at first, but it continued to meow, and finally I heard a knock on my door around 9am.

It wasn't until Queen of Sky pulled on her bathrobe (I sleep in the buff) and peered out on her patio that she realized the cat was stranded on her patio. However, the poor thing was so scared when I opened the door that it managed to climb the fence and rejoin its owner on the other side. Then I went back to bed and didn't wake up until 1pm. Could have slept longer, honestly.

Here are some other updates:

Minor Celebrity Alert!!!

Queen of Sky had a minor celebrity on board her flight to Tampa the other day. Some kind of fitness guru, apparently... Body by Burt or Bob, or something like that. Her Mile Highness had never heard of him, as she has never viewed a fitness tape.

Commuting Update:

This morning Queen of Sky got the last seat on the 8:20am flight to Bustling Base City. My friend Kim had called me last night (at 11pm!!!) to advise me that all the flights were full today since two flights cancelled yesterday because of freak severe thunderstorms in Quirksville. I was already aware that the flights were full and had booked the jumpseat on that flight. Thank goodness I didn't have to sit on it, since it's like sitting on a hard wooden bench for two hours, and you are not allowed to sleep while sitting on it. I ended up getting the very last seat on the plane—middle seat, of course.

OK, that's all the updates for now. Queen of Sky is off to Guatemala today for a short layover and then back to Panama again tomorrow.

Toodles!
—Q of S

More Delays and High Security
Filed in FLIGHT BLOGS on Sunday, 06/04

Well, of course what was supposed to be an easy trip turned into a night-mare yesterday when, after a very cumbersome although not unusual board-ing, Queen of Sky's flight to Guatemala was delayed for a mechanical. The lavatory was leaking that lovely blue fluid into the cargo hold.

After sitting onboard the full boat with those high-maintenance people for about an hour, we were finally advised that the problem could not be fixed and we would have to change airplanes. Just what the crew wanted to hear. :-(

"There goes my good night's sleep," Queen of Sky was overheard com-plaining to another crewmember.

After another cumbersome boarding (during which the same passengers had the same luggage stowage and seating problems as the first time), Queen of Sky and crew finally took off from Bustling Base City and got into Guatemala almost TWO AND A HALF HOURS LATE! This reduced our layover to about nine hours, and by the time the wheelchair passengers had finally deplaned and we had finally arrived at our five-star hotel, we only had the *potential* to get about seven hours sleep. So the captain was nice and pushed back our pick-up time to give us a little extra ZZZZs, although only by half an hour.

At the hotel, the crew was made to go through a metal detector, and then they wanted to hand-search everybody's bags. Q of S complained rather loudly to the security people, as this was not the routine at this hotel or at any hotel, for that matter. But it turns out the president of Finland was staying there that night, hence the heightened security.

What else? Well, everything else went normally, but there were a lot of Scandinavian types in the breakfast room at the hotel this morning, and in the lobby there were security guards everywhere. Queen of Sky and crew had been joking the night before that for all of the security inconvenience we had had to go through, the president of Finland should have sent a bottle of Finlandia up to each of our rooms. :-)

Unfortunately, I didn't have time to go to Duty Free this morning in the airport to look for a Guatemala pin for my sweater. I have been collecting pins from the countries I fly to of late. Going to look for a little Panama Canal pin tomorrow.

Anyway, Q of S took some pics of the volcanoes as the plane took off from Guatemala today. Will post them next week. But right now Her Mile Highness is exhausted again and has to go to Panama this evening. Am heading to the sleep room now to attempt to take a nap.

Hasta luego...
—Q of S

P.S. That Guatemalan hotel is the only hotel Queen of Sky has ever stayed in that has a TV in the bathroom (albeit a small B&W one). Unfortunately, the only channel Q of S could get on it this morning was a French channel—and she does not *parler*!

Full Moon over Panama
Filed in FLIGHT BLOGS on Monday, 06/05

Panama, oh, Panamaaaaa...

Queen of Sky remembers the good ole days several years back when Anonymous Airlines had long layovers (30 hours) in Panama. You can get in a lot of trouble in Panama for that long! Her Mile Highness had a steamy layover affair there once. :-P And a couple of times Queen of Sky and another flight attendant took a little putt-putting ferry out to Isla Toboga, a picturesque little tropical island right off the canal, and drank piña coladas out of pineapples on the beach. It was one of those layovers we called the "Anonymous Airlines Dream Vacations."

Anyway, the good ole days almost returned yesterday. After the meal service last night on the flight to Panama, Queen of Sky was in a *very* bad mood (exhausted, still PMSing MAJORLY, and so tired of saying "Chicken or beef?" and "Would you like something to drink?" that she could scream). Then the captain called to inform us that there was a problem of some sort with the engine (something to do with heating the wings to keep the ice off them), and that they would have to fly the part in from L.A., and therefore we would probably not leave on schedule the next day.

The layover was only scheduled at nine hours, which is about enough time to get six hours sleep, shower, throw your stinky uniform back on, and grab a cup of café con leche before heading back out to the airport. I was so happy when I heard we would be able to sleep in that my mood immediately improved.

Instead of a 6am pick up the next morning, we ended up having a 10am pick up :-) and Queen of Sky actually got a full night's sleep.

Then Queen of Sky and crew had to wait around at the airport for a couple of hours while the pilots tested the plane to make sure it was fixed. So we went upstairs to the employee cafeteria to have a late breakfast. But it turns out they were already serving lunch, so Queen of Sky got some fried sea bass, rice and lentils, and plantains. She got to the register, and they rung up $2. :-D Then Queen of Sky bought a big bowl of chicken soup, which was less than $2, and a tres leches cake for about the same.

It was funny because every time a crewmember went over and got a huge tray of food, it cost them $2. Reminds me of the little cafeteria near the hotel I used to eat at on the long Panama layovers back in the good ole days.

Of course, that little six-hour delay today caused Her Mile Highness to miss her early commuter flight home to Quirksville, so now, as usual, she is waiting for the 9pm flight home.

Will post pics from all of these trips tomorrow...

Guatemala Pics
Filed in PICS on Tuesday, 06/06

For Guatemala flight blog, see June 4 entry.

View of the Guatemalan volcanoes taking off from Guatemala City.

Panama Pics
Filed in PICS on Tuesday, 06/06

Sitting in the airport waiting for the plane to be fixed. Girlfriend on the left had just shopped 'til she dropped in Duty Free.

Views from Queen of Sky's hotel room. (It was low tide, so if you look closely, you can see the sewage pipes that lead right into the bay.) That's old Panama in the background. Quaint colonial district, although extremely poor and dangerous. One of those islands is Isla Toboga.

This is new Panama. Most of these buldings are empty. They're just fronts for laundering drug money.
(At least that's what I've heard.)

Aches and Planes
Filed in LIFE OF LEISURE on Wednesday, 06/07

Well, Queen of Sky is sore all over today after flying two three-day, supposedly easy, trips with only one day off in between. And guess what? My chiropractor is on his honeymoon this week in Tahiti—damn him! Could really use an adjustment right now. :-P

The Contents of Queen of Sky's Tote Bag
Filed in MISC. on Thursday, 06/08

Once in a while I go through the contents of my tote bag and clean out all the junk that seems to collect inside. Here's what I found today:

- Plenty of plastic cutlery
- One filthy apron with a mysterious white substance splattered all over it
- An assortment of boarding passes from various commuter flights

- An Spanish dictionary
- One pair of socks
- Several eye masks and earplugs
- Maps of various foreign cities
- Herbal and green tea bags in a Ziploc bag
- Travel clock with world time zones
- One miniature pillow case to fit airplane pillows
- Uniform sweater covered with souvenir pins and bits of gunk (probably chicken or beef)
- Stinky galley shoes (also covered with some sort of airplane funk)
- A stash of Handi-wipes
- Squished and half-melted individually wrapped slices of processed cheese from international coach meal trays
- Pulverized individually wrapped crackers, also from coach meal trays
- Odor Eaters foot powder
- English and Spanish onboard announcements
- The all-important digital camera to capture layover fun
- An assortment of unidentifiable supplements in a Ziploc bag
- Generic over-the-counter sleeping pills (for jetlag emergencies *only*—am not a prescription pill popper like many a disillusioned sky waitress)
- Crumpled-up cocktail napkins with locations of broken seats/reading lights/tray tables scribbled on them
- Peanuts and pretzels—two bags each (gag! For emergencies *only*!)
- Two celebrity gossip mags... one current and one week-old
- One EXTRA LARGE bottle ibuprofen

The Confrontation
Filed in MEN on Friday, 06/10

OK, so I've waited long enough. Today I finally emailed Maurizio to hear what he has to say. He should be out of the hospital by now. Fortunately I've been too busy flying this past week to think too much about the whole situation. But now I have a few days off to stew over it, so let's hope I get a response soon so I can close this chapter in my life. Buh-bye, Countess of Sky fantasy!

Anyway, in the email I basically told him that I was onto him, how could he do this, I thought he was a nice guy... yaddah, yaddah. You all know the drill.

Why is it that all the men Queen of Sky is attracted to end up being sleazeballs?

Dashed Hopes
Filed in MISC. on Saturday, 06/11

Today Queen of Sky finally drove all the way up to the local culinary academy in search of a school catalog. She has requested a catalog by phone and email four times now to no avail. So today she was determined to find the place and get that stupid catalog.

Anyhow, unlike the last time Q of S tried to find the school, today she called first to get directions. (Two weeks ago, I drove up there and found the miniscule sign for the school but then was never able to locate the school itself. I drove around and around the expansive parking lot peering at a bunch of nondescript buildings for at least half an hour.)

Well, this time I found the right building but then had quite an ordeal trying to get a catalog from the receptionist. It seems that there is an obligatory tour of the school attached to receiving a catalog. But I was *not* having that... just wanted to know the bottom line: how much the damned school costs!

I finally managed to pry a catalog and school packet out of the receptionist without going on the tour. Then, after a quick escape to my automobile, I anxiously opened the packet and searched for the fees page.

I couldn't believe what I read: "Le Cordon Rouge" Culinary Academy's tuition was almost $40K for a nine-month program!!! $38,500, to be exact.

"Ridiculous!" Q of S uttered incredulously, tossing the catalog into the backseat (where it still lies). "If I could afford to pay that much, I would go to culinary school in France!"

Oh well, c'est la vie! *shakes head*

Off to Guatemala
Filed in MY LIFE IN THE AIRPORT on Sunday, 06/12

Queen of Sky doesn't know where her six days off went. :-(She is once again in Bustling Base City today, getting ready to go back to Guatemala.

Well, gotta run now to meet some friends who are passing through BBC on their way back to Germany. Then gotta brief, so I'll catch y'all on the way back.

Protests and More Protests
Filed in LAYOVERS on Monday, 06/13

Yesterday in briefing the captain told Queen of Sky and crew that there was a security issue in Guatemala. The next day the Guatemalan authorities were expecting a BIG strike, during which strikers were expected to block the roads to the airport. This meant we could get stuck in Guatemala.

Sounded good to us. *Anonymous Airlines Dream Vacation, here we come!*

Upon our arrival in Guatemala, the Anonymous Airlines agents and the hotel desk clerk reiterated that we would probably not be able to get to the airport the next day.

Great! We changed into layover clothes and headed across the way to a nice restaurant for some drinks and food.

It was a fabulous crew—the super divas Queen of Sky and Chucha Galore were united once again. At the restaurant the whole crew had a grand old time laughing, telling jokes, drinking, talking about spouses... laughing, drinking, talking about lovers, eating, telling more jokes, and drinking some more. All the while, we knew we wouldn't be going any-where the next day and would get to sleep in.

Well, the next morning at 6am when the lead flight attendant called Queen of Sky to advise her that we needed to be downstairs at 7am in-stead of 7:15 because the roads were clear and we needed to get to the airport before that changed, our late-night drinking and taco binge didn't seem like such a good idea anymore. :-P (But it doesn't matter—Chucha would have hauled my booty out to party whether the layover was eight hours or twenty-eight hours!)

Queen of Sky dragged her tired ass out of bed, showered, and dashed upstairs for a cup of joe to go, just as her crew was leaving the breakfast room.

Anywhoo, that's all to report for now. Q of S and crew are about to head to Savannah, location of the G8 Summit *and* today's layover. Hope-fully the military choppers and Air Force jets will not disturb Her Mile High-ness' much-needed rest.

Gotta run...

—Q of S over and out!

Crappy Regional Carrier
Filed in COMMUTING on Tuesday, 06/14

OK, so Queen of Sky finished her three-day trip today. After a strenuous day of flying from Savannah to Bustling Base City to Denver and back to BBC, Queen of Sky decided to try to make her Crappy Regional Carrier flight home at 5:30pm. Problem is, we landed from Denver at about that same time. Nevertheless, I checked the board, and HALLELUJAH! The CRC flight to Quirksville was delayed twenty minutes. By this time it was 5:40, so I only had ten minutes to spare. I hustled over to Concourse X and arrived at the gate just in time for the delayed departure.

But guess what? The bitchy Crappy Regional Carrier agents told me the flight was closed, even though I could clearly see that the plane was still out there and the door was open and they were still loading bags.

So I asked again if the plane had left. Bitchy Crappy Regional Carrier agents replied again, "The flight is closed."

Her Mile Highness walked away muttering profanity and now sits in the flight attendant lounge waiting for her 9pm flight home.

Crappy Regional Carrier today changed its name to Piece of Sh*t Regional Carrier! >:-(

H-town
Filed in MISC. on Thursday, 06/16

I guess you are all wondering what happened to Queen of Sky yesterday. I finally got home at midnight (!!!) on Tuesday and then had to get up at the crack of dawn (8am) yesterday to drive to Houston (two and a half hours) to renew my passport.

While waiting for my passport, I had a couple of hours to kill in downtown H-town. Let me just say that downtown Houston is not exactly pedestrian-friendly. And there are no restaurants down there except sandwich shops and fast food. No wonder it's one of the fattest cities in America!

I ended up eating a shrimp po-boy and hushpuppies. For those of you who do not speak Cajun, that is a fried shrimp sandwich and fried cornbread. Very Atkins-friendly.

Anyhow, our heroine made it out of downtown by 3:30pm and headed to IKEA for some shopping. (Still need a rug and coffee table for living room.) Well, guess what? The stupid store is relocating, so they had NOTHING!!!

Q of S is irked that she's going to have to drive all the way back there next month to do some shopping. Q of S HATES driving.

Anyway, I had such a headache after the long drive home that I went to bed last night at 7:30 without even logging onto the internet first!

I leave you with a pic from the drive...

Exciting Stuff
Filed in MEN on Friday, 06/17

Hello, all. This is Q of S's first time posting on her new super-fast laptop, connected to HIGH-SPEED internet (as opposed to the low-speed dial-up internet I have at home) at a local Quirksville cafe/restaurant. Queen of Sky's neighbor, a techie, came over a while ago because he saw the UPS truck today and wanted to see her new computer. :-O

When he arrived, Q of S was talking on the phone with Victor, who was more interested in her new computer's specs than dancing plans for tomorrow night.

What is it with guys and computers?

Anyway, Helpful Neighbor was able to help Q of S tap into one of her neighbors' WiFi networks. Ah, the advantages of living in a condo.

Unfortunately, though, as soon as Helpful Neighbor left, Q of S lost the connection. Will try again later.

Does anyone know if it's easy to find hotspots (WiFi access) in Europe? I'm thinking of bringing my laptop with me on my Italian vacation next month.

OK, I know you all are really excited about Q of S's technological advance. So excited that you can't contain yourselves.

TAhis daMn keyboard is gonig to take a little getting used to, thouhg!

P.S. Still no word from Maurizio. I wonder if he even has the balls to write me back! >:-(

Bustling Base City
Filed in MY LIFE IN THE AIRPORT on Sunday, 06/19

OK, people are waiting for computers, so Queen of Sky can't stay. Am off to Milano this evening. Crazy Chilean Girl, who I am flying with today, said she has some friends in Milan, and they are going jet skiing on Lake Como. She wants Q of S to come too.

And when, pray tell, will Q of S get her beauty rest?

The layover is only 24 hours, and I have to make up two nights' sleep during that time, plus go to dinner, shower (twice), go grocery shopping, etc.

Anyway, will let you all know, but I'm leaning toward staying in and just meeting up with Unhappily Married Chilean Girl (aka Crazy Chilean Girl) for dinner.

Ciao!
—Q of S

Back in BBC/the 777
Filed in MY LIFE IN THE AIRPORT on Tuesday, 06/21

Well, Queen of Sky is back in Bustling Base City and pooped, as usual, after her trip to Milan. And the 5:30pm flight on POS Regional Carrier to Quirksville is full as usual, so I'll be hanging out here in the flight attendant dungeon until 9pm!!!

Please remind Q of S next time she decides to do an international trip to AVOID the 777 like THE PLAGUE! That plane is just a NIGHTMARE... too many people (220 in coach), the in-seat videos never work, and the floor plan is just impractical (no lavs in the back—only in the mid, and no cross-aisle).

Did I mention the fact that the flight attendant call bells are located on the armrest, and subsequently go off NONSTOP the ENTIRE flight as people accidentally lean on them?

Also, there is the part about everyone being miserable because they are packed in like SARDINES in the back with five across in the middle and leg room that leaves something to be desired.

Q of S had the pleasure to travel in coach last summer on the 777 from BBC to Rome as part of a working trip. The rest of her crew got to sit in business class, but Her Mile Highness, being the second most junior on the crew, got stuck in CATTLE CLASS!!! That's nine hours, folks. It was NOT pretty!

Anyway, presently I see the light at the end of the tunnel. I now have a well-deserved and well-needed week off, and if I ever get on a flight back to Texas tonight, I am HOME FREE!

Got some great pics from the Milan trip... will post them tomorrow.

A la prossima...
—Q of S

Pic du Jour
Filed in PICS on Wednesday, 06/22

June 21, Milan, Italy, on the 777 before passenger boarding.
ANONYMOUS AIRLINES' FINEST...

Queen of Sky and Erica, aka Crazy Chilean Girl

Erica used to be kind of frumpy, but then she had a mid-life crisis a couple of years back and started working out, lost her glasses, and had a boob job. I didn't even recognize her. She was hot! The only thing she didn't upgrade was her husband. :-O (She was a virgin when she married him—BIG mistake, if you ask me.)

THE END
Filed in MEN on Thursday, 06/23

Well, guess who I FINALLY got an email from? Yep, that's right—that mysterious/sleazy diplomat of mine.

He fessed up to being married.

I feel so stupid.

Remember that blue-blooded woman Maurizio told me his family had wanted him to marry? Well, it turns out that he *did* marry her after all!

But my favorite part of the email was this:

Elena, I LOVE YOU, and not my wife. Please understand I need some time to get out of my marriage. I want to be with you.

Yeah, RIGHT!!! I've heard that line too many times before from dumb flight attendants talking about their married pilot boyfriends' excuses. And they *never* leave their wives.

I'm not THAT blond!

Anyway, I was too angry to even ask if Maurizio has children. I simply replied that he is NEVER to contact me again. PERIOD. END OF STORY.

Mood: LIVID!!!
Filed in MISC. on Friday, 06/24

OK, Queen of Sky can't remember if she has mentioned the new bidding system that Anonymous International has implemented for the flight attendants starting next month. We bid for our schedules every month, and they are usually released by the 18th or 22nd of the month before, so we have time to swap and rearrange stuff if we need to.

Well, this month being the first month of the new bidding system, schedules were just released today, June 24, for July.

As you know, I'm planning to go to Rome for an Italian course next month, which I have already paid for. Even though I'm no longer dating

Maurizio, I'm still hoping to learn enough Italian to qualify as an Italian speaker at Anonymous International.

Well, I was VERY upset when I found out that Scheduling assigned me a trip the DAY AFTER my course in Rome ends, as I was hoping to have that whole week off to do some traveling after the course. In fact, my WHOLE schedule next month SUCKS!!!

In any case, it appears now that Scheduling has made a mistake—they just called to tell me they're looking into it.

Mood: a little less livid.

How is Her Mile Highness going to meet her new Italian boy toy in just one week??!!!

Talk about a Tight Fit...
Filed in PICS on Saturday, 06/25

If you were wondering where flight attendants take their crew rest on international flights, the mystery is finally solved:

Unfortunately, Q of S doesn't fit in the new "improved" crew rest area, so she doesn't get a break. :-(

A Week in the Life of Leisure
Filed in LIFE OF LEISURE on Sunday, 06/26

I'm sure you all are wondering what Queen of Sky has been up to this week.

Q of S has been off for over a week now and was going to go to Costa Rica to visit her friend Nina, whom she has not seen in a couple of years. However, since Q of S is going to Italy next month, she decided to just stay home and relax and get some stuff done this week. (Sorry, Nina!)

Anyway, here's what I have been up to on my days off:

- Sleeping late (except when people call from Germany at 6am!!! You KNOW who you are!!!)
- Rowing
- Deleting the remnants of Maurizio from my computer and cell phone (pics, email addresses, phone numbers, IM address, etc.)
- Going to yoga class
- Swimming at Barton Springs (the water wasn't as clear this week due to recent flooding)
- Eating very healthy—lots of salads and fruits and veggies
- Catching up with various friends, including <u>Booty Call Guy</u>, who called last night to tell Q of S that he has been called back from furlough. He also offered me a proposal, which I immediately rejected without hearing him through. Actually, he was trying to save Q of S some money by advising her to roll her car loan into her mortgage. But Q of S was worried that he was trying to roll *himself* into her condo as well. (That's his normal proposal.)
- Looking at rugs for my living room
- Trying to decide whether to sell my dumpy condo and get a nicer one. However, by my calculations, I am about $200K short for the house that I want. DONATIONS ARE APPRECIATED—hint, hint!

Queen of Sky Gets Her Groove Back
Filed in LIFE OF LEISURE on Monday, 06/27

OK, not *that* groove... Queen of Sky went salsa dancing last night. My friend Evan was my warm-up dance. Then, unfortunately, I couldn't seem to find any decent dancers, except of course for Victor, the Jamaican Sensation.

After a while, I tried to avoid anyone who did not have an accent, as my second dance partner (and the only one tall enough for me with my heels on) was a clumsy white guy who thought he had rhythm (the worst kind). Even after a Mexican martini, Queen of Sky couldn't follow that guy!

Anyway, by the end of the night, I had lost track of the number of men I had danced with, just as I have, through the years, lost track of the number of men I have slept with (kidding), and I left the club ALONE to return to my humble abode. Must have been still tipsy when I got home, otherwise wouldn't have taken pics like this:

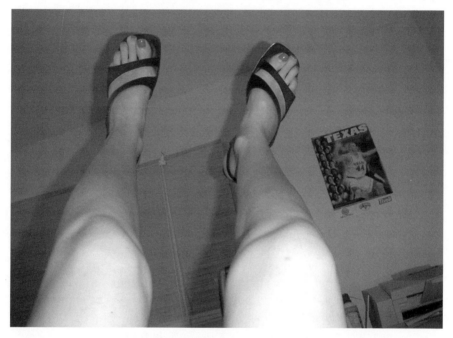

And YES, Q of S's legs *are* that white, but *no*, they're not that skinny, it's just a bad angle.

Busy Tuesday
Filed in LIFE OF LEISURE on Tuesday, 06/28

Well, Queen of Sky just got back from running errands and now has to pack, as she has to fly to Bustling Base City tonight. :-(I have an early (crappy) trip to Bogotá mañana. Yuk! Haven't even booked a hotel in BBC tonight. Am hoping for a last minute miracle (like a swap for com-mutable trip).

Anyhow, that's what's going on here. Can't chat long...

Am still mad about my schedule next month, and In-flight Scheduling is giving me the run-around. First they said they had accidentally switched my schedule with someone else's. They said they would switch it back and Q of S would get her cushy Madrid line with three weeks off in the middle of the month to go to Italy. Then they called back yesterday while Her Mile Highness was having a quiet macrobiotic lunch and said that they had made a mistake, that she was *indeed* stuck with that CRAPPY-ASS schedule with only one week off for her Italian vacation.

Needless to say, Q of S was furious and demanded that they drop the trips after her vacation, since it was their mistake. Anyway, they said they would, but I don't trust them. Won't believe it 'til I see it.

Well, gotta run...

Hasta luego!
—Q of S

Running through the Airport
Filed in MY LIFE IN THE AIRPORT on Wednesday, 06/29

Hello, all. Queen of Sky is currently mid-rotation. For those of you non-airline people out there, that means she is running from one gate to the next to work yet another FULL flight.

My flight to Bustling Base City was two hours late last night, which left me time to stop at my favorite Mexican vegetarian restaurant to pick up a to-go plate to take to the airport. Good thing I did, too, since all the restaurants in Quirksville airport close at 8pm.

Anyway, talk about comfort food... I had a chile relleno filled with mashed potatoes and corn and cheese. Not the typical greasy chile relleno. It was topped with a salsa verde... yum! Then, as my sides, I had the refried beans (no lard here), stir-fried veggies, and cucumber salad. And they top it off with a homemade corn tortilla. Sure did hit the spot as I was waiting for my Crappy Regional Carrier flight last night.

BTW, Q of S didn't get to BBC until 12:30am! And by the time she got to her hotel, it was 1am and then she had to get up at 7am. Hence, she only got about four hours sleep. :-(

Just got in from Jacksonville, FL, and now we are heading for beautiful Bogotá, Colombia, for a short layover. Good news is this is only a two-day trip, so Q of S will be home tomorrow night.

Gotta get going...

Ciao!
—Q of S

Pooped and Screwed
Filed in FLIGHT BLOGS on Thursday, 06/30

Hmm. Just got back from sunny (NOT! It's the rainy season.) Bogotá. Girlfriend on the crew yesterday jinxed Queen of Sky by mentioning how many people have trouble sleeping their first time in Bogotá because of the high altitude. It was not Q of S's first time there, but nonetheless she woke up at quarter to three last night and is not sure if she ever drifted back to sleep between angry thoughts about her schedule for next month.

At 6:45am (uggh!) I dragged my tired ass out of bed, showered, spent longer than usual in front of the mirror (am getting more and more diva-esque by the day), and finally schlepped my trusty sidekick Valigia down-stairs to the breakfast room, where my crew was already dining. I only had ten minutes left to slurp up as much caldo de carne and café con leche and gobble up as much fruta and omelets and arepas and bread and yogurt and juice as possible. I was the last one on the crew bus, as usual.

At the airport I purchased my two dozen roses from the van driver ($5) and then bought two new pins for my uniform ($2 each). One is a Colom-bian flag and the other is a green ribbon representing peace.

The flight went OK, and afterward, as Q of S and her crew were passing through the immigrations area, the lead flight attendant, Kapahana (from Hawaii), said that Q of S and another girl on the crew looked like beauty queens (at which I told them my blog name... hee, hee) strolling along with their bouquets of roses. So, we decided it would be a good idea to have a "Miss (and Mr.) Airlines USA Pageant." We started practicing our waves and walks.

A future Miss Anonymous Airlines was certainly in our midst!

Anyhow, back to the subject of this entry... Now Q of S has to wait four hours for her flight home, which is FULL, and she forgot to book the jumpseat, which are now both taken. :-(So, I may have to wait until 10pm (five hours!) for my flight home. :-((

Oh, well. The good news is, I just checked my schedule for next month, and Scheduling has indeed come through on their promise and dropped the trips after my vacation. So now I will get to spend THREE WEEKS in Italy next month, if I so choose and my pocketbook holds up. :-D

JULY

Vacation!

Daily Horoscope

Filed in MISC. on Friday, 07/01

Great news, all! Today I finally got a *good* horoscope—and just in time for my FABULOUS Italian vacation...

Things Are Looking Up

During this period there is the increased potential for fortunate circumstances. You will receive much ego gratification during this time from cultural events, artistic projects, foreign travel, and activities that expand your intellectual horizons. This is a good time to strive for your personal goals, as you will have a good chance of achieving them. But, as with all good fortune, there is the danger of excess and misuse. You may feel overconfident that things are going well and will continue so indefinitely. You may take things too much for granted and as a result, positive opportunities could pass you by. In general, however, this is a very pleasant period. Just beware of overindulgence.

Aspect: Jupiter trine Sun
Period of Influence: 7/01–7/12
Courtesy of <u>*Astro Wizards*</u>

Overindulgence? Hmm... I guess I need to leave my credit cards at home this time!

Some Days I Wish I Was a Man
Filed in COMMUTING on Saturday, 7/02

Mood: IBUPROFEN, PLEASE!

Of course, Queen of Sky was hurrying around last night trying to stuff all of the necessary items into her trusty sidekick Valigia for her three-day trip and subsequent three-week vacation in the Old Country. By the time she had shoved everything into the bag, it was already after midnight, and she had to get up at 6am. :-(

And then this morning, of course, Q of S started her "cycle" as she was cramming all items forgotten from the night before into Valigia and tote bag. It couldn't come on her day off yesterday...no, it had to come on the first day of a three-day trip—a three-leg, 11-hour duty day. :-(

On top of all of that, Q of S then had the pleasure of riding the jumpseat to work. That's almost two hours sitting on a stiff board with another stiff board for a back. Lovely.

Alas, I have finally made it to Bustling Base City, from whence I will now embark on a nonsensical journey to Boston and back and then to Baltimore, where I will stay all day tomorrow. Hope it is sunny and there is a pool at the hotel. :-)

This is the first trip on which Q of S has carried her new high-tech companion—and all I can say is five pounds, my ASS! This will probably also be the *last* time Q of S carries her laptop to work. And now I'm seriously considering *not* bringing it to Italy with me next week. It sure does take up a lot of space, not to mention the extra weight!

I may just leave it in a supervisor's office in BBC airport while I'm gone. There should be plenty of internet cafes in Italy from which to blog, anyway.

In any case, if you don't hear from Q of S later this month, it means that she has run off with an *incredibly* HOT and romantic Italian god. Please don't come looking for her, as she will be happily swigging wine, slurping pasta, and facendo l'amore in a villa somewhere by the sparkling Mediterranean Sea. ;-)

Baltimore, MD
Filed in LAYOVERS on Sunday, 7/03

Well, we finally got to Baltimore last night at 1:30am (which was on time, BTW), and Queen of Sky crashed. Don't think I have ever slept so well at a hotel.

Right now Q of S is going to meet up with a girl on her crew to go to the Baltimore Aquarium and then a late lunch/early dinner. (We have to get up at 4:30am tomorrow.)

Unfortunately, the pool here at Name Brand Hotel is indoor, so there will be no sunbathing today. Will have to do that in Italy later this month.

OK, bye for now...
—Q of S

Happy 4th!
Filed in MY LIFE IN THE AIRPORT on Monday, 7/04

Hello, all. Happy Fourth if you are stateside. Guess where Queen of Sky is spending her Fourth of July?

Well, in Bustling Base City airport, of course!

We had to get up at 4:30 this morning to go from Baltimore to BBC and then to Mexico City and back. We were delayed every leg, thus causing

Q of S to miss the flight to Rome that she was going to take this evening.

I'm exhausted anyway, so am just going to go to a commuter hotel here in Bustling Base City now and maybe catch some fireworks on TV. :-(

Will fly off to Roma tomorrow. The flights looked better today, but what can you do?

Anyhow, I'm now off until the 28th!!! So suffering through that domestic trip was worth it in the end.

OK, Her Mile Highness would presently like to vent a little about one of her coworkers this trip who was lactating and every hour or so had to go in the lavatory and pump her milk. Q of S saw those bottles of milk in girlfriend's cooler and almost gagged! But I guess Q of S is just a tad bit squeamish.

OK, enough gossiping... gotta get to my hotel and bed... ZZZZzzzzzz!

On My Way
Filed in *MY LIFE IN THE AIRPORT* on Tuesday, 7/05

Well, here I am once again in BBC airport, my home away from home. The flight to Rome looks good today. Only problem is business class is full, so Her Mile Highness will most likely have to sit in coach. :-(

Hopefully I will at least get two seats together, though.

Well, gotta go... almost boarding time.

Ci vediamo!
—Q of S

Il Volo e l'Arrivo
Filed in *LEISURE TRIPS* on Thursday, 7/07

Well, Queen of Sky arrived yesterday morning totally pooped, of course.

I got an aisle seat in coach on the flight over, which was good and bad. It was good in that I didn't have to disturb the person sitting next to me to get up and use the bathroom, but it was bad in that I had no window to rest my head against, hence no shut-eye. And the seat next to me *was* occupied, unfortunately. It ended up being a full flight.

BTW, guess who was working the flight?

Queen of Sky's old friend Booty Call Guy.

He kept passing by my seat to "check on me." Actually, though, he was just trying to cop a peek under my blanket. He mistakenly thought my nude cami-top was my nude top, period. It was hard to tell in the dark cabin.

Anyhow, all I asked BCG for was a glass of wine. And what did he give me? A glass of *coach* wine. His ass was too lazy to even go up to business class to get me some of the *good* stuff. And then, to top it off, he had the cojones to invite Q of S to stay in his room in Rome that night.

"I'm willing to share," BCG offered humbly.

I thanked him for his generosity (yeah, right!) but declined, explaining that I had booked a room at a nice hotel near the airport using my Name Brand Hotel points. I had to bite my tongue to refrain from adding that I would not share his bed with him if my life depended on it.

Anyhow, I exited the Rome airport in a jetlagged daze and somehow found a pay phone to call my hotel van. This was the advantage of staying at the airport. The disadvantage was that it wasn't convenient to get into the city. I had to take a van back to the airport and then a train from there.

The first day, I was so exhausted that I stayed in and ate at the hotel restaurant. I only have two nights to enjoy this luxury accommodation, after all. Tomorrow night I'm checking into the student residence arranged by the Italian school. I decided against staying with a host family due to prior bad experiences. Have never stayed at a student residence before, so I don't know what to expect. Supposedly I will have my own bathroom and kitchenette, though, so I have high hopes.

Well, that's all for now. I did a little museum-hopping today and now it's time to start my long trek back to the hotel. (Am presently at an internet café on the Via Veneto... left laptop back in BBC.)

A presto!
—Q of S

Rome, Part II
Filed in LEISURE TRIPS on Friday, 7/08

Oh, how I *love* Rome!

Everything is going great, except for the living situation. Today Queen of Sky checked out of her luxury hotel and checked into her new, slightly less deluxe quarters. My apartment is pretty basic, and the little bed (which doubles as a sofa) is hard as a ROCK. But at least it's clean and I have my own bathroom, and it's only for a week, so I guess I can deal with it.

When I arrived at the nondescript gray building this afternoon, I rang the doorbell and a tiny wrinkled lady named Signora Antonelli came to the door. She was friendly and (stereo-) typical. She reminded me of my Italian-American grandmother, in fact.

Signora Antonelli showed me to my room as if she was escorting me to my suite at the Ritz Carlton. For her sake, I tried not to display too much disappointment when I finally saw my room.

Well, anyway, classes don't start until Monday, so I have a couple more days to chill and try to get over my jetlag. I just love the energy of this city. In fact, I often wish I had brought my mother here. She would have loved it, too.

My mother never visited Europe. Hard to believe, since I come here at least once a month. But my mother never even had a passport until the year before she died. Her only trip abroad was a short vacation with me in Mexico two years ago.

Well, I'm going to stop rambling now. Sorry, I guess this entry kind of ended on a downer.

The Bus Ride
Filed in LEISURE TRIPS on Sunday, 7/10

Ciao belli!

Perhaps you all are wondering why you didn't hear from Queen of Sky yesterday. Well, all this sightseeing and man-seeing is keeping her very busy!

Yesterday morning I decided to go see the Appian Way and the catacombs. I hopped a bus in that direction around 10:30 and subsequently spent most of the day meandering around the Appian Way. (The Appian Way was the *original* Roman highway, in case you don't recall from your high school Latin class.) It was a warm summer's day. And the green of the countryside was a welcome relief from the gray streets of the city.

While in the area, I decided against visiting the catacombs, however, since I'm quite claustrophobic. I didn't want to waste my money on an entrance ticket when I was pretty sure I wouldn't be able to complete the tour. (Once in Cholula, Mexico, Queen of Sky bought a ticket to see the inside of a pyramid. Upon entering, however, she was seized with fear—it was a very dark and narrow tunnel—and had to rush back outside. Of course, there were no refunds. Also, on my trip to Hawaii last year with friend Raquel, we went hiking up Diamond Head one day. Upon reaching the first DARK tunnel at the top of the mountain, Q of S was again seized with panic and had to wait at the tunnel entrance while Raquel climbed to the top and took in the view.)

So anyway, by four o'clock I decided to hop on a bus from the Appian Way back to Rome center. But I was too tired to walk all the way back to the bus stop I had seen earlier. Plus, it had become quite a hot afternoon. Luckily, just then I spied a bus pulling away from the side of the road a little ways down. Queen of Sky ran toward it—her bra-less boobage flapping the whole way. (That's what I love about Europe—no bra required!)

The bus pulled back to a stop, stirring up a cloud of roadside dust. I peered inside to the handsome young bus driver's obvious pleasure. Beneath his Gucci shades, he was grinning from ear to ear. (Quite possibly my white cami-top had caught his attention.)

Q of S asked him if he was going to the "centro." He said "Sì," followed by some stuff she didn't understand.

Undaunted, she climbed aboard.

Well, that bus was driving and driving and I was not recognizing anything. In fact, it looked like we were going further away from Rome rather than toward it. Finally the bus stopped in the middle of nowhere. It was the end of the line. There were only a couple of other passengers besides Queen of Sky still onboard.

At this point, the bus driver, who I came to find out was named Davide, conveniently had fifteen minutes or so to chat up his six-foot-tall blond passenger.

He got up from his seat and my eyes were immediately drawn to his feet.

Damn, even Italian bus drivers have good shoes! Q of S mused.

Anyhow, after a very basic conversation in my broken Italian, Davide finally turned the bus around and we headed back into the city.

At thè end of the ride, Davide gave me his phone number. He was a cutie, one of those olive-skinned Italian gods, so I gave him my student residence's phone number (where I unfortunately don't have a phone in my room).

Well, at about 9pm last night Signora Antonelli came up to my room to notify me that my young suitor was on the line. I descended to the house mamma's apartment (interrupting the pasta course of the Antonelli family dinner) to take the call. During a brief and cumbersome conversation, we arranged to meet for a coffee today after my classes.

Or I think we did, anyway!

Anywho, gotta get going to class now. Will give the full report on my rendezvous with Davide the bus driver tomorrow. ;-)

First Day of School and a First Date
Filed in LEISURE TRIPS on Monday, 7/11

Well, today was my first day of class at the Italian language school. They placed Queen of Sky in an intermediate level class (although it seems like a beginner class to me... moving awfully slow). But it was *after* class that things got interesting. Time for Queen of Sky's rendezvous with the hot bus driver—and her chance to put those Italian lessons to practice!

Q of S headed to the metro station where she and Davide had planned to meet. When he showed up, she was quite surprised by his ride: a brand-new BMW!

What's up with that? A bus driver who drives a Beamer?

Q of S thinks perhaps Davide *lives* in that car.

Anyway, Davide is cute and chatty, and Q of S is rather attracted to him, even though he is quite a bit below her normal height standards.

After we had a coffee in a café near the metro stop, Davide led me to a small park nearby. I knew what he was up to. When we sat down on a bench, I strategically placed my knapsack between us. We had another basic conversation with some definite hints of tensione sessuale. :-P

Well, that was it for that little mini-date. Davide had to go to work and Q of S had to go back to the residence to do some homework. Presently I'm about to grab a bite of din-din (odds are it will be pizza or pasta), and then am to meet Davide later tonight at the Via Appia bus stop. I'm going to ride his last route with him and then we're going out. Or at least that is what I have capito.

The End of the Line
Filed in LEISURE TRIPS on Wednesday, 7/13

Hmm. There's not much to tell about my classes. There are a couple of Germans and Swedes and even a Japanese or two studying with Queen of Sky. I don't want to hang out with them, though—prefer to hang out with the locals. Speaking of locals, let me catch you all up on what happened with Davide the other night.

Monday night I met him again at the bus stop to go to the Via Appia. He wanted me to ride his last route with him. So I did, even though I was tired from my persistent jetlag coupled with my first day of school. Then we went out with some of his friends, in his Beamer, of course. Davide was quite adorable. A real cutie-pie. However, I did *not* like his friends. Two of his girlfriends were very immature.

In any case, I missed my last bus back to the student residence, so Davide conveniently offered to drive me there. After getting lost a couple of times, we finally found it.

Being the middle of the night, there was no one around. Davide parked his Beamer in the alley, and we started making out. He had already had the talk with me—the talk I have had with so many guys in so many languages. I immediately knew exactly what he was talking about.

"Senza impegni," said he.

Booty call, thought I.

I will have you know that the Queen of Sky does not hump in the front seat (or back seat, for that matter) of cars—even Beamers. So when Davide whipped out his salami, Queen of Sky yawned and remarked that it was late and she had to go.

Apparently Davide thought he was going to spend the night. :-O Nope, not at the residence where guests are not allowed and where the little house mamma has to let Queen of Sky in after midnight. That would have been rather noticeable. I told him that it would be better if we saw each other when I returned to Rome on layovers. Then I would have my own hotel room off the Via Veneto.

In any case, maybe Davide was pissed that I left him hanging (or standing, in this case), but I haven't heard back from him.

Oh, well. Hot Italian guys are a dime a dozen over here...

NEXT!

Italian Studies
Filed in LEISURE TRIPS on Saturday, 7/16

Well, a week of Italian classes was enough for Queen of Sky. Now she's going to concentrate on more important studies—namely the in-depth study of Italian men. Tomorrow I'm heading south to the Isle of Capri. I have just booked a hotel on the web in Anacapri for two nights. It says it's a three-star. I just hope it's not a dump!

Ciao tutti!

La Dolce Vita

Filed in LEISURE TRIPS on Wednesday, 7/20

Wow—I had a *great* time in Capri! I will write about that later, though. Presently Queen of Sky is here on the BEAUTIFUL Amalfi coast, livin' la dolce vita.

    I have some great pics to post when I get back...

A presto!
—Q of S

The Advantages of Traveling Alone (According to the Queen of Sky)

Filed in LEISURE TRIPS on Sunday, 7/24

1. There always seem to be single rooms available in hotels.
2. Q of S never has trouble being seated at restaurants by herself.
3. No compromises. Q of S can do as she pleases... can spend the whole day in bed if she wants.
4. You can go from restaurant to restaurant eating as much as you want, and no one will ever know. :-D (Not that Q of S has *ever* done this.)
5. Q of S is more approachable when she travels alone (see #6).
6. You can have a fling with an Italian race car driver in Amalfi, and you don't have to tell anybody! ;-)

Finally Back

Filed in MY LIFE IN THE AIRPORT on Monday, 7/25

Uggh. Queen of Sky has finally made it back to Bustling Base City. Am currently waiting for my flight back to Quirksville. I had to ride the jumpseat today from Rome to BBC. :-P That sucked, except the part when I got to sit in the business class crew rest seat while the flight attendants were not using it—about three and a half hours out of the eight-hour flight.

    Can't wait to finally be in my own LARGE CUSHY bed tonight. Am going to sleep VERY LATE tomorrow...

    Will try to post vacation pics and stories tomorrow.

—Q of S

The Troll of Capri
Filed in LEISURE TRIPS on Tuesday, 7/26

After our heroine's adventures with Davide the bus driver in Rome two weeks ago, she took a train south to Naples. From the train station, she hopped a cab to the port and then took a ferry to the isle of Capri. I had made a reservation through the internet at a three-star hotel called il Cacciasole in Anacapri.

There are two towns on Capri, Capri Town and Anacapri. Anacapri is the more remote of the two, perched high on the mountain. The island itself is extremely scenic. Everywhere you turn, you are treated with a magnificent view of greenery and sheer cliffs dropping to aquamarine waters below. It reminded me of Santorini, except Capri is much greener than that volcanic Greek isle.

Most people just make a day trip to Capri. The Queen of Sky is *not* most people. I intended to relax for a couple of days on the lush little island at my 60-euro-a-night hotel. (60 euros is about $84. This was the low range for Capri—not an island for budget travelers.)

The hotel was actually very nice. They picked me up at the port (for a fee). And there was a pool that overlooked the ocean (for a fee).

My fondest memories of Capri are of strolling around the quaint little walking paths that sometimes cut right through people's backyards and gardens, and, as I said before, always ended at some spectacular view of rocks and turquoise sea far below. I also immensely enjoyed my chair lift ride to the top of Monte Solaris. (But then, the lifts are my favorite part about skiing, too. I could ride around on them all day.) Had I had my hiking boots with me, I would have hiked the mountain. (Well, at least the way down.)

One beautiful spring evening I was sitting in the Piazzetta in Capri Town reading a book and soaking in the view of the port and the sunset below me. A man came and sat on the bench quite close to me. I could feel his eyes looking me over, and I could smell the alcohol on him before he even opened his mouth.

"Hello," he said. "Where are you from?"

I tried to ignore him, but he persisted.

"Gli Stati Uniti," I finally replied, looking up rather vexedly from my book.

I first noticed his cloudy eyes, and then my eyes were drawn to his shaggy clothing and hair. It looked like he hadn't bathed in a week. His overwhelming odor of cigarettes and alcohol took a couple of minutes to adjust to.

"Ah, you speak Italian! What's your name?"

"Elena."

"Piacere, Elena. My name is Vincenzo."

He started asking me if it was my first time in Capri, who I was traveling with, and how long I was staying.

"A couple of days," I responded to the latter.

Vincenzo then commenced to recommend to me places to visit around the island.

"Have you been to the Blue Grotto?"

"Yes, today."

Earlier that day I had taken the bus from Anacapri down to the Blue Grotto. When I realized that it was a cave with a very small entrance only accessible by rowboat, I got scared. I knew if I ventured inside, I would have a claustrophobic attack. So I made my way back up the steps to the bus stop.

"Ma dove vai?" (Where are you going?) I heard a voice yell out from below. It was one of the rowboat captains on the water below.

"Claustrofobia," I called back.

"Ah, no, vieni qua!"

He motioned for me to come down, and I hopped in the boat with him and a group of Japanese tourists.

"My name is Gianni. Don't worry. You don't have to be afraid. It is very big inside."

I paid my ticket, and we rowed into the cave, ducking our heads at the entrance. Inside it *was* rather large, and I was *not* scared. The cave gets its name from the blue light that reflects through the entrance into the waters of the grotto.

Meanwhile, Gianni invited me on a private tour of all the other grottos of the island—the Green Grotto, the Red Grotto, etc. I should just wait for him at six o'clock that evening at the Marina Grande. The Japanese group leader in the boat overheard our discussion and winked at me. Gianni was quite ugly and extremely short.

Before we left the grotto, Gianni pointed out to me the "Grotto of Love", a little cave within the cave just big enough for a rowboat to fit into. I was pretty sure that was where he wanted to take Queen of Sky later that evening.

When the tour ended, I jumped out of the boat and made my way back up to the bus stop.

"Don't forget, six o'clock at the Marina Grande!" Gianni called to me from below.

"Sure, I'll be there," I replied unconvincingly.

The heavy-set Japanese lady who had been listening in on our whole conversation said to me something along the lines of, "Hot date tonight?" *wink*

"I'm not going," Her Mile Highness clarified with a flip of the wrist. She grinned, and we parted ways.

To be continued...

Trip Pics
Filed in PICS on Tuesday, 7/26

Rome...

The Forum

View from the Vatican

The Via Appia

Capri (No pics of the troll, sorry—he would have broken my camera!)

Riding to the top of Monte Solaris

View from the top of Monte Solaris

Another view from the top of Monte Solaris

The Troll of Capri, Part II
Filed in LEISURE TRIPS on Wednesday, 7/27

So anyway, where did I leave off?

There Queen of Sky was, sitting on the bench in the Piazzetta around six in the evening, the Marina Grande far below her. A rather smelly character named Vincenzo was harassing her as she sat peacefully trying to read her book.

Then he offered to be my tour guide, and, for some reason, a light went off in my head.

"You're from Capri?"

"Sì, sono originale caprese," he boasted.

I told him I was about to have dinner, and before I knew it, he had whisked me off to a local pizzeria. Upon entering the pizzeria, Vincenzo introduced me to his mother and sister.

He seemed rather trustworthy. After all, I had already met his entire family.

We each had a pizza and some wine. Vincenzo, albeit somewhat of a troll and likely the town drunk to boot, was gentleman enough to pay for my dinner.

"I pay today, you pay tomorrow," he said.

Then we went to a bar above the Piazzetta. Queen of Sky was already cheery and rosy-cheeked from the wine. (Note: Queen of Sky is a cheap drunk.) After another glass or two of wine, Vincenzo leaned across the little bar table, grabbed my head with both hands, and tried to plant a kiss on my startled lips. I tried to pull away, but the spell of the Capri troll on the moonlit night was irresistible. (OK, not really, but it sounds good. Actually, I just couldn't wriggle away from him.)

To my surprise, Vincenzo the troll was a very good kisser.

The next thing I knew, I was plunging through the summer night on the back of Vincenzo's motorbike. We ended up at the Marina Grande, where he stole a few more kisses and showed me one of Capri's few (pebble) beaches. Drunk or not, it didn't take me long to realize why the troll had brought me there.

He wanted a piece of the Queen of Sky! :-O

"Well, it's late. I'd better be getting back to Anacapri," Her Mile Highness said with a yawn.

So back we sped on Vincenzo's motorbike to the bus stop for Anacapri. He made me promise to meet him again the next afternoon in the Piazzetta, and, with a wink directed at the bus driver, I was granted a free ride back to the top of the mountain.

The next afternoon I strolled into the Piazzetta, feeling good, excited to see Vincenzo. When I saw my little troll in the light of day, however, I deflated like a flat tire. He ran up to greet me with a hug and a kiss. I slyly looked around to see if anyone was watching.

Oh my God, I can't believe I was kissing this toad last night! I thought. *And he didn't even turn into a prince!* :-O

Embarrassed by his appearance and smell, I pushed him away. Then we started on our way up to Hadrian's Villa, which I had wanted to visit that day. Vincenzo kept trying to kiss me, and I kept pushing him away.

"Why you don't kiss me today like you did yesterday?" the heartbroken troll inquired.

"Because I'm not drunk today," Queen of Sky replied bluntly.

First Vincenzo proudly showed me the little town church. He told me he was very religious and started crossing himself.

"I'm not Catholic," said I. "I'm a strega (witch)."

On the way up the path to the villa, he wanted to stop at a friend's cafe to have a glass of wine and a cigarette. He had his friend play a song for me on his guitar. Then he tried to kiss me again as I slurped a granita di limone and chomped on a fabulous caprese salad.

"I told you he was drunk," I overheard one of his friends say.

Well, at this point, I had had about enough of my little troll, so I said goodbye and got up to leave. Of course he followed me, so I had *the talk* with him among the greenery of the footpath.

"Solo amici (just friends), Vincenzo."

I kept repeating that phrase on the way up the hill, hoping that it would sink into his alcohol-infused brain. At the top of the hill, he again winked at a friend, and I was granted free admittance to the ruins.

While I visited the site, Vincenzo passed out on a bench at the entrance. He only lifted his head once to bellow to me "I LOVE YOU!" in the way that drunk people bellow.

It was kind of amusing.

When I finished my tour, I considered slipping out without arousing Vincenzo, as he was snoring contently on his bench. But I felt a little guilty, so I waited for him to wake up. When he did, he propped his greasy little head on my lap, like a happy little boy.

On the way back down the path, the troll started getting on my nerves again. This time I decided to lose him for real. I ran ahead of him and hid in a little alley along the path. From my hiding place I spied him run past in hot pursuit, incessantly calling my name.

I felt bad. So I reappeared, upon which my troll asked meekly, "Where did you go, strega?"

I don't know when exactly it started, but at some point Vincenzo started introducing me to everyone on the island as his moglie (wife). He kept asking me when I was coming back to Capri. He said he would light a candle in the little church every day, awaiting my return.

I have to say I was quite flattered and thought that living in Capri wouldn't be such a bad deal, if it were not for the troll.

Vincenzo followed me around the island for the next couple of days like a stray cat. In fact, at one point he tried to eat some of the cheese I had bought to feed to the legions of stray Capri kitties.

Anyhow, on my last night in Capri, he invited me to his house for a feast with his family and some friends. I hoped it wasn't our wedding feast.

Vincenzo lived in a tiny two-bedroom apartment with his mother and obese sister (I guess the women share a bed) by the Marina Piccola. The apartment was so small that for two people to pass in the living area, you had to both turn sideways, like on an airplane aisle. His mother was busy making the ravioli when I arrived. About eight of us crammed around a table only meant for five, and the feast began.

First, there was prosciutto and melon. Then the homemade ravioli capresi. Vincenzo's mother insisted that I have another portion, which I did. But then she produced a whole roast chicken, french fries, and a salad. I was already stuffed, but I managed to eat a little chicken. Then there was ice cream. Vincenzo and I had had a gelato earlier, so I tried to pass. But Vincenzo's mother and sister would not have that. I was given a parfait glass with two large scoops.

The whole time, Vincenzo's friends and family were asking me when I was coming back to Capri.

"I don't know," I said.

I had told Vincenzo earlier that the winds had changed and it was time for the *strega* to depart. Of course, he was sad and tried to talk me into staying. He also tried, unsuccessfully, to talk me into "making love" to him.

"Ma e' naturale, e' naturale! (But it's natural, it's natural!)" he proclaimed, showing apparent flexibility on his devout Catholicism.

We parted ways with a kiss (on the cheek), and Q of S swooped off on her broom...

-THE END-

Next up: The Playboy of Amalfi...

On the Road Again

Filed in *MY LIFE IN THE AIRPORT* on Thursday, 7/28

Hello, all. Queen of Sky is back in Bustling Base City airport today, on her way to Lima.

I know you are all just *dying* to hear about Q of S's tryst with the Italian playboy in Amalfi last week, but you will have to just wait a little longer...got some stuff to do here in the airport now, namely change into my uniform... Oops, I just remembered—I don't kiss and tell! ;-) Sorry!

Adios!

En Vivo Desde Lima, Perú

Filed in *LAYOVERS* on Friday, 7/29

Hello, all. Queen of Sky here. Turns out that this weekend is a holiday weekend in Peru—Peruvian Independence Day was yesterday—and unfortunately, a lot of things are closed—including the HAIR SALON!!! That's the main reason Q of S kept this trip... to get her hair cut. :-(Oh, well, guess I will either have to go shaggy or get my hair cut in the States and pay four times more for a cut that's not as good.

Así es la vida...

Anyway, in other news, last night Q of S went downstairs for a drink with her crew and didn't get back to her room until 2am. The bartender, Julio or José, who is a friend of everybody's favorite barfly Chucha Galore, wanted to invite me to lunch today, but I explained to him that I already had plans with my crew to go to Al Fresco to have some fabulous seafood. To be polite, I invited him along, so we shall see.

Anyhow, there is a line for the computers at the hotel, so can't chat long. The good news is, with all this extra time from not going to the salon, Q of S has more time for her two favorite layover activities: eating and sleeping.

Plus, Q of S has a junior suite today, as she was one of the first off the bus (even though she had to collect the sangria cups from everybody), and therefore got to the front desk first and snagged a good room. The junior suite has a Jacuzzi, which is where Her Mile Highness will be shortly.

Hasta pronto...
—Q of S

Going to BED
Filed in FLIGHT BLOGS on Saturday, 7/30
Hello, all. It's 9:41am Eastern Time, and Queen of Sky just got back to Bustling Base City from Lima. We left about an hour late from Lima because a man in first class crapped his pants right after we pushed back from the gate.

Actually, I feel sorry for the guy because he may have had a heart attack, since he also peed on himself and apparently passed out briefly before going into the restroom to clean himself up. Q of S was working in the back, but the flustered flight attendant in charge (a queen of a different sort) came back to the mid galley after the incident and asked Q of S to come up to help translate to see if the guy was OK in the bathroom.

Well, turns out that the guy spoke perfect English. I tried (unsuccessfully) to excuse myself and go back to my cabin, as there was a horrible STENCH in the first class cabin (not to mention the brown stuff on the carpet at 2B). :-P

As you will remember, Q of S is always the first to disappear when body fluids are present. Anyway, we ended up returning to the gate and having the man removed for medical attention.

Everything else went smoothly last night. The main struggle on that flight is trying to stay awake. Q of S had taken a two-hour nap after her late lunch (seafood, of course) with her two crewmembers (the other two queens of sky on the flight).

As an aside, yesterday, before lunch, Q of S exited the elevator into the lobby of the hotel, and a blond girl stopped her.

"Are you the one with the Diary of a Flight Attendant?" she asked.

"Maybe..." I replied hesitantly.

"Because I saw your website in the browser history on the computer downstairs... and I was reading it, and I just have one question for you... Julio was supposed to meet me for lunch at twelve o'clock, but he didn't show. Did he go with you?"

After a little discussion, Q of S found out that the little Peruvian bartender had made a lunch date with girlfriend (who it turns out was a flight attendant for another airline) at noon and then had planned to call Q of S at 2pm. :-O

Then my friend Jesse, who had been waiting for me in the lobby and overheard the conversation, exclaimed, "Julio was supposed to meet me, too!"

Heh, heh, heh.

It was too funny... Chucha should get a kick out of this. Her little friend is quite the HOMBRE! ;-)

Thankfully, he didn't call Q of S that day. She was, however, in her room at 2pm having her hydro massage in the Jacuzzi. :-D But she wasn't really looking forward to a lunch date with a man half her size, anyway.

OK, that's all the updates for now. Q of S is off to her commuter hotel now, as she has an ASS-KICKING three-day trip to WhoKnowsWhere tomorrow and needs to get some rest. This is payback for the three weeks Her Mile Highness had off this month. :-(

Hasta mañana...
—Q of S

AUGUST

The Normal Grind

The Trip From HELL!!!

Filed in FLIGHT BLOGS on Wednesday, 8/3

I know you all have been wondering what happened to Queen of Sky. Well, for the past three days she has been in the middle of the TRIP FROM HELL!!! It really kicked my butt!

Here are some of the highlights:

Day 1: Q of S is almost late from briefing as she did not sleep well the night before due to CRAMPS. :-(

Leg 1: Bustling Base City to Mexico City. Q of S and crew have to serve hot meals to a FULL 757 with NO meal carts. :-P

Leg 2: Mexico City back to BBC. Same as leg one.

Leg 3: BBC to Washington. Q of S pulls her beverage cart down the aisle and accidentally hits an African gentleman in the knee. He winces in pain but says he is OK. He declines offers for ice for his knee.

Then, shortly before landing, Q of S sees African gentleman step out of restroom and asks him how his knee is doing. He responds, "Not too well," and asks for Q of S's contact info.

People, Her Mile Highness doesn't give out her contact info except to *really* HOT guys.

11:30pm: Q of S, her crew, and *all* the passengers (on bus to terminal) must wait for paramedics to examine "Abu's" slightly bruised knee (which, by the way, he has been walking around on with no complaints). It is obvious that he is trying to get some money from Anonymous Airlines. Q of S wishes she had hit him in the balls instead of his knee.

(The next day I got word that there was nothing wrong with the guy and that he refused offers to go to the emergency room.)

And that was just DAY 1!!!

Now you know why you haven't heard from Q of S.

Day 2 was DC to BBC to San Fran for a short layover. (We were late, so we got minimum rest... eight hours.)

Day 3 (yesterday) we did San Fran to BBC (that's a four-and-a-half hour flight right there), then sat for three hours in BBC in the *hot* flight attendant lounge where the A/C was broken, then went BBC to Orlando (full boat again, of course) and finally back to BBC at 11pm last night. :-P

Minor Celebrity Alert

Q of S had a famous (formerly obese) American weatherman in first class going to Orlando yesterday. He wasn't his normal chatty self, or maybe he was just tired, or perhaps that's just his screen persona. I wish I had some dirt on him, but he was drinking *virgin* bloody Marys.

Anyway, I went to my commuter hotel last night and crashed. Missed the last flight back to Quirksville so had to overnight in BBC. I considered sleeping in the flight attendant lounge—for about two seconds, that is. (Spending the night in a lounge chair in the airport is *not* worth saving a few bucks—you'll have to trust me here.)

The good news is, I took the Anonymous Airlines Italian test the other day and PASSED!!! I can't believe it! All those Italians—err, I mean all that Italian—I studied last month really paid off! ;-) So now Q of S can fly to Italy on a regular basis. To start off, this weekend Q of S has two Rome trips back to back... UGGGH! But if she survives that, she'll have two weeks off... Thank the Higher Power!

Gotta go find some yummy airport grub now before my flight home...

Hello Again from BBC airport
Filed in *MY LIFE IN THE AIRPORT* on Saturday, 8/6

Hello, all.

Well, it took Queen of Sky her *whole* three days off to recover from that Trip From Hell. In fact, she had to start taking antibiotics again because her old back/kidney problem flared up during that HORRIBLE trip.

The good news is, today I'm feeling better. The bad news is, today I have to go to Rome. Actually, anything is better than that domestic trip FROM HELL. (Although, after this I have another trip to Rome—eek!) By the end of it, I'll have been away from home almost a week. :-(

What else is new? Hmmm, all of a sudden, Q of S has two Italian men emailing her. Guess it's either feast or famine. One is my ex, Maurizio the deceptive diplomat, who is back in Argentina. I already told him once not to contact me, but now he says he *needs* to talk to me. I promptly deleted his email and blocked his email address.

The other man I heard from is my new Italian playboy, who BTW is a *dead ringer* for George Clooney, but taller. Q of S may see him when he's in Rome at the end of next month. ;-)

Well, not much else new... Q of S needs to go find some yummy airport grub once again before her briefing. I hope Rome is not too hot tomorrow, and I hope the A/C is working at the hotel... and, above all, I hope the lines at the gelaterias are not too long!

Toodles!
—Q of S

Roma in the Rain-a
Filed in LAYOVERS on Monday, 8/8

Well, Queen of Sky just got back from Rome and is happy to report that it was an EASY trip. Her Mile Highness is *never* going to complain about international flying again, in fact.

Today we had a break from the normal FULL FULL summer flights: We had 50 passengers misconnect in Rome and therefore had 50 empty seats in coach. :-D That is UNHEARD of this time of year.

Anyway, the layover was OK... I took a three-and-a-half hour nap when we got in (an hour late), and then left the hotel at 6pm just as a huge thunderstorm rolled into the city. Even with my umbrella I got drenched. I almost went back to the hotel, but needed to find a pharmacy to stock up on antibiotics.

On the way, I came upon a gelateria and ducked out of the rain to have some pine nut and cinnamon gelato. Then the rain let up, so I continued my quest for a pharmacy, which I eventually found. After that, I hurried to meet a crewmember that I had made plans with.

Sofia had said we should meet at the "wedding cake", aka Campidoglio, at 7pm. Queen of Sky thought this was a bad idea, as Campidoglio is a huge monument with various sides and TONS of tourists crawling around this time of year. But Sofia said we should meet on the right where the buses stop.

I arrived a little late and waited about ten minutes but didn't see Sofia. I figured the rain had scared her off. So, I headed back toward the hotel, past the Trevi fountain to the supermarket and then up to the hotel.

Since I was solo, I decided to eat at my normal restaurant, Il Pomodoro, up the street from the hotel.

At least my normal waiter Luigi will be there to talk to me, I thought as I walked over.

Well, turns out Luigi was in riposo (on vacation), so Her Mile Highness had to sit alone and didn't even have a book to read. :-(So, to compensate, she ordered course after course and stuffed her face. :-) :-P

The next morning, bright and early, Q of S learned from Sofia on the bus back to the airport that she had *indeed* been at the Campidoglio the day before at the specified hour.

Oh, well, we had planned to go to Trastevere together for dinner, ma così è la vita! (C'est la vie!)

Tomorrow Q of S is heading back to Roma. Hopefully the weather will be a little nicer and she won't have to eat dinner alone again. :-(

Off to commuter hotel now...

—Q of S

Off Again
Filed in MY LIFE IN THE AIRPORT on Tuesday, 8/9

Off to Roma again today... am flying with my drama queen friend, Ricky. I have to be careful what I say to him. My friend Christine hasn't spoken to me since she came with me on that Rome trip back in January, possibly due to Ricky's BIG boca!

Hmm, not much else to tell... slept pretty well at the commuter hotel, although I woke up many times last night. I was actually in the bed for about 14 hours but was not sleeping that whole time. Hopefully that rest will get me through this Rome trip.

Ciao, a presto!
—Q of S

Another Easy Trip
Filed in FLIGHT BLOGS on Thursday, 8/11

Wow, that was another easy Rome trip. I can't believe my luck. We only had about 100 passengers in the back going over (holds 160), and only 19 up front (half full) on the way home. (Those were the cabins Queen of Sky was working in.)

I feel like I've been released from prison. After flying my TAIL OFF the past two weeks, I finally get to go home and have TWO WEEKS OFF!!!

As usual, of course, Q of S's early commuter flight home is FULL, so she may have to wait five more hours in Bustling Base City airport and not arrive home until late tonight. Mais, c'est la vie... am going to sleep late tomorrow, the next day, the day after that, the day after that, etc.! :-D

Well, not much else to report. Ricky was tired last night (he was on his fourth trip in a row), so I went with another girl on my crew back to Il Pomodoro for dinner. Luigi was still on vacation. He will be disappointed when he finds out Q of S was there twice and he missed her. That would have been two more opportunities to give Her Mile Highness his phone number! :-O ;-)

OK, got to go change out of this STINKY prison guard uniform now...

A Typical International Flight with Queen of Sky
Filed in FLIGHT BLOGS on Friday, 8/12

Well, I haven't done a "Day in the Life" entry lately, and a lot of people have been asking me what it's really like to work a flight, so here is a detailed description of my last flight to Rome...

4:10pm, the "Flight Attendant Dungeon": The captain and the lead flight attendant brief us on the trip.

Queen of Sky scopes out the crew. It does not look good. The only person I know is Ricky.

Meanwhile we sign up for our crew positions. Q of S signs up for coach tonight.

Information taken away from briefing:

Flight time: 8:55 (That's pretty fast—good tailwinds, according to Captain Swifty.)

Today's movies: *The Titanic* (with whole ship-sinking scene edited out) and *Parent Crap II* (AIA really needs to get some better movies!)

Pick-up Time in Rome on Day Three: Too damn early!

4:35pm: Q of S and crew trudge all the way down to gate X99 to find out that the aircraft is not even here yet. It's still en route from Timbuktu.

5:00pm: Plane finally lands. Whole crew has scattered in search of caffeine and other stimulants. Plane will not be unloaded, cleaned, and catered for another forty minutes or so. It's gonna be a LONG night!

5:45pm: Crew is finally allowed onboard the 767. Q of S schleps her two-wheeled sidekick Valigia back to coach, tripping over the cleaners' vacuum cords. Q of S then hauls Valigia into overhead bin, almost throwing her back out in the process.

5:55pm: Q of S finishes checking emergency equipment and proceeds to start counting meals in the aft galley. We decide to hold off on distributing headsets, since we are not full.

6:00pm: Gate agent is *eager* to board (as usual), since we are already forty minutes past departure time. Lead flight attendant pages for boarding flight attendant.

Guess who is boarding flight attendant today?

Yep. Queen of Sky.

6:05pm: Q of S quickly changes from "concourse shoes" to "smelly airplane shoes" and stumbles up to the boarding door. Lead flight attendant has already paged for her two more times.

6:06-6:35pm: "Hello, do you know where you're seated? Buona sera, sa il suo numero di posto?"

Passengers consistently ignore Q of S and make their way down the wrong aisle. Q of S could care less. Q of S HATES boarding.

6:17pm: Passenger with very LARGE box (like three feet square) asks Q of S if he can put his box in the closet.

"I don't think that will even *fit* in the closet, but let me ask the lead," Q of S replies. (This is why Q of S doesn't fly lead.)

Lead flight attendant takes one look at that box and points to the jetway. "You'll have to check it," she snarls.

"But it's *very* fragile—it's crystal for my daughter's wedding in Tuscany," the concerned man replies.

Just then I note the word *FRAGILE* in big letters on the side of the box.

But lead flight attendant obviously woke up on the wrong side of the bed this morning.

"Well, where do you want me to put it? Under my fanny?" she snaps, opening the forward coat closet, which is only about two and a half feet wide and packed with coats and her luggage.

The man reluctantly exits the airplane and leaves the box in the jetway. Then, as he re-boards, he turns to me (lead F/A has already left the area) and snarls:

"I'm gonna *sue* you if *one* piece of my crystal breaks!"

Lovely.

I roll my eyes and do my best to feign a smile, "Do you know where you're seated, sir?"

6:35pm: Agents finally shut door. Q of S fumbles through her Italian announcements ("the door is closed... please be seated," etc.) and once again heads to the back of the plane, this time tripping over people's feet and half-stowed luggage and closing overhead bins along the way. (This is about as much multi-tasking as Q of S can do.)

6:36-7:29pm: We sit on the taxi-way in traffic waiting to take off.

7:30pm: Capt. Swifty comes over the PA and promises to make up some of our delay time in flight.

7:45pm: As soon as seatbelt sign goes off, we start setting up our cumbersome beverage carts.

8:01-8:27pm:
"Would you like something to drink?"
Blank stare.
"Would you like something to drink, sir?"
"What do you have?"
(Multiply this by 100.)

8:28-8:45pm: Q of S picks up dirty cups while her aisle partner, Butch Betty, sets up the meal cart and restocks the beverage cart.

8:46-9:20pm: Q of S slings hash while Butch Betty slings bevies.
Q of S: "Chicken or beef?"
Passenger, removing headphones: "What are the choices?"
Q of S: "Chicken or beef."
Passenger: "Do you have anything low-cal?"
Q of S: "CHICKEN OR BEEF."
Q of S drops mystery meat on tray table and moves to the next row.
Q of S: "Chicken or beef?"
Passenger: "Me, my hubby, and six chil'rens *all* want chicken."
Q of S: "Well, I only have one chicken left, so who gets it?"
Passenger: "Oh no! Little Johnny and Jimmy and Billy and Bobby and Edna and Mary-Jean are gonna be *so* disappointed!"
Q of S: "So sorry. Here's your slop."
Next row:
Q of S: "Chicken or beef?"
Passenger: "I'm gonna *sue* you if *one* piece of my crystal breaks! I'll take the chicken."
Q of S: "Oops, sorry—I only have beef left."
Man starts to turn red. Q of S throws tray down, releases brake from cart, and takes off for back galley.

8:46-8:59pm: "Coffee, tea or me?"

9:00-9:25pm: Pick up people's half-digested meals and snotty napkins *without* the aid of rubber gloves. Butch Betty can't be bothered and lets Q of S do most of the work.

9:26-9:28pm: Two-minute break to eat some left-over crackers from somebody's nasty tray and slurp down some water (the aircraft cabin is drier than the Sahara) before Q of S's next task: Duty Free Sales.

9:29-10:06pm: Push burdensomely heavy Duty Free cart through now-darkened cabin with my Duty Free partner, Tiny Tina. We almost take out some unsuspecting people's knees and elbows along the way. (They apparently weren't expecting any more carts in the aisle for a while.) After about half an hour of going around in circles yelling "Duty Free—get your Duty Free!" at the top of our lungs, we finally sell one pack of cigarettes.

Great! The 50-cent commission we'll get for that lone sale almost makes it all worthwhile—even the ridiculous amount of paperwork that now lies before us! Q of S muses sarcastically.

10:07-10:25pm: Fill out burdensome Duty Free paperwork, look for change for $100 bill that cigarettes guy gave us. Tiny Tina finally goes up to the cockpit to get change. (Q of S does not dare, after what happened the last time she went up there for change.)

10:26pm: Q of S is so hungry she *devours* some of the disgusting coach beef, even though she does not normally eat red meat. Then she meanders to business class in search of a salad and a sundae.

10:45-11:59pm: Tiny Tina and Q of S kill time reading girlie mags, passing out water, and stuffing buns in the oven for the breakfast service.

Midnight-2:30am: Finally—BREAK TIME! (The grouchy lead was at least nice enough to divide our break period into two blocks instead of the standard three.)

2:30am: Am awoken from a not-so-deep sleep in the extremely uncomfortable crew rest seats. (A little kid was kicking the back of my seat for most of the first hour.) Q of S barely has time to tinkle and tame bed-hair before breakfast service. Apparently we made better time than Capt.

Swifty originally thought and are now landing in an hour instead of an hour and a half.

2:32-3:04am (8:32-9:04am Rome time): Sling hot buns and coffee, then rush back through cabin with second coffees and teas.

3:05am (9:05am local): Skip hand towelette service. (*Darn!*) Time to snatch half-eaten bagels up. We are descending FAST!

3:15am (9:15am local): "Please raise your seatbacks and tray tables and make sure that your seatbelts are securely fastened, because this *bitch* is ready to *land*!"

3:35am (9:35am local): THUD! Touchdown. *Rough one, boys!*

3:37am (9:37am local): Q of S fumbles both English *and* Italian landing PAs.

3:50am (9:50am local): HALLELUJAH! The door is open and the flight is officially over!

3:55am (9:55am local): Angry passenger comes back to galley to reiterate one last time:
"If *one* piece of my crystal broke, I'm gonna *sue* you!"

3:56am (9:56am local): Angry passenger turns and marches out of galley. Butch Betty flips him off behind his back. We chuckle.

3:57am (9:57am local): Q of S and crew search for their bags and drag them off the plane in a jetlagged daze. Valigia seems to have somehow gained weight during the flight.

Now it's time for our sweet reward: The Layover. :-D

Ask Queen of Sky a Question, Take II
Filed in LIFE OF LEISURE on Saturday, 8/13

Guess what, kids? Yep, it's time again for *Ask Queen of Sky a Question*! This time, due to my slight jump in readership, I'm going to request that each person only ask one question... Don't be greedy now!

First Questions Answered
Filed in ABOUT ME on Sunday, 8/14

Anonymous asks:

I noticed your PayPal button. Why do you think people should donate you money? :-) Do you not make enough earnings where you currently work? I would think that work would be kind of lucrative.

QueenofSky replies:

People should donate Queen of Sky money so she can fly less and blog more (and shop more). :-)

Airline jobs lucrative??!! I'll be lucky if I have a job a year from now. And who is going to pay for my shopping habit then??

EyeOfTheTiger asks:

Are you a member of the Mile High Club?

QueenofSky replies:

Of course. I have the official pin. ChuchaGalore, the president and founder of the MHC, gave it to me. ;-)

Anonymous asks:

How come, of all occupations, you chose Flight Attendant? Stewardess? Queen of the Sky? What would you do if you weren't a flight attendant?

QueenofSky replies:

Queen of Sky really wanted to be an anthropologist, but seeing as that required advanced university degrees and then there was little chance of finding a job, she instead opted for the glamorous career of Waitress in the Sky. Along the way, Q of S has learned much more about human nature than she ever would have in a classroom or on some remote island in the South Pacific.

As to your second question, this is something I've been thinking about a lot lately. If Q of S weren't a flight attendant, she would probably be a chef or run her own catering business. Q of S LOVES food!

JuanCarlitos asks:

Do you have an accent? If so, is it a southern drawl or what?

QueenofSky replies:

People often are surprised when they ask Queen of Sky where she is from, and she responds, "North Carolina."

"But you have *no* accent!" they say.

But of course, if you want Q of S to have an accent, she can have one. ;-)

Low Morale
Filed in My Life in the Airport on Monday, 8/15

Queen of Sky's employee morale is at an all-time low today, since she had to get up at FIVE AM(!!!!) to come to Bustling Base City to hear upper management feed her a bunch of BS and company propaganda. Apparently they are trying to dispel rumors of upcoming pay cuts, layoffs, mergers, etc., and meanwhile boost our morale.

The powers that be are forcing ALL 15,000-plus flight attendants (and none of the other employee groups, BTW) to attend these meetings. And I've heard that discussions have gotten so heated at some of them that people have had to be escorted out. Making flight attendants fly to work on their off-days and meanwhile wasting a WHOLE LOT of the company's money is not exactly a great way to boost morale.

In any case, Queen of Sky plans to sleep through the entire four-hour pep talk. That would about make up for the sleep I lost last night. So much for two uninterrupted weeks off!

Perturbedly yours,
—Q of S

More Questions Answered
Filed in ABOUT ME on Tuesday, 8/16

I'm not going to vent anymore about what a waste of time yesterday was. Let's just say Queen of Sky read a couple of magazines and did her bids while at the mandatory meeting. Anyway, back to a much more interesting topic: reader questions...

Anonymous asks:
Have you ever dated a pilot? If yes, would you do it again? If no, why?
QueenofSky replies:
I gather a pilot is asking this question? :-O

No, Queen of Sky has never dated a pilot. And if this is the pilot whose wife left him for a lesbian, the answer is NO, she would *not* date a pilot. For everybody else, the answer is the same... Q of S DOES NOT DATE PILOTS!

...unless, of course, it was a very special pilot who had a blog called "Diary of a Dysfunctional Pilot." :-D

CaveMan asks:
Why do you refer to yourself in the third person when answering some of the questions here?
QueenofSky replies:
Because Queen of Sky has multiple personalities.

Mickey-Dee asks:
How many times have you joined the Mile High Club in the past year?
QueenofSky replies:
Sorry, Queen of Sky has lost track.   ;-)

Anonymous asks:
Have you ever had any celebrities on your flights and, if so, did they do anything weird? Dish dish and name names, girl!
QueenofSky replies:
Back in the days when Anonymous Airlines still had first class (and not just business class like we have now), Queen of Sky had Sean Lennon on a flight from NY to somewhere in Europe. He was with a girlfriend and was very nice.

Out of Bustling Base City, Q of S NEVER gets celebrities, unless you count the "Body by Greg" guy, whom she had on her flight to Tampa a couple of weeks ago.

However, Q of S has heard plenty of stories from flight attendants who've had celebrities on their flights... including the likes of JFK Jr., Melanie Griffith, Prince Albert, Angelina Jolie, etc. If you wish to hear about these instances, Q of S will gladly relate them, but it will be second-hand gossip.

Even More Questions Answered
Filed in ABOUT ME on Thursday, 8/18

Anonymous asks:
How tall is Q of S?
QueenofSky replies:
Queen of Sky is just over six feet tall (183 cm).

Anonymous asks:
I have an interview for an airline this month to become a flight attendant. If you don't mind me asking, how much do you make?
QueenofSky replies:
The more you fly, the more you make. Queen of Sky doesn't fly very much, so she makes about $35K. Also, she's not at the highest pay scale at her airline.

Anonymous asks:

Do you wear panties under your F/A uniform? if so what brand? Thong or granny panties?

QueenofSky replies:

Granny panties, of course... the biggest, ugliest ones I can find! Ask my friend ChuchaGalore. I'm sure she wears a thong, if anything! :-O

Anonymous asks:

Do people actually donate money to you? I see that you ask for it, but I wonder if you actually get much (money that is—as gorgeous as you are I'm sure you get your share of the rest). :-)

QueenofSky replies:

Good Question... So far Queen of Sky has received ONE donation in the amount of $5. She is still waiting for the "big donation" so that she can retire and live a quiet life on an island somewhere in the South Pacific.

Bob asks:

Peanuts or pretzels?

QueenofSky replies:

None of the above! :-P

Cajun01 asks:

I'm an everyday normal passenger. I'm not starting fights, getting drunk, or trying to feel you up. There are a hundred of me on every single flight. What is the one thing that I do every flight that irritates the hell out of Queen of Sky?

QueenofSky replies:

Ask for a drink when we just did a beverage service... and then ask for that same drink from another flight attendant, so we both bring it to you. Meanwhile, ask for a pillow or blanket midway through a four-hour flight, when you are sitting on an aisle seat and could have easily gotten one yourself at the beginning of the flight. (Ring your call bell in each of these cases.) And then come back to the galley while the flight attendants are eating their meals and try to make small talk with them. They will be your new best friends!

Anonymous asks:

Where is 'Bustling Base City'??

QueenofSky replies:

Somewhere on the East Coast of the USA. That would give away the identity of Anonymous Airlines, and Queen of Sky doesn't need any stalkers.

Happy Hour
Filed in LIFE OF LEISURE on Friday, 8/19

OK, enough questions! Queen of Sky is off to happy hour now. This may be my only socializing with *real* people this weekend, so I will enjoy! Can already taste that margarita and queso!

—Q of S

EDIT: I deleted the jerk who left the nasty comments under this entry *and* in my Guestbook (and YES, I know both entries in the Guestbook were from the same jerk.)

Here's a tip for you, LOSER... if you don't like my blog, DON'T READ IT!

The Hottest Pilots
Filed in LIFE OF LEISURE on Saturday, 8/20

Hello, all. Funny thing happened yesterday. Queen of Sky was looking at her blog's referrer stats and noticed a large number of hits coming from some kind of message board. Turns out it is a pilot message board entitled "The Hottest Flight Attendants."

Heh, heh, heh.

Through a little reading, Q of S discovered her site was mentioned on the message board.

Her Mile Highness has decided to start her own feature, entitled "The Hottest Pilots." Submissions are welcome!

HELLOOOO Greenland!
Filed in PICS on Sunday, 8/21

Summer in Greenland.

Taken on the way back from Rome earlier this month.
(Had to crawl over a passenger to get this shot.)

RANK THIS PILOT
Filed in LIFE OF LEISURE on Monday, 8/22

Hello all, Queen of Sky has her first submission for the "Hottest Pilot" contest. Please leave your rating of him on a scale of one to ten in the comments below.

JT is a pilot for an unspecified airline...

Not bad, eh? See girls, you never know who is reading your blog. ;-)

P.S. Q of S will publish JT's ratings after she has at least ten comments.

Update: The above pilot claims to be 6'2" and 25 years old and says that that was his first flight as captain, which is why he looks like he is constipated.

More Pics of Contestant #1
Filed in LIFE OF LEISURE on Tuesday, 8/23

Queen of Sky took these from JT's homepage:

Who could score this poor little guy a "6"?

Q of S agrees with her readers that JT needs to submit some naked pics to be judged fairly. ;-)

P.S. If you all keep bashing poor JT and hurting his feelings, Q of S will have no choice but to make it up to him by taking him out for a drink the next time he is laying over in Texas. ;-) (May have to make an exception to the "No Pilots" rule.)

Update: OK, scores have been tabulated... here they are:
AndiRack: 7.8
SwissJet: 5 (a little low, Swiss... we can't all be PERFECT!)
Lisette: 7
Anonymous: 7
Funfish: 8
Tamalito: 6
WizardofOz: 9
Airplanejunkie: 9
ChuchaGalore: 8
QueenofSky: 9.75 (.25 deduction for being a pilot)

Q of S threw out the highest and the lowest scores, leaving her with an average of 7.725 (someone had better check my math!)
Congratulations, JT!
We are currently looking for more competitors; if no one else enters, JT wins by default!

Lima Pics
Filed in PICS on Wednesday, 8/24

Here are some pics from Queen of Sky's Lima trip at the end of last month...

Crew Canoodling

Working Hard...

Special Indian Market for Independence Day
Unfortunately, they all had the same sh*t!

Life of Leisure Comes to an End
Filed in LIFE OF LEISURE on Thursday, 8/25

OK, all... Queen of Sky has been lounging around for two weeks now (minus that one torturous day of management BS)... In fact, this past week she actually got so bored that she started to clean her apartment (didn't get very far, though).

Anywhoooo, tomorrow I have to go back to work. :-P This time it is to the fashion capital of Italy, MILAN.

Just checked the weather, and it looks nice for this weekend. Just hope all the Italians are not still on vacation. :-O Otherwise there will be nothing to do (except maybe make a quick stop at H&M). Perhaps the Italian that signed Q of S's Guestbook today has some suggestions?

Well, what else is new?

Hmmm, Q of S is embarrassed to say that last night she went to the local mall for the sole purpose of eating at the Ruby's all-you-can-eat buffet. :-O I was starving since I hadn't eaten lunch, and none of my friends was available for dinner in a pinch, so Ruby's was calling my name.

I have to admit that Ruby's has the best fried chicken in town. And you can eat all of it you want, plus roast beef, sausage, veggies, dessert, etc., for $7.99! What a deal!

Unfortunately, the buffet seems to be catching on, as it was full of families with screaming kids last night. :-(Q of S sat in a corner (on the far side of the room from the clown—yes, there was a clown making balloon animals for the screaming kids) so that no one would see her scarping down two huge plates of food.

I have a soft spot for pecan pie, which I do not indulge very often. But last night it was calling my name, along with the coconut cream pie. :-D

And guess where Her Mile Highness ate today?

The Indian buffet.

That is two buffets in a row. Need to go do some exercise now... :-O

Off to See the Wizard!
Filed in MY LIFE IN THE AIRPORT on Friday, 8/26

Queen of Sky is off to Italy today. While she's gone, please *behave* and if you haven't signed my Guestbook yet, DO IT!

Q of S dropped two of her Milan trips and now has WAY too few hours next month... am scrambling to pick up time... am even considering picking up a domestic trip (YUK!) to go to see the winner of our Hottest Pilot Contest :-D in an unspecified northern city.

Anyway, after Milan, I'm going to Lima. (Just got this trip off the swap board today!) Hopefully my little bonsai plant will still be alive when I get home. (And I hope I packed enough underwear! Am gonna freeze in Lima— it's still winter down there.)

Toodles!
—Q of S

Back in BBC
Filed in FLIGHT BLOGS on Sunday, 8/28

Hi, all. Queen of Sky here. Just got back from Milan. Easy flight today, except for the usual crew cattiness. These "senior mamas" always seem to have personality conflicts amongst themselves. These women have known each other for 30 years, and they still hate each other. Oh, well, their prob! Così è la vita. Q of S just hides or blames it on somebody else if she is involved in one of their conflicts. :-O

Anyway, it was a successful layover yesterday. I flew with my crazy Chilean friend Erica (whom some of you may know as "Overhead Bin Girl"). So I went out with her and her friend Pietro on the layover. Pietro brought along a Sicilian friend, Massimo, who acted as our bodyguard for the evening. Will post pics next week.

Q of S recently got a request for more pics on the airplane showing LOTS of leg... so those will be posted next week as well.

Right now Q of S is going to her commuter hotel here in Bustling Base City and is going to swig a little airplane wine and nibble on a little airplane cheese (both first class, of course), and then pass out. Then it's off to Lima tomorrow. :-D Fun, fun, fun!

Hasta luego...
—Q of S

Ho-Hum
Filed in MY LIFE IN THE AIRPORT on Monday, 8/29

Happy Monday, everybody!

Queen of Sky is once again in Bustling Base City airport. Unfortunately, Commuter Hotel's checkout time is noon, and check-in time for my flight today is not until 3pm. So I get to while away three lovely hours in the flight attendant dungeon (aka "the lounge"). At some point I will leave the dungeon to fetch some tasty airport grub, though.

Let's see, what will it be today? The greasy fried chicken from Mopeyes... or perhaps a veggie-burger flopper from Burger Queen... or maybe a sandwich with wilted veggies and soggy bread from yet another five-star airport eatery? Ahh, the gourmet dining possibilities are limitless in this airport!

Anyway, flight time yesterday from Milan was around ten hours. Flight time today to Lima should be around six and a half... piece of cake! And we only do *one* meal service. (And *no* duty free sales... although that will be changing soon.)

Word up to everyone who is coming to this site in search of info about how to be a flight attendant: Q of S would like to know that info too, in the likely event of a furlough at Anonymous Airlines. Unfortunately, all, Anonymous Airlines and most other major US carriers have hiring freezes right now. Nonetheless, I'll post tips for finding an airline job in an entry in the near future.

Adios!
—Q of S

P.S. If you are one of the Googlers coming to this site in search of "Naked Stewardesses" and "Flight Attendant Porn," sorry to disappoint!

Hola Desde Perú
Filed in LAYOVERS on Tuesday, 8/30

Hello, all, Queen of Sky here, LIVE from Lima, Peru! Just had breakfast with the crew (free buffet... the whole crew is guaranteed to show up, although Her Mile Highness is always the last one to arrive.) Had some fried yucca, fried sweet potatoes, a Peruvian tamale, an omelet with tomatoes and onions, and some greasy potatoes, all of which I ate with a Peruvian yellow pepper hot sauce—yum!

Next up, Q of S has an appointment to get her hair cut at 12:30pm. (As my regular readers know, I'm so cheap, I do this Lima trip every other month just to get the $12 haircut.) Then Q of S is meeting a couple of her crewmembers for a late lunch of FABULOUS Peruvian seafood. :-D

Not much else to report here. As usual, there is a line to use the computers here at the hotel.

Toodles!
—Q of S

Feel Like I Was Hit by a Truck
Filed in FLIGHT BLOGS on Wednesday, 8/31

9:30am EDT

Helloooo, all! Queen of Sky just got in from Lima and would like to vent for a moment.

That was the WORST Lima crew I've had in a while!

First off, nobody made sangria for the ride to the hotel the other day. Let's see, what else? Well, Q of S was not a designated Spanish speaker on the trip but still ended up doing most of the Spanish PAs, because the two Spanish speakers were flat-out LAZY! Neither of them (who BTW were both native speakers) made the landing PA this morning, so Q of S had to schlep her bag down from the overhead bin and pull out her announcement book, lest she say half the PA in Italian (as she often does of late).

Also, the Lazy Ladies did not seem to know how to do a meal service and just did as they pleased. Somehow we ended up with only two people on the left aisle and four on the right by the end of the service!! This is common sense, people, and definitely something someone flying over six years should know: If you have six people working in the back, three work on each side—it's simple division!

OK, enough venting about work...

This morning, after rushing through US Immigrations and Customs (BTW, one of the pilots was smuggling in a couple of Cuban cigars this morning. Her Mile Highness asked him where he put them—heh, heh!), Q of S of course dashed over to Concourse X to catch her commuter flight back to Quirksville, which was showing as delayed on the board, and the Piece of Crap Regional Carrier agents informed her that it had already departed. Well, if they had taken it off the board like they were supposed to, I wouldn't have rushed all the way over there! Apparently they love to tease commuting flight attendants who are desperate to get home. >:-(

Anyhow, now I get to wait here in the flight attendant lounge until NOON for the next flight to Quirksville. Oh, JOY! I have been invited to an event this evening, but it looks like I won't make it. I need to get some serious ZZZZzzzzs when I get home. Too bad, because I was just thinking how I need to be more social.

Well, Her Mile Highness is off to drink martinis and lounge around in her sexy lingerie now. (This is what flight attendants do in the flight attendant lounge, according to Chucha Galore.)

Hopefully I will be in a better mood later...

Ciao!
—Q of S

SEPTEMBER

The Queen is Dethroned

Overhead Bin Girl is BACK!!!

Filed in PICS on Thursday, 9/1

Overhead Bin Girl is BACK—and better than ever!!!

Queen of Sky performs a balancing act...

Later Queen of Sky tried to climb into the overhead bin, too...

Maybe I would have fit if I hadn't crammed down that HUGE slice of pizza for breakfast (hey, they have good pizza in Milan Malpensa Airport!)...

...and maybe I should have skipped that LARGE cone of gelato
the night before, as well (that's whipped cream on top)...
(In foreground: Q of S's Sicilian bodyguard,
Massimo, protecting her gelato.)

Daily Horoscope
Filed in MISC. on Friday, 09/02

Hmmm. This is a little scary. I don't need any more problems in my life
right now...

Profound Changes

This is a time of great change and upheaval in your life. During this ex-
tended period your self-awareness will be heightened and you will experi-
ence a strong drive for recognition and power. This power should not be
used for selfish means, however, or you risk touching upon the dark side of
this influence: death (symbolic or literal).

The less extreme result of this influence is that circumstances may
force you to come face to face with your shadow. You cannot hide from
who you really are during this time. If your inner demons surface, you
must battle them.

The positive potential of this period is for total life transformation for
the better. If these energies are used wisely, you could emerge a more

focused and powerful person. It is a chance for positive change by taking control of your life.

You cannot escape the transformational powers of Pluto, but you can harness them to fit your destiny. If you stay true to yourself, this influence will show you how to reach your full potential as a human being. In the meantime, beware of speeding buses and falling buildings.

Aspect: Pluto conjunct Sun
Period of Influence: Starts this week and lasts approximately a year and a half.
Courtesy of Astro Wizards

Come to think of it, this sounds kind of like what that fortune teller in Buenos Aires told me a couple of months back—eek! :-O

Of Hurricanes and Rodent Pee and Trips to Spain
Filed in MY LIFE IN THE AIRPORT on Saturday, 9/3

Hello, all. Hope you are all keeping dry (especially those of you in Florida) and cool this weekend.

Queen of Sky only had two days off and is headed to sunny Barcelona, Spain, today. :-D The only good thing that came out of missing my commuter flight the other day was that I saw this Barcelona trip on the swap board and quickly grabbed it. I had just put it through in the computer when I overheard the flamer at the computer behind me pondering aloud:

"Hmmm... should I pick up that Barcelona trip?"

Q of S: "Too late, I already put it through."

Flamer: "I'll fight you for it!"

Q of S: "Too late, it's already on my schedule."

Flamer: "Well, I'll mess up your hair then!"

Q of S: "That won't work—my hair's already messed up!" (Had just gotten in from Lima all-nighter.)

Anyhow, Q of S got home finally Wednesday afternoon, and when she opened the door to her condo, she smelled a FUNK that hit her like a brick wall! :-O Q of S, rather delirious from having been up all night, spent the next hour or so searching for the source of the stench. Did something die in here? (Keep in mind that Q of S had been out of town for six days.)

Finally I concluded that a raccoon had gotten into my condo somehow and peed everywhere, because that's what it smelled like: raccoon/rodent pee. I cautiously peered into my closets and under my beds, but couldn't find the culprits.

Somehow I took a nap with that stench, despite an anxious feeling that a gang of raccoons would attack me at any moment. In the evening when I woke up, I finally realized that it was not rodent pee after all but a leaky toilet tank that had been dripping for over a week and had soaked through the bathroom wall and into the carpet in my bedroom, thus producing the lovely moldy carpet/rodent pee smell.

To make a long story short, I didn't have two restful days off as I had planned. I had to clean up my other bedroom so I could sleep in there, call various handymen, none of whom were available this week, and go to Home Depot to pick up supplies and look at carpet (will have to replace the carpet in that bedroom). Fun, fun, fun!

Meanwhile, I put a large Tupperware container under the dripping toilet and had to empty that out every few hours. This is when a MAN would have come in handy. While it is a simple problem and easy to fix, Q of S knows she would botch it and end up flooding her whole house. :-O

Anyway, all that's on Q of S's mind right now is the SANGRIA and TAPAS she will be partaking of tomorrow in Spain. :-D And since this HURRICANE looks to be headed straight for Bustling Base City by Monday, Her Mile Highness has packed extra underpants in hopes that she will get an extra day in Spain. :-)))

Happy long weekend!
—Q of S

P.S. Please send Leaky Toilet Relief Funds to Queen of Sky's PayPal account. Much obliged!

STRANDED BY HURRICANE!
Filed in MY LIFE IN THE AIRPORT on Monday, 9/5

HELP!

Just as I had feared, I made it to Bustling Base City from Barcelona today and now a hurricane is hovering right above and all flights out are delayed.

Does not look like Queen of Sky will make it back to Quirksville tonight. In fact, looks like she will be spending the night in her comfy PJs in the flight attendant lounge here in the airport. :-(

Am exhausted and just want to go home. :-((And of course, all the hotels near BBC airport are full tonight.

Uggh!

Anyway, the trip went smoothly, except for one little incident on the way over. Q of S was working in coach, and after we lowered the lights following the dinner service, word got back to us that someone's dog had gotten out of its carrier and was loose in the cabin.

Q of S promptly led a search party armed with flashlights through the now-darkened cabin. It didn't take long to find his trail: a pile of fresh poop lay mid-way up the left aisle, which apparently an unsuspecting passenger had already stepped in. (This is one of the many reasons you should NEVER go barefoot in an airplane cabin.)

We finally caught the little rascal crawling under a middle row of seats sniffing carry on bags. The piercing scream of a Spanish woman awoken by a moist tongue on her bare feet alerted us to his position.

Not much to report from the layover. I wasn't feeling that great when we got to Spain, so I almost stayed in and ordered room service. But a friend of mine was on the crew, so I ended up going to dinner with her.

Well, off to try for a flight now...

Crisis Averted/New Haircut
Filed in PICS on Tuesday, 9/6

Don't worry, all, Queen of Sky did finally make it back to Quirksville last night around 1am. The flight was surprisingly smooth, but I had to sit on the jumpseat, as it was a full boat. :-(

Here's a pic from Lima last week after my $12 haircut (remember, $12 is a small fortune in Peru).

Changes in the Air
Filed in *MY LIFE IN THE AIRPORT* on *Wednesday, 9/7*

Well, as you all may or may not have heard, Anonymous Airlines has announced some BIG restructuring plans today. The highlights include:

- Pay Cuts
- Staffing Cuts
- Benefits Cuts

Just what Queen of Sky wanted to hear.

Actually, rumors have been flying for weeks now around Anonymous Airlines galleys that there was going to be a buyout offer. They said it would be $5K or $10K per year of service. That would have given Q of S $40K or $80K in severance.

Well, needless to say, I would have jumped ALL OVER that! After all, as you may or may not know, it is my dream to attend culinary school abroad. Afterward I could start a catering/party planning business with some other flight attendant friends.

But alas, it seems that it was just a rumor.

The good news is, if Her Mile Highness *does* get laid off, it won't be for a while, so she will have time to start cooking school here in Texas, although she'll have to take out MASSIVE loans to do so. But then perhaps she can even get her catering business up and running beforehand.

Let's see, what else is new?

I spent the last two days shampooing and steam-cleaning my carpets, as advised by someone on my crew this week. And it seems to have worked. The rodent pee smell is gone. May not have to replace the carpet after all! :-D

The Ogre and the Rat
Filed in *LIFE OF LEISURE* on *Thursday, 9/8*

Queen of Sky would like to tell a true story of an ogre and a rat.

Today Q of S called her local exterminator, since she has been hearing suspicious noises coming from her ceiling again lately. A short while later, Edward, a large, jolly, ogre-like man with no front teeth, showed up at her door.

Edward the jolly ogre proceeded to Q of S's patio, where he set traps in the eave above through a rotted-out hole that had been covered with wire mesh. Then, a short while later, Edward interrupted Q of S's telephone call to motion her out to the patio.

Once on the patio, Edward the Ogre produced a perfectly preserved rat skeleton in an old rat trap that he had found in the hole. It was gross but rather fascinating. The little carcass had obviously been there a while, since there was no sign of meat on the bones.

Anyhow, Edward did me a favor before he left by installing the flap to seal the HUGE gap under my front door to prevent bugs and possibly that dead rat's cousins from coming in. Her Mile Highness has had that flap for at least six months but had not gotten around to installing it. Actually, she doesn't even own a drill.

Q of S rewarded the pot-bellied jolly ogre with a Bud Light. He was much obliged, but then she thought he would never leave once he found out she was a flight attendant. It seems that this profession enthralls men, especially the blue-collar sort. Edward the Ogre kept coming up with more and more questions.

In other news, my toilet tank has spontaneously stopped dripping... but meanwhile, a pipe in my A/C closet has spontaneously *started* dripping. :-(And, while cleaning out my bedroom last week, I discovered yet *more* water damage in one of my closets—and a coating of black mold. GREAT. :-(

All this and pay cuts coming up soon. Please DONATE to Q of S's mold and rodent and leaky pipe fund ASAP!

Gracias!
—Q of S

The Rome Cruisers
Filed in FLIGHT BLOGS on Monday, 9/12

Hello, all. Queen of Sky is in Bustling Base City. Just got back from Roma. Exhausted as usual and waiting for commuter flight home to Quirksville, which is FULL as usual.

The flight to Rome was AWFUL the other day. Q of S was working in coach, which was full of needy old people heading for their pampering cruise vacations. They didn't seem to understand that they were not on the cruise ship yet and the airplane is not an all-inclusive, all-you-can-eat outfit.

Q of S suspects we had a whole Florida retirement home on the flight that day. And that retirement home was probably located somewhere between Fort Lauderdale and West Palm Beach. We're talkin' retired New Yorkers... yes, the best kind of passengers. Like doing a nine-hour long NY-Ft Lauderdale flight. Tons of fun, believe you me.

On a lighter note, toward the end of the breakfast service, Q of S noticed a horrible stench in the cabin. She scoped out the nearby passengers for the souce of the odor, which smelled of rotten eggs and potato salad. Her eyes met those of a large scantily clad woman in the center seat of row 36.

"Don't look at me," the woman declared, pointing an accusatory finger at the man on her right, "I saw him tilt!"

Anyway, on the way home today, we had another cruise group. But this time it was the Special Meal group. Q of S was working coach once again, and everybody back there had ordered either a vegetarian, low-salt, low-cal, low-fat, low-taste, gluten-free, kosher, Muslim, Hindu, Buddhist, New Age, atheist, or born-again-Christian meal.

Oh, joy. Flight attendants LOVE special meal requests. But this group was actually much better than the retirement home group. At least today's crowd said "please" and "thank you" when they ordered their six beverages apiece.

On that note, I have decided to start a new feature called "How to Be a Good Airline Passenger." (Personally, I feel there should be a mandatory video with the same title for passengers to watch before they are ever allowed onboard an airplane.)

Anyway, coming up next are Q of S's first tips. :-)

How to be a Good Airline Passenger
Filed in MISC. on Tuesday, 9/13

(From Queen of Sky's soon to be released book: *Airplane Etiquette for People with No Manners, No Common Sense, and No Clue Whatsoever.*)

Rule #1: NEVER ask a flight attendant to lift your heavy-ass bag. If you can't lift it, you should've checked it.

Rule #2: Remove your headphones when the flight attendant is talking to you. We just LOVE repeating "What would you like to drink?" or "Chicken or beef?" ten times while you jam to your music.

More Little Known Facts About Q of S
Filed in ABOUT ME on Wednesday, 9/14

1. Queen of Sky uses her own pillowcases in ALL hotel beds, even five-star properties. (Hey, some people carry their own sheets!)

2. The first and last time Q of S ever ate caviar was in first class on Anonymous International. Back in the day when we had international first class, we always had two tins of caviar aboard each flight. But we rarely used the second tin, so it was commonly referred to as "crew caviar." (Remember, perishable items are tossed out after each international flight, so we were just preventing waste.) ;-)

3. Speaking of food, Q of S was a vegetarian before she started flying. But at her first airline, Reich international, the only options were chicken or beef, so it was either starve or convert!

4. Q of S has low morale, along with about 99.9% of the rest of Anonymous Airlines flight attendants.

5. The one WHOLE day of useless but mandatory "training" (during which we were told a pack of lies, like that there would be no pay or staffing cuts) that Q of S went to last month (at a pay rate of less than $2/hour, no less) did NOTHING to improve Q of S's morale. In fact, just thinking about it makes Q of S's morale plummet! The only thing boosted that day was Q of S's drive to get AIA flight attendants unionized, so we won't have to sit through such useless wastes of time and money EVER AGAIN!

6. Today is the first anniversary of my mother's death.

Feliz Diez y Seis de Septiembre!
Filed in MISC. on Friday, 9/16

Happy Mexican Independence Day!

We need to embrace all holidays that offer another excuse to drink margaritas. :-D Although, if your name is Chucha Galore, you don't need an excuse!

Week in the Life of Leisure
Filed in LIFE OF LEISURE on Saturday, 9/17

Nothing much going on here... Today Queen of Sky finally got her toilet fixed and her new garbage disposal installed. (It's only not been working for five years now.) Then she headed to a local veg-head hangout for a macrobiotic lunch. At Veg-Head Central, Q of S ran into a New Age acquaintance who hooked her up with a contact for her new business idea. Q of S has decided that she and some of her other soon-to-be-furloughed flight attendant friends in town should start a party-planning business. We *do* know how to party, if nothing else.

Anyhow, we shall see how that goes.

Then Q of S drove by some houses listed for sale on the internet. I am SO SICK of my crappy condo and dealing with the homeowners association and my upstairs neighbor, who has *yet* to call me about sending someone to look at the damage that *his* leaking A/C drainpipe caused in my apartment! Would love to have a house and be able to deal with problems without all this red tape. Also, a yard would be nice. And a washer and dryer on site.

Anyway, I need to pick up a trip for more hours but am waiting 'til this new hurricane clears the East Coast so that I don't get stuck somewhere unpleasant (like Bustling Base City!).

How to be a Good Airline Passenger
Filed in MISC. on Sunday, 9/18

Rule #3: Do not try to make small talk with the flight attendants while they are eating.

P.S. Good news, all! Got a Rome trip on Tuesday... am going to meet up with my hot Italian race car driver. He's visiting his family in Rome this week.

LEGAL HELP NEEDED ASAP!
Filed in MISC. on Monday, 9/19

Queen of Sky suspects her employer is trying to FIRE her for posting pics of herself in uniform on the web.

IF YOU ARE A LAWYER or can give legal advice, please send me an email ASAP!!!!

Thanks!
—Q of S

9/22 Update: Thanks for all the support, everybody! Hopefully this will be resolved this week. Keep those outrage and support emails coming!   ;-) GRACIAS!

9/26 Update: I have been suspended WITHOUT pay and WITHOUT explanation. Will update when I know what is going on. <:-(

9/28 Update: :-X :-/

OCTOBER

Media Storm

Big Brother is Watching You
Filed in PICS on Sunday, 10/2

Turbulent Emotions
Filed in MISC. on Monday, 10/3

Background music: "Fallen" by Sarah McLachlan

This morning I woke up with a knot in my stomach.

I have only experienced this range of emotions once in my life—last year as my mother lay dying of cancer.

In fact, it was her death that pushed me to blog.

I'm sorry if I have offended anyone with my writing (much of which is fiction).

If you are offended by this blog, there are many other blogs you should *not* read. In fact, you shouldn't be on the internet at all!

—The downtrodden and distressed Queen of Sky

THE QUEEN OF SKY UPDATE
Filed in MISC. on Friday, 10/7

DISCLAIMER: This entry, along with most of this blog, is a fictitious account. Any resemblance to real people, places, or events is purely coincidental.
The poor, powerless, downtrodden, and distressed Queen of Sky finally

met with the omniscient and omnipotent Mighty Management yesterday. They INTERROGATED her about her blog and then told her that her suspension WITHOUT PAY and WITHOUT BENEFITS was continued until further notice.

MM said Q of S was suspended because of some "inappropriate" (???) pictures on her blog. In about two weeks, MM said they will tell Q of S her fate (i.e., show her the door).

Hmm, they could have given me a warning and a chance to remove the pictures before suspending me, Q of S mused to herself afterward. *So much for freedom of speech! And what's this business about being suspended WITHOUT pay for weeks on end?*

Q of S will let her readers make their own judgment about Anonymous Airlines' Management.

In the meantime, with all this time off, Q of S will be entertaining the following offers:

- Offers for guest appearances on Mexican telenovelas (as the bitchy gringa)
- Offers of all-expense-paid vacations to remote and pristine tropical islands
- Offers to be Q of S's pro bono legal team
- Offers to write advice columns for trendy men's magazines
- Offers of full scholarships to cooking schools in France
- Offers of large sums of money toward the Queen of Sky Campaign
- Offers for book deals, movie deals, etc.

Please send above offers to me at queenofsky@blogacres.com. THANK YOU!!!

—Q of S

"Inappropriate" Photos
Filed in MISC. on Saturday, 10/8

OK, people keep asking me about the "inappropriate" photos. Queen of Sky does not know what "inappropriate" means, as Mighty Management didn't define it for her, but she supposes that MM had a problem with some very TAME pics of Q of S posing on the airplane with no passengers on board (which Q of S has since removed from her blog).

The most revealing photo shows Q of S with a couple of buttons of her uniform shirt undone. :-O If the Pope is still reading her blog (see Guest-book), Q of S thinks even *he* would approve of these pics.

QueenofSky-gate
Filed in LIFE OF LEISURE. on Monday, 10/10

Well, as news of QueenofSky-gate spreads throughout the world via cyberspace and the blogosphere, our heroine continues her life of leisure in peace. Queen of Sky is presently looking for a personal trainer and a styl-ist. Oh, and a hairdresser and makeup artist... and a bodyguard and per-sonal assistant... Heck, Q of S needs a whole ENTOURAGE!!! Being a Blog Super Diva takes maintenance, you know!

It's a good thing I'm independently wealthy! (Yeah, right!)

Queen of Sky's Weekly Update
Filed in LIFE OF LEISURE. on Wednesday, 10/12

1. Queen of Sky filed a sex discrimination complaint with the Equal Employment Opportunity Commission against her employer last week after finding MANY pics of male Anonymous Airlines employ-ees in uniform on the web. (What a double standard!)

2. Q of S has been on the Queso and Quesadilla Diet this week (aka the South Texas Diet). She needs to find a personal trainer ASAP!

3. Yesterday Q of S consulted with her psychic advisors (actually, they're alternative therapists I started seeing last month for undealt-with grief issues). They told her not to be afraid of what life has to offer and to pursue the path that she is most drawn to. They also told Q of S she should take up painting. :-)

4. While Q of S is sitting around on suspension, she has decided to do something useful and volunteer in her community. Unfortunately, she missed the deadline to volunteer for the Lance Armstrong Foundation's Ride for the Roses this weekend.

5. Let's see, what else? Hmmm. Well, Q of S might go salsa dancing tonight. That is BIG news. She might go to yoga class, too. :-D

Behind the Scenes (PRIVATE)
Filed in LIFE OF LEISURE. on Thursday, 10/13

I just figured out that I can post "private" blog entries that only I can read. Geez! I wish I had known about this feature a couple months ago. Maybe I wouldn't have gotten in all this trouble in the first place. So anyway, this is my first "private" entry to record for my poor memory what's going on behind the scenes at the Queen of Sky Campaign Headquarters.

At the moment I'm still *desperately* searching for a lawyer. Most of them hang up on me as soon as they find out I'm not represented by a union. I voted for the union—it's not my fault none of those company kool-aid drinking senior mamas did!

When I started this blog, it felt so good, so liberating. It quickly became my friend, my confidant, and my therapist. But I never thought in a million years that my blog could liberate me of my job. How ironic is that!?

Anyhow, as soon as I got the call from the supervisor last month saying that I couldn't fly my trip the next day because of some "pictures on the web," I immediately deleted all pictures of myself and others in the Legacy Airlines uniform from my blog. So I don't get what the problem still is. I'm expecting Legacy to call me any day now to tell me I can come back to work. They surely wouldn't fire me (with no disciplinary history) over something so trivial!

On the other hand, I did get a pretty bad vibe from management last week. When I met with my supervisor and a human resources representative (both EXTREMELY unsympathetic) without a witness (they wouldn't allow my friend Victor in the room with us) last Friday, not only did they intimidate and harass me about my blog, but they also tried to get poor "Overhead Bin Girl's" name out of me. I guess they wanted to go after her, too. Of course I told them I couldn't remember her name.

Meanwhile, a reporter from the *Wall Street Observer* emailed me and told me to call him. I was skeptical at first but eventually did decide to call him back. I was even more skeptical when he asked me for my full name. :-O But finally I gave it to him, since he said Legacy wouldn't fire me if they knew the press was watching.

Then, a couple of days later, someone from the British News Network in London emailed me. I gave her my number, and she called and interviewed me over the phone. I am really nervous about this. I told her the *WSO* had already interviewed me but had not published the story yet.

In the meantime, my readership is really starting to pick up. Instead of a hundred or less daily hits, I'm now getting several hundred. I guess my story is spreading around the web. In fact, I have been writing to various online media sites to ensure that it does.

Unfortunately, all this trauma and stress has made my old urinary tract problems flare up again. I feel like crap most days but have resolved to take NO MORE antibiotics. They just make me feel worse at this point.

And as for my social life, not much to speak of at the moment. Giulio, the Italian race car driver I met in Amalfi a couple months back, has been emailing me nonstop wanting to know why I didn't hook up with him in Rome last month. At first I wasn't sure what to tell him, but I finally replied the other day, trying to explain my predicament to him in my poor Italian. Not sure if what I said made sense. Actually, I know it didn't. I can't even explain my predicament in English!

Oh, well. If I lose my free flights, I guess I can't have any more long distance relationships. Not that what I had with Giulio was a relationship anyway... more like him trying to constantly jump me and me feeling like a piece of meat for the whole two days that we were together. Hmm. He was handsome, but totally full of himself—talked about himself constantly. However, he *did* cook me dinner one night, which earned him some booty call bonus points. ;-)

Q&A with Q of S
Filed in ABOUT ME on Friday, 10/14

Well, people have been asking me a lot of questions lately, so I've decided to try to answer some of them, since I'm just sitting at home these days twiddling my thumbs and waiting for AIA management to tell me my fate...

Anonymous asks:
If you wanted one, how difficult would it be to carry on a full time relationship with a lover who's not in the industry?
QueenofSky replies:
Queen of Sky has always dated men outside the airline industry. It's not hard. You just have to trust each other, something that's necessary in any relationship.

Bubba asks:
I saw a couple of lovely F/As on a recent flight. Do F/As enjoy being flirted with/asked out?
QueenofSky replies:
If they are single and you are hot, HECK YEAH!

Paranoid asks:

If you got on a flight and saw ten young Arab men sitting together up front, what would you do? Assume furtive glances amongst them.

QueenofSky replies:

This would be a GREAT question for the "Miss Flight Attendant World Pageant"! Unfortunately, said pageant doesn't exist.

Let's see... Actually, hopefully someone would have noticed this on the ground and reported it to the captain. Then it is his/her decision to remove or not remove the suspicious passengers from the flight.

Q of S did commute home one day with a WHOLE Tunisian basketball team on her flight. Talk about young (tall and handsome!) Arab men! Didn't bother Q of S except for the B.O. that they were emitting.

Anonymous asks:

I assume I travel quite a bit on Anonymous Airlines (assumption is that I travel on AA, not that I travel a lot). Why are all of my F/As so unattractive when you are so very good looking!?

QueenofSky replies:

Because Anonymous Airlines FIRES or INDEFINITELY SUSPENDS all of its good looking flight attendants. :-(They prefer them fat and ugly.

Anonymous asks:

Are you single and would you consider moving to california for a relationship?

QueenofSky replies:

Queen of Sky is INDEED single. However, unless your name is Brad Pitt, she's not moving anywhere for a relationship at the moment. The only reason Q of S would be relocating presently would be for JOB PROSPECTS!

Concerned Colleagues (PRIVATE)
Filed in MISC. on Saturday, 10/15

Private Entry, Take II:

I've been getting a lot of phone calls from concerned flight attendant friends lately. Apparently there are all kinds of rumors going around Legacy about why I was suspended. Most of them are lies, probably spread by Legacy management.

The best rumor I have heard came from my friend Ricky. He called me the other day and told me there is a story circulating around Legacy's galleys about a flight attendant who was fired because she was going around sleeping with all these guys on layovers in Europe and South America.

"Hmm, but *you* haven't been fired or suspended, Ricky," I teased after hearing the story.

"Yeah, it does kind of sound like me, doesn't it?" he replied proudly.

A couple of days ago out of the blue, I got a call from my friend Christine, who hasn't spoken to me since she came on my Rome layover with me back in January.

"Elena?" she began timidly.

"Christine?" I was surprised, but comforted to hear my old friend's voice.

"How are you? I can't *believe* what happened to you!"

"I know, but I'm hanging in there. How about you? It's been a long time."

We caught up a little. She told me she had gotten a new dog and then filled me in on some gossip about our mutual friend Gloria: She's pregnant by the now-divorced pilot!

"Wow! Well, good for her, I guess," I said. "I hope that's what she wanted. I think three kids would be enough for me, but if she can handle four, more power to her! I hope she's happy."

"She seems very happy," Christine replied. "They're planning to get married—no date set yet, though."

"Hopefully marriage numero dos will be better for both of them." I said skeptically.

I do sincerely wish them the best, but, at the same time, sincerely doubt it will last.

Christine went on to tell me a story she had heard recently about one of the international in-flight managers at Legacy. He had been caught with his pants down—literally. He was having an affair with a female supervisor, and someone walked in on them doing the deed in his office.

"And guess what happened to him?" Christine continued dramatically. "He was demoted... but the *female* supervisor was *fired*!"

"Why doesn't that surprise me?" I said calmly, meanwhile boiling on the inside.

Anyway, I guess this means Christine and I are friends again, so that's cool.

I also heard from Nelly, aka Chucha Galore, and Erica, aka Overhead Bin Girl, this week. They were both very worried for me and for themselves. I told Erica not to fret, as I didn't give up her name and had long since deleted her pictures. She told me she's about had it with her husband, and she really needs her job if she is finally going to muster up the courage to leave him.

Meanwhile, Nelly told me she has pulled the plug on her blog. Too bad—I really enjoyed reading about her nightly rock n' roll debaucheries.

We can't all be married to rock stars, after all. And she has an incredibly endearing and unfailing joie de vivre that comes across in her writing (pretty amazing, considering her perma-hangover).

Well, the blogosphere will miss "Chucha" dearly. But after what happened to me, I can't say that I blame her.

Recap
Filed in MISC. on Sunday, 10/16

I have now been suspended *without* pay and *without* benefits for a full month.

Anonymous International Airlines (AIA) discontinued my medical insurance two weeks ago. This means Q of S is now one of America's MANY uninsured.

AIA says it's still investigating me. After all, fun-loving, attractive front-line employees with a sense of humor and a willingness to work every holiday are a THREAT to the stability of Anonymous Airlines. (Q of S suspects that AIA will find a way to blame its financial problems on her, too.)

From what I understand, AIA will leave me on unpaid suspension indefinitely, in hopes that I will quit. This is AIA's M.O. I will NOT quit.

Meanwhile, Q of S's story has spread to the far corners of the web and has been translated into at least three languages. My story has generated quite a bit of interest from the international press, as well.

Q of S has no choice at this time but to continue her life of leisure and see how things unfold. Anonymous Airlines can't legally fire her, since that would be retaliation after she filed that discrimination complaint with the EEOC.

Q of S is still open to offers, <u>as mentioned previously.</u>

Crazy Stuff (PRIVATE)
Filed in MISC. on Monday, 10/17

Oh my God! The British News Network Online story came out today! I didn't realize it would be this BIG!

Someone called me from England this morning (at 6:45am!) wanting to interview me on the radio. That's how I found out that the story had been published. Then I checked my blog—I had already gotten 20,000 hits, and it was only 9am. And then I checked my emails. I had at least 100 emails of support (mostly from Brits), and they just keep coming! This is SURREAL!!!

Queen of Sky's Webolution
Filed in LIFE OF LEISURE on Monday, 10/17

Hullooooo, BNN readers!!!

Queen of Sky is a little flustered right now. I was out late last night and then my phone started ringing this morning at quarter to seven.

Here's how the rest of Q of S's day looks:

7am-4:30pm: Sit in bathrobe and bunny slippers with blinds drawn, lights turned off, phone unplugged, a helmet on her head, and a stunned look on her face. Santeria candles burn in the corner and "I Will Survive" plays in the background.

4:30pm: Yoga class.

6pm: See 7am-4:30pm.

7pm: BNN party at Q of S's place (and the address on the web is wrong... sorry!).

P.S. Hello, Denmark, Hungary, and anybody else who may be reading this, as well! Little did you Europeans know that we have royalty in the USA, too! ;-)

P.P.S. Q of S is trying to answer her emails as quickly as possible!

More Q&A with Q of S
Filed in ABOUT ME on Tuesday, 10/18

Hi, all. I'm still hanging in there and recovering from my BIG news story yesterday. Now back to our regularly scheduled program: Reader Questions.

Anonymous asks:
Is flight attendant training difficult?
QueenofSky replies:
That depends on your definition of difficult. It is challenging if you think memorizing city codes and airline regulations and struggling into a slippery life raft from a swimming pool with everybody in your class looking at your butt and your flailing legs sounds daunting. Oh, and all the meanwhile you have to keep your hair and makeup perfect. :-O

But you'll never know 'til you try. ;-)

Anonymous asks:

What advice do you have for a 18 yr old college girl who wants to become a flight attendant? Should she complete her 4 yrs of college first or apply as soon as possible to be a flight attendant? I am asking this because I am worried about the money.

QueenofSky replies:

Many airlines won't hire an 18-year-old. Anonymous Airlines' minimum age is 21. So check around. Find out first if the airlines you want to work for are hiring, then, whether you meet the age requirements. It wouldn't hurt to apply for the job now if you meet the requirements. You can always finish your degree later. That's what I did. I finished my degree just a couple of years ago while I was flying full time.

Good luck!

Anonymous asks:

Do you belong to a union, and if not, why not?

QueenofSky replies:

Anonymous Airlines flight attendants are non-union. Queen of Sky voted for the union a couple of years back, but the naïve senior flight attendants did not. Therefore, Q of S has to defend herself against Mighty Management with no protection.

faraway asks:

I am considering a position at Taliban travel, but the form asks if I sleep with goats. Can I lie to protect my furry friends?

QueenofSky replies:

Taliban Airlines does background checks, so be careful before you lie on your application. And it wouldn't hurt to wear a burka to the interview. ;-)

Anonymous asks:

Why does the seat belt chime/light go on and off during ascent and descent? Wouldn't once be enough, or are the pilots just goofing around?

QueenofSky replies:

The seatbelt sign is a TOP SECRET signal. It means the flight attendants can now read their *People* magazines. ;-)

BigBurt asks:

People must forget stuff they left on the plane. Why can't people remember... it's right above them? Do flight attendants make sure everything gets out before people leave the plane?

QueenofSky replies:

Queen of Sky is the only flight attendant who is tall enough to see into the overhead bins, therefore it is Q of S's *sole* responsibility to check them post-flight.

One time Q of S found a pair of pants that a little Japanese lady had soiled (and we're not talking about a soda stain) and left in the overhead bin after a Lima flight. Had to tell the cleaners to put on the *GLOVES* for that one.   :-P

It's Over
Filed in PICS on Wednesday, 10/19

2:37pm CT

Queen of Sky was just FIRED from Legacy Airlines, aka Anonymous Airlines, for posting the following pics on her blog (back by popular demand):

Overhead bin check.

Breakfast in Milan.

R.I.P. Freedom of Expression and the Rights of the Little Guy (or Gal, in this case). Apparently employees, especially *female* employees, don't have a right to a life outside of work in this country. Nor do they have a right to fair treatment from their employers.

Quick Update
Filed in MISC. on Thursday, 10/20

1. Yes, you read correctly. I was fired yesterday from Legacy Airlines, and over the phone, no less! They generously gave me two days' time to think about sending in my resignation letter. Yeah, RIGHT!!! Big blunder on Legacy's part, if you ask me. (See #2.)
2. Q of S is considering hiring a PR firm, as she has received so many interview requests.
3. A BIG lawsuit is coming for Legacy Airlines.
4. Q of S and her team are working on T-shirts to support her cause. Also, Q of S is thinking about going on a "laptop-signing" tour. :-) But that does not mean, as one of her fans suggested, that she will be sitting on top of your lap as she signs. :-O

Join the Queen of Sky Campaign!!!

Filed in PICS on Friday, 10/21

Hello, everybody! This pic comes to Queen of Sky from one of her readers in jolly old England...

Now that is a TRUE Q of S supporter! Thanks, B!

—Q of S

More Behind the Scenes Stuff (PRIVATE)

Filed in MISC. on Friday, 10/21

Well, I finally found a lawyer to take my case with no retainer. He was recommended to me by the Human Rights Commission where I filed my discrimination complaint. When I first called the lawyer's office to talk to them about my case, I got the legal assistant. I was in the middle of telling him my story when he said:

"Hmmm, I read about a case like that on the BNN website the other day."

"That was me," I replied.

"You live here in Austin?" He sounded perplexed.

"Yep, right down the street."

Needless to say, I got an appointment right away.

Anyway, meanwhile, the *NY Chronicle* interviewed me the other day, and I think the BNN is planning a follow-up, now that I have been fired. The reporter told me that the first story about me was *extremely* popular on their site, probably because they posted one of my uniform pics on the news front page.

Who knows where all this will lead? All I know is it's just crazy!!! In fact, Booty Call Guy called me the other day to find out who was going to play him in *Queen of Sky* the movie! I told him I was open to suggestions, and he started running down a list that started with Colin Farrell and ended with Vin Diesel. Brad Pitt was somewhere in the middle.

"Keep dreaming, Ralph," I managed to choke out after picking the phone up off the floor.

PRESS INQUIRIES
Filed in MISC. on Saturday, 10/22

HI EVERYBODY!

IF YOU ARE A MEMBER OF THE PRESS, PLEASE SEND ME AN EMAIL REQUEST AT QUEENOFSKY@BLOGACRES.COM.

THANKS FOR YOUR PATIENCE... I AM VERY OVERWHELMED WITH EVERYTHING THAT IS HAPPENING TO ME RIGHT NOW!!!

—Elena, aka Q of S

Misc.
Filed in MISC. on Sunday, 10/23

Hi again, everybody! Sorry, but Queen of Sky's DSL is down tonight. That plus the INCREDIBLE amount of fan mail she has received today means that she will unfortunately be unable to return emails today. If I don't get back to you, consider posting your message in my Guestbook for all to read.

Also, please, if anyone comes across pictures of Legacy employees on the web in uniform (including those in profiles on dating sites), please forward the URLs to Q of S. The more evidence the better!

Thanks... I'd better sign off now before President Bush outlaws blogging (or specifically Q of S's blog)!

Media Inquiries
Filed in MISC. on Monday, 10/24

Due to today's *NY Chronicle* article, I've been getting a LOT of media inquiries today.

If you are a member of the media and interested in my story, once again, please send me an email including your phone number, and I will get back with you ASAP.

—Q of S

P.S. See my <u>Oct. 19 entry</u> for the now-infamous uniform pics.

Of Media and Mediums
Filed in LIFE OF LEISURE on Tuesday, 10/25

Hi, all. Queen of Sky just got back from a meeting with her psychic advisors. They told her how to deal with this new celebrity and then did some intuitive healing on her.

Anyhow, now it's off to the hairdresser. The interview onslaught starts tomorrow... will try to keep everyone up to date.

—Q of S

An Interesting Poll
Filed in MISC. on Wednesday, 10/26

I thought you all would find this interesting. Seems there is a poll about Queen of Sky over at *What's That? Forums*. According to the latest results, approx. 75% of those polled favor Q of S (in one way or another!)...

Regarding the fired Flight Attendant:

- Legacy was right to fire her... people should *never* post in a blog, *ever*. **15.41%**
- She should not have been fired. It's her right to post whatever she wants. **46.12%**
- She's a dog! That's reason enough to can her ass. **10.10%**
- I'd like her to introduce me to the "Mile High Club". Hubba-hubba! **24.08%**
- I'm smitten. She had me at "Buh-bye". **4.29%**
- Total: 980 votes **100%**

Media Blitz
Filed in MISC. on Thursday, 10/27

Well, today Queen of Sky is going to her lawyer's office for a shoot for a local TV station. I've been giving all kinds of interviews lately...too many to keep track of. Here are the main ones scheduled for next week: *The Morning Show*, *On Target*, *Inside Story*, the local news in Houston, and several radio shows.

Luckily, today I'm having one of those *extremely rare* good hair days. Hope the hair holds out for the shoot. :-P Unfortunately, though, all the makeup Q of S has piled on today cannot hide the stress bags under her eyes. Am going to go buy one of those massage chairs tonight to sit in during my little downtime this week.

Tah!
—Q of S

Ricky Rings (PRIVATE)
Filed in MISC. on Friday, 10/28

My friend Ricky called me today to congratulate me on all my publicity.

"You *go,* girrrl! You *work* your fifteen minutes of fame!" He could hardly contain his excitement.

"Fifteen minutes *my ass*, Ricky! This is just the beginning..." I replied smugly.

"Hmm. You've become quite the drama queen, Elena."

"Well, *hellooooo*—I learned from the *best*!"

He then proceeded to tell me how Captain Bill, aka Captain Sleaze, had recently been written up for sexual harassment.

"God, will he ever learn?" I said, rolling my eyes.

"Yeah, well, it gets better—all he got was a slap on the wrist. He didn't even get any downtime or anything. He is already back flying to his normal hooker hotspots."

"Figures!" I felt my blood pressure rising. "I post a harmless picture of myself in uniform and get canned, while Legacy men get away with every trick in the book!"

"That's true. I know. I've done about every trick, honey," Ricky replied teasingly.

"Well, the Good Ole Boys that run Legacy are about to get a wake-up call!"

Newspaper Article
Filed in ABOUT ME on Saturday, 10/29

There is a very good article about Queen of Sky and her dilemmas in today's Austin (aka "Quirksville") paper.

Queen of Sky out of her Element
Filed in MISC. on Sunday, 10/30

This may surprise you all, but Queen of Sky's alter ego, Elena Guaio, is actually very shy. In fact, she is TERRIFIED of being on national TV. That, coupled with the fact that Elena is not a morning person, means that she will look like a deer in headlights on the *Morning Show* tomorrow. :-O

So I guess you all should tune in to see how I do!

—Q of S

Update: It should be on the first hour of the *Morning Show*, which is 7-8am Eastern time. Am probably going to wear a dark suit, and am probably going to have to do my own hair and makeup... Eeek!

OK, Peeps...
Filed in MISC. on Monday, 10/31

If you want to see more of Queen of Sky, the deer in headlights, tune in to *Inside Story* today. Check your local listings. Also, if you are in Houston, tune into the 10pm news on channel 12.

I don't know why people don't believe me when I say my blog is therapy for me. It's true.

Also, PLEASE, if you do not know me, do NOT try to call me at home. In fact, I'm not taking any phone calls today. If you wish to say something to me, leave a comment or sign my Guestbook.

If you are a member of the media and interested in my story, please send me an email including your phone number.

Am going to take a nap now...

—Q of S

P.S. In the midst of this media roller coaster, I almost forgot to wish you all a very Happy Halloween!

The Morning Show

Filed in MISC. on Monday, 10/31

Well, I finally got up the courage to watch the *Morning Show* tape this evening. :-O Not only do I look like a deer in headlights, but I can tell that I've gained weight in the past month, and I look like I have no lips. :-O Gotta work on the lip lining next time! Other than that, I am proud of myself for just being able to formulate complete sentences. I'm the one who always hid in the galley when I had to make PAs on the airplane. And even then my voice stuttered.

OK, in regards to all of the nasty comments today, I don't understand why people would go out of their way to leave comments on my blog unless they had something to gain from it (like certain ex-employers).

I will NOT be intimidated.

—Elena, aka Q of S

P.S. It looks like the *Inside Story* piece will run later this week. And next up is *On Target*! Stay tuned!

NOVEMBER

The Clouds Open

Stressed Out (PRIVATE)
Filed in MISC. on Tuesday, 11/1

Well, that was very stressful yesterday. Not only was I scared TO DEATH to be on LIVE national TV, but to top it off, the interviewer ended up being a jerk! He must have woken up on the wrong side of the bed.

The worst part was when he asked me condescendingly what I had been thinking when I posted the uniform pictures on my blog. I was attempting to explain that I had just lost my mother and grandmother, but he cut me off:

"Are you saying you posted these pictures because your grandmother died? You don't look very sad there."

Oh, well, what's done is done. Better luck next time!

All these interviews are stressing me out. :-(

Bewitched
Filed in PICS on Tuesday, 11/1

Saturday night Queen of Sky went to a good old fashioned American Halloween party. :-D She dressed as Cher (I LOVE YOU, CHER!!!); however, she ended up looking more like the tall, sexy witch that she is (note the broom).

Incidentally, yesterday would have been Queen of Sky's eight-year anniversary with Legacy Airlines. See what happens when you hire a witch on Halloween!!!! *evil laugh*

P.S. One of my readers told me in an email yesterday that Legacy management's attitude toward my photos matched that of the MIDDLE EASTERN carrier he works for. :-O Draw your own conclusions there. Maybe the burka should be the new Legacy flight attendant uniform!

No Update Today
Filed in PICS on Wednesday, 11/2

Sorry, everybody, Queen of Sky has been conferring with her legal team all day today.

It's amazing that a poor little flight attendant trying to have a little innocent fun could cause a HUGE international controversy!

Will answer some pressing questions tomorrow.

FAQ
Filed in ABOUT ME on Thursday, 11/3

Here are some frequently asked questions about Queen of Sky's *Morning Show* appearance:

Q: *Elena's lawyer is now William Paxley. I wonder what happened to George Waite. Did he drop her case given its lack of merit?*
A: My legal team consists of three attorneys. They couldn't all be present for the taping.

Q: *Elena appeared sedated, almost as if she was drugged. She was not the vivacious, gregarious Queen of Sky that I imagined. Perhaps she was just intimidated by the fancy cameras and backdrop.*
A: I am NOT a morning person, and I'm also very shy. If you noticed, I was trembling. This was my first time on LIVE NATIONAL TV, folks! :-O

Q: *Elena and Will were filmed in Austin, rather than in the Morning Show studio. Why is that?*
A: The *Morning Show* did offer to fly me to NY, but I was stressed out enough being on live national TV as it was.

Q: *Elena really played up the pity angle. There was a bizarre story about how she recently lost both mother and grandmother, and the photos were posted for therapeutic reasons. The story did not hold together well... it came off as very contrived.*
A: My blog is therapy to me, and the photos are part of that therapy. I don't understand why people don't believe this. I lost my mother and my maternal grandmother within six months of each other. It has been a stressful year (even more so now), and my blog lets me let off steam and have fun. I am NOT a public speaker, and I understand that I did not convey this very well in the *Morning Show* interview.

Q: *Unlike in her website photos, Elena sported eyeglasses for the appearance, as well as a conservative business suit. I think she's pretty attractive, and I retract my "fugly" comment from an earlier post.*

A: I *do* actually wear glasses. I just take them off when I work (and of course for pictures). Thanks for the compliment—I thought I looked awful!

Q: *Why didn't Elena just read her employment contract? Then she would have known that she had violated the rules.*

A: I don't *have* an employment contract. Legacy flight attendants are *non*-union. How many times do I have to say this? And Legacy Airlines does NOT provide its employees with copies of its HR policies. Incidentally, I have yet to be shown a rule in black and white that I violated.

On Target
Filed in MISC. on Friday, 11/4

Hello, all! Queen of Sky gets another chance today to do LIVE national TV. At 6pm EST, I will be on *On Target* on DNBC. Actually, I'll probably be on the second half of the one-hour show.

Keep your fingers crossed that I don't have any brain farts or other embarrassing moments!

—Q of S

Queen of Sky's Bug
Filed in LIFE OF LEISURE on Saturday, 11/5

Thanks, everybody, for your well-wishes for the show yesterday. I was VERY proud of myself afterward. Even though I was sick, I was feeling much more confident, and it showed!

As for my bug, well, it had to do with a little place called La Panza Bakery...

Last Saturday night I had nachos and margaritas with my friend Monica. Afterward, we made the foolish decision to stop at La Panza Bakery, a 24-hour operation on South First Street, for some cinnamony Mexican hot chocolate, which I had been craving.

To my delight, they had some hot chocolate (probably left over from the morning), so we bought two and went back to Monica's place to watch a movie.

Well, that hot chocolate was more like lukewarm chocolate with crusty little pieces of milk skin floating all through it. Monica had a sip and turned her nose up at it. I drank some, then filtered it to remove the lumps, and drank some more, ignoring my good sense and forgetting about my bad experience the last time I ate at La Panza Bakery. (That time I had Mexican eggs at three in the morning with some salsa that had been sitting out for who-knows-how-many days, and ended up with a horrible stomachache and case of the runs the next day *and* the day after.)

Of course, the next day (Sunday), I felt like I had been run over by a truck. My kidneys ached and my stomach growled. And this week the bug has slowly progressed into a full-blown head and chest cold, which is what I am now left with.

Fun, fun, fun! And no health insurance, to boot! :-(

So the moral of the story is: no more La Panza Bakery for me! Am going to have some soup now...

Dazed and Confused (PRIVATE)
Filed in MISC. on Sunday, 11/6

Well, the media frenzy continues... I'm mentioned in *Current* magazine this week! Go figure!

Queen of Sky, Newsmaker—who'd a thunk it?

The *On Target* interview the other day went a lot better than the *Morning Show*. Maybe I have some potential as a public speaker after all.

I am still feeling completely dazed by all of this. I mean—where the HELL is my life going? And why was I suddenly thrust into the limelight?

Sometimes I wonder what my mother would have thought of all this. She was a good Southern woman who never stood up for herself. What would she have advised me?

I have to screen my phone calls now, because I get weirdos calling me at all hours. I had to subscribe to the call block service, too.

Oh, well. As my friend Nina says, "People only throw stones at ripe fruit!"

Queen of Sky Story Summary
Filed in ABOUT ME on Sunday, 11/6

I've noticed a new influx of readers, partly because of the *Current* and *CyberNet* articles. I know they are mainly coming in search of the now infamous uniform pics. See my <u>Oct. 19 entry</u> for some of those pics.

Now, something I want to get off my chest... I have heard some people call my pics "*Playmate*-like." Well, apparently these people have never seen a *Playmate* magazine. If you think my pics are similar to *Playmate*'s, then there is something wrong with you.

My pictures are innocent and playful representations of a 29-year-old who is going through some tough emotional times.

Now let me summarize things a little bit...

- I NEVER named my airline or my base city (Atlanta) in my blog prior to being fired.

- Perhaps a handful of my 100 or so core readers knew what airline I flew for (and most of those were other airline employees). My blog was, after all, a semi-fictitious account of life as a flight attendant.

- I would still be flying, or at least guaranteed a *fair* appeal, if Legacy flight attendants were unionized.

- Legacy has repeatedly refused to tell me what "inappropriate" means and which of my pictures (and/or comments) they deemed "inappropriate" enough to fire me for.

- Remember, I had removed all of the uniform pics from my blog once Legacy suspended me without warning (on Sept. 19), and they still fired me a month later.

- I had also filed a sex discrimination complaint with the EEOC two weeks *prior* to being fired. That's called retaliation, folks.

- There are TONS of male Legacy employees in uniform on the web, none of whom have been disciplined. Legacy's firing policies are arbitrary and discriminatory.

- My blog is therapy to me. I lost my mother last year to cancer and my grandmother to Alzheimer's in April. My blog makes me feel good. Legacy management knew about my recent losses. The first time I met my most recent supervisor was at my mother's funeral. (They switched my supervisor right before my mother died.)

- Sexism is ALIVE and WELL in 21st century America—and civil liberties are DEAD and BURIED!!!

Fight the Power! (PRIVATE)
Filed in MISC. on Monday, 11/7

It makes me angry that people make judgments and presumptions about me based on a few light-hearted and spontaneous snapshots that I posted on my blog.

But it makes me even angrier that some of those people are trying to beat down my will by leaving me nasty comments. Why is it so disturbing to people that a woman should stand up for her rights? Is there something wrong with that?

And the fact is, I DIDN'T DO ANYTHING WRONG!!! I didn't violate any rules or regulations at Legacy and I surely was not given fair warning for whatever I did that offended upper management. If personal expression is something to be ashamed of, then please SHOOT ME NOW!

There was NO greater premeditated meaning to those pics, even though people try to assign one to them. I was not trying to portray flight attendants or my airline in a particular way. The pics are what they are—goofy snapshots taken on a whim during my downtime. But it doesn't matter. Corporations like Legacy don't want to employ individuals with personalities and lives—NO, they prefer mindless drones and lackeys who only live to work and never complain.

Although, perhaps men are allowed to have a life—at least at Legacy, where it's OK for male employees to have dating profiles, personal web pages, etc. But I guess men in general are freer and less judged in this society. I have a feeling that if I were a man and felt that I had been wronged, nobody would be calling me an "attention-seeking whore." And nobody would be telling me to give up my fight and "get a job at McDonald's where you belong."

There's also an equally disgusting faction of commentators that assumes because I'm an attractive, fun-loving female, my goal in life is to pose naked or—worse yet—star in porno movies.

It's a good thing I'm thick-skinned. In truth I've never been a good Southern girl who does as she's told and says "yes, sir" and "yes, ma'am" to everyone and everything. And through this ordeal I have learned that if you don't stand up for yourself, nobody else will.

I mean, who knew how much resistance I, a wrongfully terminated female at-will employee, would face?

But, in the end, the naysayers actually make me stronger. I believe in myself and my cause more and more each day. Besides, I'm not just fighting this battle for me—I'm fighting for the rights of women and bloggers the world over. And when I succeed, I will dedicate my victory to my poor mother, may she rest in peace. She never believed in herself enough to reach for the things that she deserved, like self-respect and the respect of others. So I'm fighting this battle above all for her.

A Victory Against the Legacy Lynch Men
Filed in MISC. on Tuesday, 11/8

Hello, all. Yesterday I had my first victory against Legacy: The Texas Department of Labor granted me unemployment benefits.

The reasoning for their determining in my favor was as follows:

> *Your employer terminated you for violation of a reasonable and known policy. The available facts show that you were **not** aware of the rule, policy, or requirement. The facts show that you did **not** fail to follow employer's rules, orders, or instructions. Therefore, you **can** be paid benefits.*

I couldn't wish for a better pre-30th birthday present (OK, maybe there is *one* thing...).

—Q of S

Vague Update
Filed in MISC. on Wednesday, 11/9

Hello, all. Am feeling much better today. I'm on my way to a party but just wanted to give a brief update.

The last correspondence I received from Legacy was very VAGUE, to say the least. In fact, their correspondences are getting vaguer by the day!

This one says that not only did I allegedly post "inappropriate" photos but also "inappropriate" *comments* on my website *and* on other websites. Boy, that's *not* what I was told before, and I can PROVE that. Looks like they're just making up reasons for my termination as they go along!

I have once again requested that Legacy provide copies of the policies that I allegedly violated, so we shall see. I would really like to see Legacy's unabridged code of conduct. There must be a BIG section on blogging and picture taking in there. (Yeah, right!)

Hasta luego...
—Elena aka Q of S

Daily Horoscope
Filed in MISC. on Thursday, 11/10

Finally a good horoscope!

Removing obstacles
This is a fortunate period in your life. It is a time to free yourself from restrictions imposed on you by others—restrictions you may not even know exist. Circumstances during this influence may lead to great achievements or the accomplishment of goals that you have been striving for through hard work and patience for some time. The key is to remain focused. Another possible outcome is an easing of the burden of responsibilities in your life. The ultimate rewards of this influence, however, are the divine gifts of wisdom and maturity.

Aspect: Jupiter conjunct Saturn
Period of Influence: 11/9-11/21
Courtesy of Astro Wizards

Mixed Emotions (PRIVATE)
Filed in MISC. on Friday, 11/11

I have a feeling good things will happen this week, and it's not just because my horoscope was good yesterday. I have a *deep* feeling that things will turn out OK.

Meanwhile, though, I'm really frustrated that Legacy HR is giving me the run-around. Our emails just keep going in circles. I keep asking the same questions, and they keep giving me the same *vague* non-answers.

This reminds me of what one reporter told me about the Legacy Airlines Corporate Communications Department:

"They need to change their name," she said, "because the *last* thing they do is communicate. In fact, they do everything possible *not* to answer your questions."

Well, that's the way I feel about Legacy HR about now.

Oh, well, there's no use venting to myself. Am going to go do some yoga and think some positive thoughts now...

Busy
Filed in *LIFE OF LEISURE* on *Saturday, 11/12*

Let's see... here's the quick update... I've been busy at social engagements all weekend. It's tough being a famous fired flight attendant!

Anyhow, I'm still trying to secure a hearing with Legacy to appeal my termination. They're giving me the run-around, as usual. Legacy told me they have no formal appeal process and nothing in writing that I can see (ah—the joys of having no contract). They also told me I can't bring my lawyers with me to such a hearing (although they will probably have theirs present), *and* they still refuse to tell me which Legacy policy I allegedly violated to justify my termination.

I guess by now they know about the tape. Yes, that's right, I RECORDED the phone conversation during which my supervisor fired me (and *yes*, it *is* legal to record a phone conversation in the state of Texas). I'm still waiting to hear what policy they have that backs up my termination. And what, pray tell, is the definition of "inappropriate"?

Inquiring minds want to know!

—Q of S

War Zone
Filed in *MISC.* on *Sunday, 11/13*

There has been movement in the enemy camp. *sneaky sideways glances* Looks like the "appeal hearing" will take place this week... Will try to keep you all updated... must go now... think I hear enemy fire... *dives behind breakfast bar*

Forward Movement (PRIVATE)
Filed in *MISC.* on *Monday, 11/14*

Well, Legacy management has finally agreed to meet with me *and* my lawyers. So on Wednesday we're flying to Atlanta to meet with them. I'm so nervous that I'm making myself sick! Don't know what to expect. Will they offer me my job back? Will they continue to intimidate and harass me about my blog? Or will they give me the boot for good?

I really miss my flight attendant friends, not to mention my trips, but I *especially* miss my free flight benefits. :-) Anyway, now that my lawyers are going with me, at least I don't have to worry about Legacy management strong-arming me.

There are plenty of other things to fret about, though...

Top Secret Meeting
Filed in MISC. on Tuesday, 11/15

Tomorrow morning, bright and early, I am headed to Atlanta, aka Bustling Base City, with my lawyers for a TOP SECRET meeting at Legacy Airlines Headquarters.

Please keep your fingers crossed for me, all!

The Clouds Open (PRIVATE)
Filed in MISC. on Thursday, 11/17

7:35pm

Well, I just got in from Atlanta. Utterly exhausted but completely *overwhelmed* with JOY!

On Wednesday, my three lawyers and I touched down in Atlanta and hopped a cab over to Legacy HQ, where we were shown into a boardroom filled with a bunch of suits. There wasn't a single female among them, so I was sure I was screwed. The Good Ole Boys were all there, and the mood was very somber.

The suits started off by going over all the elements of my blog that they had had a problem with. My lawyers answered back with evidence of all of the other Legacy employees' websites. Why hadn't *they* been disciplined?

Then my lawyers further questioned why Legacy management didn't follow their *own* policies of progressive discipline in my case. Why didn't they at least give me a warning before taking such drastic steps?

This arguing went on back and forth for hours. But somehow, by the end of the day, my lawyers—my FAB-U-LOUS lawyers—were able to turn the meeting around. They started negotiating, not about my punishment or getting my job back, but for just compensation for all of the stress, suffering, humiliation, etc., that I have faced as a result of losing my job.

Then there was the matter of ruining my career. Some numbers were thrown around—how many years I would have had left until retirement at Legacy had I not been fired, etc. Finally, there was a stalemate, and we retired to the hotel for the night to start negotiations again early the next morning.

Day Two of Operation Queen of Sky Settlement started about as badly as the night before had ended. But, by 11am, my lawyers had not let up, and the numbers that were passed back and forth across the table finally met nods on both sides. Then there were the handshakes, and finally the documents were drawn up.

Around 2pm, we were on our way back to the airport, settlement agreement in hand. I was so excited, I bought George, Will, and Doug a round of champagne in a bar in Concourse A before our flight.

Well, I haven't slept in three days, so I'm going to retire now. I am so excited, though, I don't think I'll be able to sleep!

YAAAAAAAAAAAY!!!!

THANK YOU, AVIATION GODS!!!
Filed in MISC. on Friday, 11/18

Words cannot even express what I feel right now. But the closest thing is RELIEF and outright ELATION!

Yesterday, after a day and a half of negotiations with my BRILLIANT legal team, Legacy Airlines offered me an *undisclosed* settlement. So generous of them! I take back all those bad things I said (or thought) about Legacy management.

I guess everything happens for a reason. Now I am *free* to start a new life!!!!

Wow
Filed in MISC. on Saturday, 11/19

Today I'm just in shock. I've been on the phone all day with family and friends. And the media have been calling, too. They are trying to get the details of my settlement, but unfortunately, I can't disclose that info. All I can do is direct them to my lawyers or to Legacy Corporate Communications. (And good luck!) Just know that I am content and will be set for a long time at my current lifestyle level.

Well, my phone is ringing *again*... gotta run!

Buh-Bye, Twenties!
Filed in LIFE OF LEISURE on Sunday, 11/20

Hi, all!

Tomorrow I turn the big 3-0. This is going to be the BEST birthday I've had in a *long* time. I have, after all, already received the best gift I could hope for. This year I truly have something to celebrate.

237

I'm leaving behind my twenties, and with them my turbulent (pun intended) eight-year career as a flight attendant. It's time to move on to bigger and better things. I've been thinking a lot about my future this week and am starting to formulate a plan—so stay tuned!

Thanks to all of you who supported me during this rough year, especially the past two months. There are a lot of nasty people out there, as well, who have been leaving me ugly comments of late saying I deserved to be fired. Well, to those people I say: GET A LIFE!

Anyway, I'm having a nice quiet dinner with friends tomorrow in honor of the big day. It should be really nice.

Daily Horoscope
Filed in MISC. on Monday, 11/21

Happy Birthday!
Today the sun returns to its natal position in your chart. It's your day to shine. You will receive a natural ego boost. Accordingly, you should surround yourself with friends and loved ones. And remember, the events that occur today will mirror the whole year until your next birthday, so make sure to have a good one!

Aspect: Sun conjunct Sun
Period of Influence: 11/21
Courtesy of Astro Wizards

I sure will! Thanks, Astro Wizards!
—Q of S

Old Woman, New Life (PRIVATE)
Filed in MISC. on Tuesday, 11/21

This morning when I woke up, for the first time in a really long time, I felt truly *good*. Coincidentally, today I'm officially 30 years old. Am going out tonight to celebrate my birthday *and* my settlement with Legacy. I may be out of a job and a career, but I just came into a lot of money. :-D And this money will allow me to pursue the career path I thought I would only be able to dream about: culinary school abroad. Right now I'm trying to decide between France, Italy, Spain, and maybe even Peru!

Decisions, decisions!

Birthday Wishes (PRIVATE)
Filed in LIFE OF LEISURE on Wednesday, 11/22

My birthday celebration was really lovely last night. Kim and Monica and Jesse and the rest of the Austin commuters all managed to make it. It's so hard to get my flight attendant friends together, but they were all there, so it was really special.

Victor stopped by, too, later in the evening to congratulate me and to find out what I was planning for the future. I told him and the gang about my dream of going to culinary school in Europe or South America. They said they couldn't wait until I got back, seeing as I was already such a good cook. I promised to throw a big dinner party upon my return.

Anyway, at various times during the night I felt a special presence—like a hand on my shoulder, accompanied by a warm fuzzy feeling. At first I brushed it off, but a little while later it returned. I finally realized that my mother wanted to be there with me on that special night. She must have known that my victory was dedicated to her.

Well, I'm about to make a BIG announcement here on the blog. When I got home late last night, I started thinking about my future again. I decided that in the spirit of a fresh start, I should pull the plug on "Diary of a Dysfunctional Flight Attendant." And, seeing as I will be going back home to North Carolina to visit my father today and won't be able to post very often this coming week, I have decided to say my goodbyes today.

Ah, the future is bright... I feel freer than I have ever felt before!

Goodbye, Farewell, Auf Wiedersehen, AdieUUUU!!!!
Filed in MISC. on Wednesday, 11/22

Hello, everybody! I'm preparing to head back East for Thanksgiving today. As I do so, I have some good news and some bad news to tell you all.

First the bad news... As you may have guessed from the title of this entry, the "Queen of Sky" is about to embark on a new journey. The start of that journey, as with any journey, includes saying some goodbyes.

Yes, I'm afraid it's true. The Queen of Sky as you know her is now officially gone—or transformed, rather. She has hung up her wings, retired her lesbian prison guard uniform, and thrown away her Coke can opener for good.

No need for tears and all that nonsense, however, because the good news is... (drum roll, please!)... you can follow the further adventures of the former Queen of Sky in her new incarnation, the "Queen of Cuisine," at her new world-premiere blog, "Diary of a Dysfunctional Foodie." ;-D The new blog is also located right here at BlogAcres, just in a different plot.

Yep, that's right. I've decided to use my settlement money to pursue my dream of attending culinary school—preferably somewhere on a distant and mysterious continent, where I will likely get into plenty more trouble with dashing young men with exotic accents and a penchant for casual sexual encounters.

Anyway, I leave you all with these final closing thoughts...

Peace and Love and FOOD! BLOG ON!!!

—The diva formerly known as Queen of Sky

P.S. Don't forget to drop by and visit me at my new blog!